Familiar

Familiar

By David L. Carter

RESOURCE *Publications* · Eugene, Oregon

FAMILIAR

Resource Publications
An Imprint of Wipf and Stock Publishers
199 W. 8th Ave., Suite 3
Eugene, OR 97401

www.wipfandstock.com

PAPERBACK ISBN: 978-1-5326-0001-2
HARDCOVER ISBN: 978-1-5326-0003-6
EBOOK ISBN: 978-1-5326-0002-9

JUNE 3, 2026

For Carolyn Frank, RN

Number 1!

Contents

familiar
(fəˈmɪlɪə)

noun

1. (Classical Myth & Legend) Also called: *familiar spirit,* a supernatural spirit often assuming animal form, supposed to attend and aid a witch, wizard, etc.

2. (Roman Catholic Church) a person, attached to the household of a pope or bishop, who renders service in return for support.

3. (Roman Catholic Church) an officer of the Inquisition who arrested accused persons.

4. A friend or frequent companion.

Chapter One

Metanoia

IT ALL STARTED THE day that Niniane nearly choked to death on a disk of pepperoni in the middle of her crowded high school cafeteria.

She would never forget that moment. She was sitting across the table from her boyfriend, Dillis, noting that lenses of his glasses were filthy. She was just about to ask him how he could see anything out of them when the greasy piece of pepperoni on the bite of pizza she'd just taken slipped down her throat, lodged in her windpipe and would not allow her to breathe. She stood up, knocking her chair backwards, and her hands clutched her throat. Her vision clouded but she could see a blurry Dillis still sitting down across from her, gawking at her but not moving.

She realized furiously that she wouldn't get any help from him. She turned and ran to the cafeteria exit and when a kid from her calculus class named Oscar saw her clutching her throat, he stood up, grabbed her around the waist, pressed his joined hands up and under her ribcage and the disc of pepperoni popped out of her mouth and through the air in a perfect arc to land on the filthy cafeteria floor ten feet in front of her. Niniane took in several shuddering, desperate breaths, then burst into tears and ran out of the cafeteria into the nearest girls' room.

↩

"Dillis!" She said after school. "Why didn't you help me? I almost died!"

Dillis shrugged. "I didn't know what was wrong."

"You couldn't see that I was choking to death?"

"You didn't give me a chance . . . " He said.

"I didn't give you a *chance*?!" Niniane didn't know why she was bothering. But it bothered *her*, not a little, that it had been a relative stranger who had literally saved her life instead of Dillis, her boyfriend of almost nine months. They were sitting in Dillis' old Plymouth in front of her house, as Dillis was dropping her off before going to his part time job at a deli near downtown.

Niniane rolled her eyes. There was a lot about Dillis that was not up to par. He wasn't all that good looking, with his mop of brown hair, his lanky, toneless body, and his big nose. He had no ambition, his grades were awful, and he smoked too much pot. But he had a very sweet, large toothed simian smile, and she had to admit that she liked being around him even though he wasn't what she wanted him to be.

Dillis was used to Niniane's exasperated sighs and eye-rolls. They didn't bother him. "Well, you're all right now, right? He said. "That's what counts." He reached for her hand. She hit him lightly with it, and he gave up.

Niniane opened the passenger door. It still bothered her that it had been a random classmate, and not Dillis, who was sufficiently in touch with what was going on around him to save her from death. But maybe she was making too much of it. She leaned in and kissed his cheek. "Pay more attention next time." She said. "What would you do without me?"

⌒

Niniane N. Westvane lived in a nice split level home in a quiet residential neighborhood in a rapidly growing city in the southeastern United States with her mother and father, who had adopted her when she was not even a year old and when they were already a childless middle aged couple. The fact that she was adopted very rarely crossed Niniane's mind, as she could not imagine her life being any different from what it was. But that afternoon, after Dillis dropped her off and she let herself into the house that was the only house she could remember living in, with the only parents she could remember being raised by, she found herself thinking that, if it wasn't for any number of twists of fate, she would not be here. For one thing, if her original parents had not died in a fire, she would certainly have remained with them. For another, if her classmate Oscar hadn't noticed her distress in time, she would have choked to death in the middle of the high school cafeteria. Niniane was not normally given to morbid philosophical speculation, but her near death experience had rattled her.

Normally Niniane came home from school and attacked her homework, but that day she left her book bag on the kitchen counter and went upstairs to her bedroom to lay down. Both her mother and father were at work, her mother at the public library where she worked in the Children's Room, and her father at the office where he managed a home and auto insurance agency. Niniane stared up at the popcorn ceiling of her bedroom and felt very odd . . . she didn't feel like herself, and yet in a way she felt more like herself than ever. "I almost died." She said aloud in the silent room in the quiet house in the peaceful neighborhood. She closed her eyes and allowed her mind to bring the moment back, the helplessness, the fear, the furious despair that overcame her when she realized that Dillis was not going to do anything to save her. And the terrible sense of having her airway blocked by a greasy disc of processed meat. In that moment it was as if her own body was punishing her for some unconscious, thoughtless insult. It would have been such an embarrassing, undignified way to die, beneath her sense of who she was and of the graceful mechanisms of her healthy young flesh.

Niniane's eyes opened wide. She sat up, as if to assume a position as far from that of a corpse as she could. "No. She said aloud, from the very core of her consciousness. She wanted nothing to do with death, absolutely nothing. She coughed, as if the disc of pepperoni was still in some sense blocking her airway. I will never put a piece of pepperoni in my mouth again, ever, she told herself. And immediately in her mind's eye she beheld a vision of a narrow, gated enclosure, crowded with terrified and recalcitrant livestock, snuffling, snorting pigs, lowing cattle, squawking poultry, all being herded by some unseen and relentless human figure from behind into a long, low, windowless, barrackslike enclosure where they were all slaughtered in some unimaginable and inhumane manner. I'll never eat *any* kind of meat again, she declared. Nothing should die to keep something else alive. It's wrong.

Niniane scrambled off her bed and walked over to her dresser and looked into the mirror attached to the top. There she was, her face, her hair, her torso; behind her the walls of her bedroom, the headboard of her bed, the window that looked out over the backyard to her old swingset. Nothing looked different, but everything had changed. She could do something to keep suffering and death at bay, and the time was now.

↜

After Niniane and her parents finished their supper of baked lasagna, Niniane made her announcement. "That was excellent, Mama." She said. "But that's the last time I'm ever going to eat meat. From now on, I'm a vegan."

And as if to emphasize her point, she placed her knife, fork, and napkin on her plate, and pushed it forward.

Her mother and father looked at one another, then at Niniane. "What brought this on?" Her mother said, a bit tentatively, as if she wasn't sure she wanted to hear the answer.

Niniane opened her mouth to answer, but no words came. She closed her mouth and looked down at her plate, and felt foolish. What brought this on? Coming face to face with death brought it on, but did she really want her parents to know that? And was it as simple as that, after all? Lots of people choked on food, but they didn't necessarily change their lives because of it. Niniane knew that if she told her parents about the pepperoni that her father, at least, would make a crack about it, and her mother would get upset about nearly losing her, and tell her to be more careful, which would infuriate Niniane.

"It's something I've been thinking about for a while." She said, still looking at her plate instead of at her mother. "And I've been doing some research, you know, about the meat industry, and . . . " She pushed her plate a bit further away, still feeling foolish. "It's just something I have to do." With that, she looked up squarely at her mother.

"You know there was ground beef in that lasagna," her father said, indicating her plate.

"I *know* that, Daddy!" Niniane said. "I said from now *on* I'm not eating meat. Would you please be serious? I'm *serious* about this."

Niniane's mother leaned forward placatingly. "Honey, we're just a little surprised. This just seems sudden. I know a lot of kids are doing it these days, and I know there's a lot of information about it at the library, but I do think this is something to think about carefully. How are you going to get the protein you need?"

Niniane hadn't had time, of course, to think through details like that, so she waved them away. "There are lots of things that have protein. Don't worry about it, Mama, I know what I'm doing. And I know that I'll have to be responsible for my meals. It's only fair."

Niniane's mother leaned back, her soft chin tucked in and her lips pursed as if to hold in some fresh concern, and Niniane's father's forehead corrugated with real consternation. "What about Thanksgiving and Christmas? You aren't going to have turkey with the family?"

"No, Daddy. I'll just have something else. Don't worry about it."

"Well, what about bacon? You know you're crazy about bacon and eggs. And what about fish? You aren't going to eat fish anymore? Not even at the beach?"

"No, Daddy! I'm not going to eat turkey, I'm not going to eat bacon and eggs, I'm not going to eat fish! How many times do I have to explain it? I'm vegan, I'm not eating meat, or wearing leather, or anything like that! It's really not that hard to understand."

"Horace . . . " Niniane's mother interrupted her husband before he could respond with another question, for she knew he loved to tease their high-strung daughter. But Horace Westvane was genuinely perplexed.

"Well, what about the farm? What in the world do you think you'll eat when you go down to the farm this summer, Nin? Because you can't just pick and choose what your Aunt May is going to cook. You know that . . . "

Niniane blinked. Her father, she assumed, was baiting her, but he also had a point. Every summer, for as long as she could remember, she spent eight weeks with her Aunt May and her Aunt May's partner Irene on their small family farm in the middle of nowhere in the southeastern region of the state. The farm had been in Niniane's mother's family for many generations, and Niniane's mother had grown up there. For the past ten years, since the death of Niniane's grandfather, Aunts May and Irene had taken over the running of the place, to the relief of Niniane's mother, and it had gone from a tobacco monocrop to a few acres each of cotton, soybeans, rice, a number of orchards and a full range of livestock that included cattle, hogs, chickens and sheep. There Niniane's aunts lived as much as possible off of their own land; they grew, raised and slaughtered much of what they ate. Niniane had indeed not thought about the farm, and the farm was not a detail she could dismiss.

Horace Westvane cleared his throat nervously. Niniane looked just like she'd swallowed a bug. He hadn't really meant to upset her.

"I guess I won't go to the farm this summer." She said.

Her parents looked at one another. "Niniane . . . " Her mother said. "You can't . . . You have to go to the farm this summer."

"Why?" Said Niniane. "I mean, I wish I could, but Daddy's right . . . May and Irene aren't going to like having a vegan there, so . . . I'll just stay here. I'll just get a job somewhere, and rack up a little more money for study abroad."

"Niniane . . . " Her mother said. "Honey, you can't. You can't stay here, because your father and I aren't going to be here. We were going to tell you later, when we know all the details, but . . . I guess now is just as good a time as any . . . we're going to Europe for our second honeymoon. Daddy's company has offered to pay for a cruise. Isn't that something? Just in time for our silver anniversary. I've always wanted to go to Rome, and we're going to have four days there . . . We'll see the coliseum, and the Sistine Chapel. I can't wait!" Her mother beamed beneath her powder and foundation.

"Rome!" Niniane was thunderstruck. Her parents, her solid, more than middle-aged, affectionate but hardly passionate parents, taking a whirlwind trip across the globe to Europe without her? She felt as uncomfortable as if she'd caught them nude. As if to make the prospect seem all the more outrageous, her parents winked at one another and intertwined their fingers.

"I can stay here by myself." Niniane said determinedly.

Her fifty-six year old father had an exasperating habit, particularly when he was in a good mood, of adopting what he thought was contemporary youthful slang. "In your dreams." He said.

"I can't believe this." Niniane said. She stood up, took her plate to the kitchen, and then marched up the stairs to her bedroom, unable to keep herself from not quite slamming the door. She threw herself face down upon her bed, then turned over and scowled at the popcorn ceiling. A cobweb strand hanging from the rim of her overhead light cover swung in the disturbance she created in the air with her sudden entrance. Her furious gaze drifted after awhile from that to the window overlooking the back yard. And just at that moment, seemingly out of nowhere, a small brown bird, perhaps a sparrow, perched on the windowsill, sang a few shrill, cheerful notes, then disappeared. Even for a staunch agnostic like Niniane, it seemed to be a sign from above. She sat up, her determination and sense of purpose renewed. Of course the world was not going to make it easy for her to live by her convictions. Of course she was bound to be misunderstood, even by those she loved. The truth was on her side, and that was all that mattered. Knowing that, she could stand her ground, anywhere, with anyone, even at the farm.

The next day Niniane went to school determined that if Dillis in any way made light of her new commitment to animal welfare she would immediately end their relationship. She was not a little irritated, then, that he was yet again absent from school. At lunch period she slipped outside and called him. "Where are you!" She said.

"Home." It was obvious that he'd been sleeping when she called.

"Why?"

There was no answer.

"Dillis!" She raised her voice. "What's going on?! Are you sick?"

"No." He said after a moment. Then, "Niniane, I quit."

For a split second she felt cold, for her first thought that was that he was breaking up with her! Then it occurred to her that he must be talking about his job at the deli. "Well, hallelujah." She said.

She could hear Dillis grunt with surprise. "You're not upset?"

She laughed. "Of course not! You need to pay more attention to school, anyway. You know that. And you can always find another job once you're caught up . . . "

There was a rustling noise on Dillis' end of the line, as if her were sitting up in bed. "Niniane, I mean I quit school. I was gonna tell you later today . . . they offered me a full time shift manager position at the deli. It pays benefits and everything. After a while I can even move up to district manager, if I'm good. And this means I can get my own place and everything. But I can't work full time and go to school too, so . . . " Dillis' voice became uncharacteristically emphatic. "So, I'm dropping out."

Niniane was too shocked to speak. She gripped her phone so tightly that her knuckles cracked. "Dillis, you can't drop out of school to work in a deli. That's . . . " She spluttered, unable find words for such foolishness. "You'll ruin your entire life."

Dillis had the nerve to laugh out loud.

"I'm serious, Dillis. You can't just work in a deli for the rest of your life."

"Why not? It's good money, Niniane. And it's decent work. What's wrong with it?"

"It's . . . " Niniane made herself take her phone in her other hand and put it to her other ear. " Dillis, don't do this. I mean it."

"Niniane," Dillis said wearily. "It's already done. I told them last night I'd take the job. Jesus, even my mom isn't freaking out as bad as you are. What's the big deal, Niniane? I can get my GED after a while, and that's as good as a high school diploma. It's not like I'm going to college, I suck at school and you know it. Everyone's not like you Niniane. I work hard at my job, I got a nice promotion, and I'm going to take it! The least you can do is be happy for me."

Niniane felt for a moment as if she might be losing her sanity. Could it really be that Dillis was so dimwitted, or that he knew her so little, that he could honestly expect for her to be happy that he was going to be working full time in a deli? She stared unseeing across the boulevard beyond the school parking lot and made herself wait before she spoke again. "Dillis," She said in as calm a voice as she could muster. "I think we need to talk. Can you pick me up after school?"

Was she imagining that he sounded reluctant? "Yeah." He said. "I just have to be at work by five."

"That's fine." She said. "It won't take that long."

꙰

After a rainy late April morning, that afternoon was bright, sunny, crisp and refreshing, and Niniane found it hard to maintain her determination to be cool to Dillis. He picked her up in front of the school, drove to her house, pulled into the driveway, rolled down the windows, turned off the ignition, and turned to her. "So you're breaking up with me." He said. "Go ahead. Let's get it over with."

Niniane did, of course, have every intention of breaking up with him, but she wasn't going to give him the satisfaction of knowing that. "Oh, don't be so dramatic." She said. "We just need to talk."

"Niniane, nothing you say is going to make me change my mind. I got offered a good job, and I'm going to take it. I was flunking most of my classes anyway, and you know it. If you don't like it, or you're too embarrassed or whatever to have a high school dropout for a boyfriend, well, I guess that's the way it is. This is what I need to do, and I'm doing it." Dillis looked her right in the eye through glasses that were still unbelievably smudged.

It was not lost on Niniane that his words were very much like the words she'd used the night before to defend her own decision. "Dillis," she said. "I just . . . " Her eyes began to sting, and fill, and she turned away and looked out of the window at the well-trimmed lawn her father mowed with the environmentally unsound riding lawnmower that he took such a childlike pleasure in riding.

Dillis's eyes widened behind his smudged eyeglass lenses. She was actually crying. For the first time since they'd been dating Dillis felt as if he really mattered. His stomach flipped and he gripped the steering wheel to keep from grabbing her and putting his lips to those unexpected and precious tears.

"Niniane," He said, and his voice cracked like a twelve year old boy's. "I . . . "

"I like you so much." She interrupted. Dillis caught his breath.

"I like you so much," She said again. "But I don't think this is healthy, Dillis. We're really different . . . more that you realize, I think. I mean . . . you know I'm going to college next year, Dillis, I'm going all the way to New Jersey, and . . . "

"I know." Said Dillis. "We've talked about all that."

"It's not just that, though, Dillis." Niniane looked down at her lap, where the passenger seatbelt was still fastened. "There's some things going on with me that . . . I just don't think you'll understand. I don't think I understand them myself."

Just as intensely as Dillis had felt overjoyed by her tears, he now felt a sickening dread. She was going to tell him that she wasn't attracted to him, that there was another guy, or girl, or whatever. He was gripped by an urge to punch a hole through his windshield. Never had he felt such a queer, unfamiliar, devastating pain. I'm in love, he realized.

"Niniane." He said. "You're a good person. I mean it."

She looked at him, evidently surprised. There were still tears on her lower lashes, and Dillis was maddened by the desire to taste them. He made himself nod reassuringly. He wanted to tell her he loved her, but he didn't want to make her feel worse. "I care about you no matter what." He said.

Niniane unbuckled her seatbelt and wrapped her arms around Dillis, pressing her cheek to his narrow bony shoulder and closing her eyes. She could not see that Dillis's face was a grimace of exquisite pain and longing. He stroked her hair until she pulled away and smiled at him as if nothing was wrong. "I'm a vegan now." She said. "So you can understand why I'm a little freaked out that you're dropping out of school to cut meat. But as long as you can respect my decisions, I guess I can respect yours . . . I just worry about your future, that's all, Dillis."

Dillis felt as if his brain were a pinball being ricocheted against bumper after bumper. "You're vegan?" He said. "Is that it?"

"What do you mean, is that *it*?" She said, her familiar, difficult self once more. "I'm *serious* about this, Dillis! It means a lot to me!" She reached for her book bag on his floorboard. "But I guess a little bit of encouragement is too much to ask. I thought you gave a damn about what's going on with me . . . "

"I do!" He cried. "I do!" He was dizzy with relief. He took off his glasses, wiped them ineffectually with his shirttail, and put them back on. "It's great!" He said. "I'm proud of you! It's terrible what they do to animals!"

Niniane's expression was that of a person accepting a suspicious package.

"I could never go without meat." He said. "But I know you can. You're amazing."

"Thanks." Niniane was happy that she was finally getting some credit for doing something difficult. She hugged Dillis again. "Call me later." She said. All was forgiven.

⌒

Niniane graduated magna cum laude, and Dillis attended the ceremony along with her parents and joined them all at the restaurant afterwards where he and Niniane shared a bland but filling vegan casserole dish. Niniane was to leave for the farm the very next Monday, and Dillis was scheduled to work overtime at the deli, so that evening was the last chance they had to spend time with one another. They drove around for a while in Dillis' car, and then walked around the empty, well-lit streets of Niniane's subdivision, occasionally arm in arm. "Are you going to miss me?" Said Niniane.

"Yeah."

"Even though I'm a vegan and a nag?"

"Well, I won't miss you nagging me." He said, even though he would.

"It's just because I care."

"I know."

They walked in silence for a while, thinking their own thoughts. A firefly lit up just above Dillis head, and reflexively he reached for it, caught it, opened his hand to look at it on his palm, then flicked it away.

"Don't hurt him!" Niniane cried.

Dillis rolled his eyes in the dark. "Oh, I didn't hurt him." He said. "He's a tough little bug."

"You don't know that." Said Niniane. "How would you like someone grabbing you out of the air and then flicking you away?"

"He started it." Said Dillis.

Niniane stopped suddenly, and her arm slipped out of Dillis'. He turned around.

"Sorry." She said in a thick voice. "I know you didn't mean to hurt him. I'm just sad. I wish I wasn't going away."

"I wish you weren't either."

They started to walk together again, unattached. "Actually, I wish you could come with me. You'd like the farm, Dillis, it's . . . special."

"I'll come visit." He said. "When I can get a few days off work."

"Oh . . . " Niniane made a wistful sound. "Oh, I really wish you could. But I don't think so, Dillis. My aunts . . . they're just really careful about who can be there . . . and they don't allow any men at all, unless they've known them forever, it took them a long time to even let my dad stay there, and you know how sweet he is. They have a kind of off and on thing going there during the year, they provide work, and shelter for women in trouble, who've been raped, or battered or stuff like that, and so they can't let just anyone know where it is . . . So . . . "

"Wow." Said Dillis.

"I'll try to convince them, Dillis, but I just don't know. They're really nice, and I know they'd like you, it's just . . . "

"It's all right." Said Dillis. "I understand."

"I'll really try." She said again, and then she laughed.

"What?" Said Dillis.

"I can just see you coming up the driveway and my Aunt Irene meeting you with her shotgun. Because that's what would happen if you just showed up."

"Well, that's not very vegan." Said Dillis.

Niniane punched him lightly on the shoulder, then kissed him. "I'll make them come around." She said. "I promise."

Chapter Two

The Middle of Nowhere

THE FARM, KNOWN FOR decades as "The Middle of Nowhere" by members of Niniane's mother's family, was an hour and a half's drive east from the city. Niniane knew the way because all of her life she paid close attention to where she was going. Several times during the drive she was obliged to redirect her father.

"Left, Daddy! Remember? It's always left turns once you cross the Robeson County line."

The aunts must have heard Horace Westvane's Buick crunching up their steep gravel driveway long before it reached the end, for by the time the farmhouse came into Niniane's view her aunts were standing on the porch steps.

Niniane ran first to Aunt May, her mother's younger sister. May was a tall, fat woman with long hair that she always wore in a grayish brown braid as thick as one of her soft, freckled forearms. She had a wide, ruddy face and an enormous bosom which Niniane was pressed into before running over to hug her long-limbed, hatchet faced Aunt Irene, May's partner, who wore her own white hair very short.

Irene grunted her greeting and placed a quick dry kiss on Niniane's forehead. Strangers were intimidated by Irene's tendency not to talk, but except for the women that her aunts sheltered, strangers seldom came to the middle of nowhere.

Niniane rushed her father and her Irene, who were shaking hands. "Let's go inside!" Niniane urged. "I'm hot."

They went inside. The familiar scent of oil soap and coffee laced with the faint, unmistakable odor of manure from Irene's boots by the washer and dryer cheered Niniane as she entered the house. She took a deep breath, then sat down at the round kitchen table.

Irene pointed to each person in turn and said, "Drink?"

"Tea." Said Niniane.

Irene pointed at Horace. "Beer?"

"No, thanks Irene. I've got my orders to get back to the city, soon as we get all of Niniane's stuff out of the car. And that's probably going to take an hour!"

Niniane peered at her father. "Why are you in such a hurry, Daddy?"

May spoke up. "Horace, at lease have something . . . it's a long drive."

"Not this time, May." Horace Westvane's clean, pink face and forehead corrugated as he grinned. "Tonight me and Thelma are going to have us a nice steak . . . It's been a long time since we've been able to have one without the meat police here giving us a hard time." He winked at Niniane, who scowled.

"We're heaving steak too." Said May, as if there was nothing wrong with that. "Too bad Thelma didn't come along. You could have saved your money."

Niniane bolted out of her seat. "May! You *promised* that you were going to be *considerate!*"

May folded her meaty arms against her meaty chest and turned to Niniane. "I promised . . . " She said. "That you wouldn't have to eat anything you don't want to eat. We have plenty of options here. And I seem to remember making it clear that you understood that your decision would be respected here, but that you would not dictate to anyone else what she will eat. Am I to understand something different now? Because, if so . . . "

"Sugar . . . " Horace Westvane's round face reddened and he shrugged and winked at May as he reached for his daughter's hand. "Don't give your aunts a hard time, now, okay? You want to be reasonable . . ."

Niniane shook off her father's hand. "I'm *being* reasonable! I'm just . . . " She hung her head so that her long hair hung down and forward to cover much of her face. She had not, of course, expected that her aunts would alter their own menu for the entire summer. May had been very clear about her own convictions regarding the vegan diet, which she considered to be unsustainable and in the long-term, unhealthy, though admirable in its attempt to foster a less hierarchical view of the organization of species. But Niniane would have thought, that on her *very first day!*

She felt her chin pucker, and she gritted her teeth.

"You can't force your lifestyle on other people." May said softly.

I *have* to! Niniane thought furiously. "I know that!" she said out loud.

The silence was heavy. Horace lifted it by saying he thought he might as well go ahead and bring Niniane's luggage in. Irene moved to assist him, and just as they were walking through the door the quiet of the farm was broken by an unusually loud and triumphant crow from one of the roosters in the chicken yard beyond the far wall of the kitchen.

"Now, that's odd." May commented. "What's he crowing for? It's almost four o'clock in the afternoon."

"That old rooster." Irene spoke out of one side of her mouth. "He's crazy."

"Wouldn't you be crazy . . . " Snapped Niniane before she could stop herself. "If you saw your wives and children butchered and eaten every day of your life?"

Her father and aunts exchanged amused glances with each other, but that was to be expected. Rome, she told herself, wasn't built in a day. "*I'll* get my luggage. Sit down, Daddy." She said, and she broke through them and beat them to the car.

꒰

Not long after that first supper, during which her aunts seemed to make a point of enjoying their cow's flesh while Niniane dutifully ate a square of grilled tofu and artichokes, Niniane excused herself. Her aunts seemed to have dismissed the earlier conflict, but Niniane had not. Though she was glad to be with her aunts, she could not help but feel that her vacation was already tainted with a new tension. It was a shame. This summer would not be like other summers at the farm, free of any real lasting disagreement. Like meat itself, those playful, lazy summers were all in the past, the unappreciated fringe benefits of childhood and dependence, where one's values and decisions were based upon those of the people around you who looked out for you at the expense, she could now see, of all who had no one to look out for them.

Niniane examined her own bereft expression as she washed her face in the upstairs bathroom. Sometimes it seemed so futile, the struggle to do something good for the world . . . maybe she was going about it the wrong way. After all, if May and Irene, who were, after all, the most socially conscious members of her family couldn't see the obvious truth, then what hope was there? Her parents' lack of understanding was one thing, and Dillis was just as complacent, but May and Irene! She felt like a failure. She pulled back her hair and slipped a hair tie around it and rinsed her face. When she covered her face with a cloth to pat it dry, in the darkness, with her mind's eye, she saw the face of Mercedes Hernandez.

Mercedes. Mercedes understood, even if no one else did. Mercedes Hernandez was the special education resource instructor at Niniane's high school, and the only other vegan Niniane knew. It was Mercedes Hernandez who took time during her planning period to answer Niniane's questions, who never made light of Niniane's sudden and selfish conversion, and who made Niniane feel as if her choice mattered. Mercedes Hernandez was an angel.

For her school service project, Niniane was assigned to report to Mercedes Hernandez' classroom for one period a day as a student aide. Her first choice had been to work on the newspaper, but all of those positions were filled. She'd entered the special education classroom the first day with not a little nervousness, half expecting some sort of juvenile bedlam, but after being welcomed by Mercedes and greeted with polite indifference by five students with what seemed to be mild intellectual deficits and who were clearly eager to please their slim, young and gorgeous teacher by behaving with far more self-control and focus than most other students in the school, Niniane soon looked forward to her special education period as the best part of her day. Her job was simply to be there and observe, and help the students with their schoolwork if their first choice of helper, Ms. Hernandez, was helping someone else. It wasn't long before Niniane became just as besotted with Mercedes Hernandez as her students were.

Mercedes Hernandez was half Dominican and half Swiss, with an MA in Special Education and a near PhD in International Studies. Mercedes Hernandez was the woman Niniane wanted to be. Only Mercedes bothered to listen to her and then help her to place her new conviction into a broader perspective without discouraging her. "It's all interconnected . . ." Mercedes told her, looking right into her eyes that fateful afternoon of the pizza incident. "The meat industry, the degradation of the earth, the Middle East conflicts, sexism, racism, homophobia, American Imperialism. It all stems from the same root . . . corporate greed. They keep us under control by convincing us we need what they have to give . . . but we don't! What we need is respect! A voice! It's not selfish to realize that you're choking to death on privilege! It's selfish not to!"

Niniane left the special education classroom that day feeling more adult than ever before in what she now recognized to be an obscenely insulated life. She knew now that she could make her own choices, and so make a positive difference in what Mercedes revealed as a terribly unjust world. Here and there throughout their time together Mercedes had told her of the atrocities she'd seen in her travels, she'd worked with a group of nuns who had been raped by soldiers at their TB Clinic in Liberia, she'd translated for the mothers of disappeared children in Chile, she'd rescued child prostitutes in Sri Lanka. "They want us to get discouraged and give up when we can't get past their traps," She told Niniane one day when Niniane was feeling the strain of having to balance her convictions with her desire to keep the peace with her family when she was obliged to go along with them to the Longhorn Steakhouse for her father's birthday.

"Who's *they*?" Niniane asked. She thought of her father, her easygoing, bald and potbellied father, who teased her for her beliefs, but who would never trap her into betraying them. He honestly believed that if she just had a salad everything would be okay. Was he 'they?' And Dillis, too?

Mercedes looked away, but Niniane could see that her aggrieved expression was that of a person who was also sad. "Anyone who tries to tell you that their way is the only way." She said. And she told Niniane that her own father ran a textile factory in the Dominican Republic, which paid its Haitian workers less than two dollars a day, and when she found out and confronted him, he had her sent to boarding school in Connecticut. "He knows he's causing misery." She said. "But he doesn't care. As long as he can drive around like a big shot in his . . . " She sighed. "Vintage Mercedes."

Niniane patted her face dry of a refreshing astringent she'd brought from home. The sharp, cold, clean smell was nice and familiar and she felt better. No, her parents and Dillis and her aunts weren't Them. And that was a beginning.

Chapter Three

Exterminator!

"MAY . . . "

The morning sunlight beamed eagerly through the window above the shallow porcelain kitchen sink as Niniane, without being prompted, helped her aunt gather and wash the breakfast dishes.

"Yes?" Said May, inspecting the pan that Niniane had just rinsed and handed to her.

"You remember the guy I told you about over Christmas?"

"I believe you did mention a guy from school. Dylan?"

Niniane looked down at the dirty utensils lying at the bottom of the sink. "Dillis."

"That's right. Dillis. With an 'i.' You know, Dilys, with a 'y' is a feminine name. It's quite common among women around my age in the British Isles . . . "

Niniane reached for a bread knife lying at the bottom of the sink, scrubbed it, rinsed it, and handed it to her aunt. "Well, he's not a woman around your age in the British Isles. He's a seventeen year old idiot in North Carolina, and he's about to ruin his whole life."

"Drugs?"

Niniane snorted. Dillis' marijuana habit didn't bother her. She would rather he gave up his deli job than give up smoking marijuana. "No. He's dropping out of school."

"Oh," said May. "Well, that doesn't sound good. What does he think he'll do? Take the GED?"

Niniane shook her head. "Who knows? He doesn't know. All he wants to do is work in a disgusting deli. He just decided, literally on the last day of school, that he wasn't going to go back next year. Can you believe that? And he expects me not to care." She glanced up at her aunt. "He's so stupid."

"Well, I'm surprised. I had no idea you were that serious about anyone."

"I'm not serious. We're just good friends."

"And that's not serious? What do your parents think about him?"

"Oh . . . He's nervous around them, so Thelma thinks he's 'sweet . . .' You know how she is . . . and Daddy asked me if he was 'slow.' They're just relieved that I finally have a boyfriend, if you know what I mean . . . "

"I know what you mean. What do they think about him dropping out of school?"

"I haven't told them."

"Oh."

Niniane rinsed a butter knife and looked out the window over the sink "I've got to talk him out of it, May. I can't stand it! I mean, I if I'm going to . . . be in a relationship or whatever with somebody, I have to respect them . . . "

May laughed. "Baby, you're seventeen! What difference does it make? It's not like you're gonna *marry* this boy . . . are you?"

"Of course not!"

"Well, then don't worry about it. Enjoy yourself. You're not his mother. If dropping out of school is the only stupid thing he wants to do, you should thank the Goddess!"

Niniane squeezed the sponge pad in her hand. If there was one thing she hated, it was being told that something she *knew* to be a big deal wasn't such a big deal. "So I should just be happy that all my boyfriend wants to do with his life is slice meat?"

"I'm sure that's not all he wants to do," said May, winking.

Niniane groaned. That was exactly the sort of silly, dismissive comment her father would make. She was suddenly depressed again.

May laughed. She put her arm around Niniane's shoulders and drew her in. "It really bothers you that much . . . ?"

Niniane nodded. "It does, May. I can't help it. It bugs me," she drew back and looked her aunt in the eye. "And that's why I was wondering . . . "

May looked back warily at her niece. "Wondering?"

"I thought it might be good if he could come stay here for a couple of days."

"Oh, no."

"Come on, May. I told you he was a nice guy . . . you can ask Mama . . . "

"She'd say no and you know it."

"Well, you should take my word for it. May, it would only be for a few days . . . I just want to have the chance to figure out *why* he's being so stupid."

"Niniane . . ."

"May, please? It's hard being out here away from everything."

May crossed her arms over her chest. "Bull."

"May! Put yourself in my shoes."

"Put yourself in mine and Irene's," said May. "You know how the people around here feel about us. And you want to have some boy come and stay! Goddess only knows what people will think. And what makes you think his parents would even allow it . . . what are they like?"

"His father's not around." Niniane said. "His mother's . . . liberal. She won't care." Niniane had never felt comfortable around Dillis' mother. She was a frail, distracted, frizzy haired woman who didn't seem to have a job.

May scowled. "Have you told him about Irene and me?"

"What's to tell? He's from *Boston*, May."

"That doesn't mean anything." May said, darkly.

Niniane sighed. Irene's breakfast plate, upon which remained half a slice of cold bacon, still sat on the counter beside the sink. Niniane had made a point of avoiding contact with this defiled dish. Now she made a point of reaching for it and scraping it, without complaint, into the old ceramic jar they used for compost. She looked at her aunt to see if this registered.

It had. "We'll see," said May. "I don't think it's such a good idea, but we'll talk to Irene, and we'll see."

Niniane knew better than to press her advantage. She nodded and the two of them finished the breakfast dishes in peace.

⌒

By the end of the morning, however, she almost lost all the ground that she gained, as right before lunchtime, the exterminator came.

The moment she saw that ridiculous vehicle, with its anthropomorphic cockroach with x's for eyes lying on its back on top of the van, Niniane knew that if she saw either one of her aunts speaking to that killer she would be unable to keep her mouth shut. That drove her to the chicken yard, which was shaded at that time in the afternoon by a large poplar tree.

She sat herself on the dusty ground of the chicken yard with her back against one of the wooden stakes that held the fence in place. She rested her chin on her knees and felt like crying. Confronting May or Irene would only ensure that Dillis never set foot on the farm. Niniane knew, anyway, what May and Irene would say to her, wielding their unanswerable carnivore logic. Termites, if there were in fact termites, would destroy the barn, and thus leave them without a space to store food for the livestock. The potential and potentially doomed termites, acting in accordance with their own nature, were themselves destroyers. If it weren't the barn they were burrowing into, it would be a tree, perhaps. Trees are also living things.

Niniane sighed. Looking into the coop, she could see that a hen sat within, its beak pointed straight at her. The expression of that hen, perched as she was so solidly on a shallow pile of straw, was territorial and hostile. Niniane felt inexplicably threatened. She bent her head and attempted to read the silly teen fashion magazine that she'd snuck along with her out of the house and into the chicken yard, but her mind wandered and she kept looking over at the hen. Niniane didn't want anyone, especially May and Irene, to know that she read these stupid magazines. It was her greatest shame. But she was addicted to them. She read every article with contempt, but she helplessly, compulsively devoured and retained the celebrity gossip, the dating tips, the formulaic articles. She groaned at the sight of the anorexic models, but her small, sharp eyes lingered over their rawboned, gaunt, empty, and yet striking faces as she tried to imagine how powerful it must make one feel to be so noticeable. Niniane had been given most of the subscriptions back when she was a loudmouthed, yet dreamy, meat-eating, chubby little girl as a gift from her grandmother Blattery. She told herself sometimes that she kept the subscriptions up out of respect for the memory of the sweet old lady, who had died of cancer when Niniane was seven. Niniane had liked her grandmother, and perhaps that was the reason that these magazines, even though she hated them, somehow cheered her up whenever she felt, as she felt that day the exterminator came, as if she were all alone in the world.

She checked on the hen, whom, she now noticed, was surrounded by a number of what appeared to be fairly recently hatched chicks, to whom their mother seemed to be paying hardly any attention. In fact, it seemed to Niniane as if the hen's attention was focused solely upon Niniane!

Despite the heat of the day, Niniane shivered. She leaned back against a post to steady herself, and as she did so it seemed to her that the hen shifted its position upon her pile of hay. It was then that Niniane caught a glimpse of the unhatched egg still lying underneath that intimidating bird. It seemed smaller than most chicken eggs, and that made it seem vaguely repulsive. Niniane felt sorry for it.

Did her feelings show on her face? Maybe they did, for the hen stood up suddenly, as if offended, and Niniane could see her thin purple legs. Niniane rose and stepped forward and watched as a tiny crack in the egg's shell lengthened, then widened, then narrowed again into invisibility.

Niniane tried to swallow, and her throat made a clicking sound. How long, she thought, was it supposed to take? To her, the struggle between the container and the contained seemed horribly suspended. Was the shell of the egg too strong? Or was the tiny life within that shell just too weak? That unfriendly hen took a step towards the egg as if to poke it with her beak, and Niniane stepped forward and reached her hand in over the egg reflexively.

The hen made a gargling sound, and Niniane snatched her hand back. But within the split second of her attempt at interference, a tiny darkness emerged from the hairline crack in the egg, withdrew, then emerged again, with an increment more of itself showing. A moment later a few shards of eggshell broke away to form a distinct hole, and out of that a tiny point appeared, withdrew, appeared again, then there was a bigger hole. There was a wobble, then the crack in the egg widened, then gaped, and then out of it fell a wet and bedraggled baby chicken, which immediately collapsed onto the hay.

Niniane exhaled against the palm of her hand that was still covering her mouth. Her fear of the hen and her dismay over the visit of the exterminator had been completely eclipsed by the sight of that monumental struggle. She started to reach into the coop to touch the newborn thing, but stopped herself almost immediately. The baby chick was so fragile looking; so naked and unfeathered. Its breathing was so rapid and shallow that she wondered if perhaps the struggle of its birth might have been too much for it. But after a few moments the damp, bedraggled thing rose upon its matchstick legs and staggered over toward its mother, who with one grand, sweeping motion of her wing, brushed it over to where the other tiny chicks, all of whom were covered with pale down and who were noticeably larger than this one, were gathered together, peeping and scratching about on the floor of the coop. Once again, Niniane felt a surge of pity that raised a lump in her throat and brought tears to her eyes. She glared at the heartless mother hen. For a moment Niniane loathed that hen with a loathing so visceral that it made her dizzy. In that moment she would gladly have seen that hen dismembered, plucked, fried, and served in a bucket. She gathered her magazines, stepped over the chicken wire fence, and walked towards the house.

As she approached the screen door of the kitchen, the exterminator came through it and winked at her. "Hey there, little lady." He drawled, and because Niniane was caught off guard, she smiled distractedly at him. As she did so a feeling of incredible loneliness seized her. Then the momentousness of witnessing the chicken hatch settled on her like a burden. What would it mean to such a man if she told him what she'd seen just then? Nothing. Even Irene and May, she knew, wouldn't share the intensity of her feelings. Something was hatched or born or killed every day of their lives on the farm. Even the little chickens' own mother couldn't care less, it seemed. It was difficult, trying to live alone amongst unbelievers.

This is a brutal, selfish world, she said to the image of the little hatchling in her head. But you'll never have anything to fear from me, she promised.

At lunch that afternoon, Niniane affected a nonchalant tone to inform her aunts that she'd witnessed the hatching of a baby chicken.

"Good for you," said Irene. "Stick around and you'll see it get its neck wrung one day."

"I'd rather see you get yours wrung!" snapped Niniane.

Irene just smiled.

Niniane glared at Irene, then May. She took her plate to the sink, pointedly avoiding eye contact with either aunt, then went outside and wandered around aimlessly for a while, until she found herself climbing back into the chicken coop to reassure herself that she really had seen something wonderful.

Chapter Four

Exploited?

As THE BRIGHT, HOT summer days went by, Niniane fell into the habit of visiting the coop in the mornings after her chores. Usually she took a magazine or her stationary along and would spend an hour or so reading and writing to Dillis or Mercedes. May noticed that Niniane was spending time in the coop, and so suggested that she might as well take on the responsibility for the chicken's care and feeding. It wasn't long before Niniane observed that the smallest chicken, whose entry into the world she had witnessed, wasn't as energetic or robust as the other hatchlings in the coop.

Niniane decided to feed him out of her own hand, cupping the feed in one upturned palm and holding him in the other. Once she started doing that, she felt that there was some improvement in the little chick's appearance. At any rate, he grew larger and steadier, and was soon gratifyingly coated in thick, yellow down. Niniane loved to feel his little heart thrumming within him when she held him in her hand, and she felt sure that she was a better mother to him than the forbidding hen who sat unblinking in her compartment in the coop for most of the day doing nothing but producing and perching on more eggs.

↬

The little chick, for his part, came to know, and to rely upon, Niniane's presence every morning. Though he hadn't the words to say or even to think so, he felt Niniane to be, despite the more constant presence of his mother the hen, the source for him of all that was vital and sustaining. The other chicks, male and female, were all stronger and more aggressive than he was, and whenever he managed to find a seed or a grub to eat, one of his brothers or sisters would rush up with all of the blithe confidence that comes of superior physical capability, and snatch it right out of his beak. With inarticulate cheeps, he would voice his distress to his mother, but she only stared into the distance, showing no more concern or even sentience than a rock. It was only on account of those soft, warm, gigantic hands from beyond the coop that the littlest chicken ever got cared for.

≈

As Charlie, (as Niniane, for lack of imagination and for the sake of alliteration, began to call him), rapidly matured, Niniane began to take him out of the coop to sit in her lap or on her shoulder as she read and wrote each morning in the peaceful and shaded, if a bit smelly, enclosure of the fenced in chicken yard. As a result of this regular break from the relentless struggle to survive among the fittest, Charlie became all the more attached to Niniane. As is usual when one creature assumes responsibility for the well-being of another, Niniane grew to depend upon the runt chick. She found herself talking to him. She read aloud from the letters that her parents sent her from Europe, she read him infrequent and maddeningly short and poorly spelled letters from Dillis, and she read from her stash of magazines. Before long she was telling him everything that came into her head. He nestled in her lap and gazed up at her with such unblinking attention that it was almost as if he understood her. It felt nice.

≈

Niniane did not imagine for one moment, of course, that the chicken could really comprehend. But one day, when the little, runt chicken was beginning to develop little spots of darkness and symmetry in his yellow down, she asked him, as conversationally as she would have asked a human being, what she should do about Dillis. "He's so frustrating, Charlie!"

At first, Niniane thought nothing of it when the chicken hopped down from her lap into the dirt. It did seem strange that he was moving himself back and forth with his beak on the ground and raising little clouds of dust. It looked as if he was trying to scratch an itch on his head. But as he paused every second or so and moved not just up and down, but incrementally from left to right, Niniane' s brow wrinkled. "Well, look at that!" She said to herself, out loud. "If I didn't know any better, I'd swear you just made the letter 'K', Charlie!"

Niniane smiled to herself and imagined that she was a guest on a television talk show discussing how she had discovered a means by which humans and non-human animals could communicate. "It wasn't long," She imagined herself saying to the interviewer "before I realized that this chicken could become a spokesperson–well, spokeschicken, for the entire animal-rights movement. By the end of the summer, we were testifying before a senate sub-committee—and it wasn't easy, but we were able to bring down the meat industry eventually . . . "

"Just think, Charlie," she said now, out loud. "We could make the world a safer place for all beings. Wouldn't that be wonderful? " Niniane smiled and wondered why the movement had never come up with such a gimmick–why not take a parrot, say, and teach him to say something like "Don't exploit me!" and take it along to marches and protests.

Niniane's brow wrinkled. But, she considered, that in itself could be exploitative.

"Hey Charlie . . . " she said to the little bird, who now stood stock still on the gravel, facing her with his left eye. " If I could teach you how to write, "Don't exploit me" in front of a Senate Subcommittee, would you feel exploited?"

The chicken turned around again and appeared to repeat the above performance. But this time Niniane watched him with real attention. Now that she had imagined it, it became difficult not to imagine that indeed, the chicken was scratching letters into the dusty ground of the chicken yard enclosure.

"What . . . " she breathed out loud, speaking with increasing amazement as the chicken moved from left to right, revealing his thought. "What . . . does . . . x . . . xploy . . . xployted mean . . . "

The chicken, incredibly, nodded his small head.

Niniane blinked.

"What does exploited mean?! What does exploited mean?!" Niniane read the letters in the dust over and over again.

Niniane stood up, and her notebook and her magazine tumbled onto the dirt. "I'm going crazy," she whispered.

She closed her eyes and rubbed them. Opening them again, she looked at the chicken, who stood in the gravel with his tiny head cocked, peering up at her with one unblinking eye. I'm imagining things, she thought. I'm dreaming.

Niniane felt a lurch in the pit of her stomach, and she covered her mouth with her hands. I have to get inside. Out of this sun, it's the sun; I'm having a stroke; I have to get inside the house. She turned and scrambled over the chicken-wire fence, but even as she did so, her vision swept once again across the lines written in the dust, registering for the first time the meaning of the first line, written above the second, which, she realized, the chicken had scratched out in answer to the question she'd asked him about what to do about Dillis.

In the spirit of the magazines that he and Niniane spent so many hours reading, the chicken had written, in emphatic, uneven letters, "Kick him to the curb, girl!"

⌒

Niniane ran into the house, up the stairs, and threw herself face down on her unmade bed.

⌒

But after only a second she got off of the bed, clenched her fists, and began pacing the length of the small room. She locked the door.

She turned and looked across the sunlit room out of the screened window. Outside a large black bird flew across her line of vision from one tree into another. She stared between these trees, into the distant woods, and tried to reason with herself.

Now, I can't be going crazy. I wouldn't question what I saw if I was crazy. So maybe I did see it, and there's a reasonable explanation.

She realized that her breathing was shallow, and forced herself to breathe deeply.

Maybe he was just copying me. He's seen me write, and maybe I've used those words together, and I just can't remember.

She shook her head like one troubled by a fly. Her mind mercilessly prodded her. She knew that she'd never, all this summer, spoken or written or even read the word "exploited." It was a word that meant a lot to her, and one not often encountered, particularly within teen magazines. She would have remembered using that word, she was sure of that.

So the chicken had, of its own accord, asked her a question.

What does xployted mean?

Niniane sat down on the very edge of her bed and continued to stare out the window. She gazed, thinking of nothing for a long time, until, inexplicably, her aunt Irene's teasing hatchet face appeared to her mind's eye. Despite a real loss of confidence in her own grasp upon reality, Niniane began, without realizing it, to scheme. If chickens, or even one chicken, were capable of even the simulation of conversation, then even that thoroughly unsentimental Irene would hesitate to take the life of such an exceptional animal. It would be like killing a parrot, or a dolphin, or a monkey. It occurred to Niniane that if she could convince her aunts that their coop contained such a smart chicken, it might lead them to think twice about what they were doing.

The possibility of finally triumphing over her aunts' complacency galvanized her. She unlocked her door and scrambled down the stairs and out the kitchen door to the chicken yard, hoping, now, with all of her heart, to accept the reality that just a moment ago she'd feared.

In the meantime, left alone and vulnerable on the ground of the chicken yard, the chicken called Charlie realized that his attempt at communication had backfired. He hopped instinctively back into the coop and back to the side of his mother, who continued to stare, sphinx like, into the distance as the rest of her brood played and slept and fought and fed all around her.

But Charlie, as soon as he rejoined them, felt, to his alarm, that he was returning, not to familiar surroundings, but to a shadowy, silent netherworld. Once again he stood apart, feeling vulnerable and conspicuous as never before as he regarded his own family. He saw, now, as they did not, the transience of their actions. He saw himself, as if he were still one of them, scrabbling about the henhouse, nuzzling the mother, preening his fledgling feathers, pecking at the leftover chicken feed seeds scattered among the sawdust of the coop. Even if he could survive there now, what of it? The one who had reached for him and who made him special had gone away. He had frightened her. He now had thoughts to express, but no one to express them to. For his own kind, even for his silent mother, it was enough to feel—self-expression was unnecessary. But something more had been shared with him, something meant to be shared with another. He knew he had been given a name: his name was Charlie. But to whom did it matter now? Not to these other chickens, for whom he was just a harmless irritant.

The littlest chicken regarded the huge forest in the distance. He knew, by recalling an article Niniane had read to him earlier in the week that these feelings of hopelessness, isolation, and depersonalization were characteristic of a state of mind called depression. He blinked several times and longed for the warmth, quiet, dimness, and simplicity of the egg he had fought his way out of not long ago.

Charlie folded his skinny legs underneath his abdomen and perched in this position at the edge of the henhouse. He saw in his mind's eye the giant coop out of which the girl with the soft, warm hands came to him every morning. It was hard, he found, to put into words and images those feelings that her advent, presence, and even her absence aroused in him. He likened them now vaguely to a breeze coursing across his feathers or the slosh of a recent swallow of cool water in his gizzard. The warmth of her hands, the murmur and lilt of her voice, her sharp, sanitized, mammalian scent, the miracle of her affection for and gentleness with him, all this was beyond his power to describe even to himself. He could only recall, only feel them. He wanted these things as he remembered once wanting feed, water and the closeness of his mother. But he had no power to have them, for the girl had run across a vast expanse of ground into an enormous coop that he would never be able to reach, let alone enter. He was as doomed now as if he had been taken from the chicken yard and flung into the forest. He was lost without her. His head drooped. Why had she done it? Why had she chosen him out of all the others and read to him if she didn't want him to understand and respond? In answering her question to him, had he committed some unforgivable transgression? Was one meant, once granted the ability to speak one's heart, to despite that ability, keep it to oneself? Was the self to be the self's alone?

But she talked to me! Charlie thought. It isn't right! It isn't fair!

Charlie shut his eyes, trying, in this naive fashion, to cut off his capacity for thought. But all that shutting his eyes did was to blind him to the fact that the girl was running back to him—it was not until he heard her footsteps in the gravel and smelled her excited perspiration that he realized that he had been remembered.

⁊

She held him up to her face for a long time, and stared at him. Back in the coop, facing the impossible reality of him, his smallness—he did not even fill her palm-, his face incapable of expression, his tiny head which couldn't conceivably harbor a brain large or sophisticated enough for language, Niniane once again began to doubt her sanity. She closed her own eyes for a moment and, taking a breath; she bent and set him on the ground in front of the chicken coop. Then she knelt and spoke, as one might with a deaf person or a foreigner, with exaggerated enunciation. "Charlie. I want you to write something for me. Something that will show that you're not just copying. I need to know that you really understand what you're doing. Can you write something like that? Anything! Please . . . "

Charlie's beak was already moving in the dust. Niniane's jaw hung as she breathed out the words forming on the ground before her. It was a phrase that Charlie had no doubt seen in one of the teen magazines, but she knew that he understood them and that they were meant for her.

Will you go out with me?

～

Niniane and Charlie sat down together, right there in the dirt of the chicken coop. Niniane spoke freely, and every once in a while Charlie would scratch a question into the gravel, for there were still many things that Charlie, despite the teen magazines, did not understand.

So. He scratched. *I'm what's called a chicken. And you're what's called a woman. And that's why you won't go out with me?*

"Charlie!" exclaimed Niniane. "Do you even realize what going out with someone means?"

From the magazines, Charlie had gathered that 'going out' with someone entailed unrestricted access to their time and attention. But perhaps there was even more to it than that. *What does it mean?*

"It means . . . " Niniane searched the cloudless sky. "It means . . . that you want to be . . . intimate with someone . . . in all kinds of ways." She frowned. "It means, to be honest, that at least at some point, you want to . . . Oh, Charlie, this is impossible. Just trust me. You don't want to 'go out' with me. We're different species."

What's species?

"Oh, God. I don't know, exactly. It just means that we're two different kinds of animal, that we can't . . . well, basically, we can't reproduce. We can't come together, like . . . like a man and a woman, or a rooster and a hen, to make little combinations of ourselves."

That's what people in the magazines want to do?

"Charlie, those magazines aren't important. Don't pay any attention to them. They're just . . . propaganda." She could anticipate his question. "They're just trying to sell you . . . or women . . . the idea that you aren't good enough as you are, that you have to look different, or act different, or buy certain things to make yourself attractive. They're lies, Charlie, nothing but lies." She felt suddenly exhilarated, having enlightened the little chicken thus. "I don't know why I bother reading them. I won't read them any more, I can tell you that. I've had it with their narrow, racist . . . *speciesist* standards of beauty."

Charlie knew what that word meant, having come across it in every magazine. Inspiration struck him.

You're beautiful.

Niniane blushed. "Oh, my God, how funny! You're trying to flatter me ..."

Flatter? Charlie naturally associated the term with the quality of flatness, and so was puzzled. There was certainly nothing flat about Niniane.

"Never mind ..." Niniane regarded the chicken with affection tinged with not a little alarm. For such a baby chicken he certainly had chutzpah. Clearly it was time to broaden his sphere of acquaintance.

"Charlie." She said. "Let me ask you something. If I promise you that nothing bad will happen ... that you'll be safe ... will you write to other people the way you write to me? I swear you can trust them; they're my aunts ... they're my family. They won't do anything to hurt you."

Charlie's response was immediate. *If you want me to.* He scratched.

Niniane felt once again that spark of alarm that comes of knowing that one is being trusted. She took another deep breath. "All right. Get ready to meet May and Irene."

Chapter Five

The Encyclopedia

WHENEVER HE WAS ASKED, later on, about what it was like to all of a sudden find himself out of the world of the chicken coop and in the world of human society, Charlie would always remark that it was no more strange than hatching from his shell into the dangerous world beyond. But at the time that Niniane swept him up off the gravel into her arms and bounded with him out of the coop, across the front yard and into the farmhouse, Charlie was terrified. The scenery around him changed so suddenly and rapidly that he had no time to collect his bearings before Niniane had plopped him down on the kitchen table. He sat there for a moment, too dizzy to take note at all of his surroundings while Niniane bolted out of the kitchen to summon her aunts.

"Hey!" she called. She caught her breath, swallowed. "Get in here! You're not going to believe it, but it's true!" She came back into the kitchen with two much larger human beings right behind her. Somehow Charlie had an innate sense that the expressions on their faces meant that they were not particularly happy to be interrupted from whatever it was they had been doing.

"Look at that baby chicken." Niniane indicated Charlie. "Well, guess what! He can *write!*"

Niniane, her eyes shining, regarded her aunts with an expression of absolute triumph, patted Charlie's head, then grabbed each aunt by the wrist and led them to the kitchen table. With the sunlight from the large kitchen windows streaming past them, the three women formed one dark mass, and for the first time since coming inside Charlie was afraid. Niniane by herself, even in the beginning, had been a lovely, fragrant, life-giving if enormous presence, but this collection of female humanity, of which she seemed so absolutely a part, was terrifying in its bulk in comparison to himself. Charlie felt an overwhelming urge to retreat. He backed away, to the furthest perimeter of the round breakfast table, and stuck his head under a woven placemat. Niniane backed out of the envelope of her aunts, and came around to him, lifted up the placemat, and guided his eye to meet hers.

"What's the matter, Charlie?" she said.

Charlie stood up and trotted closer to her. Niniane picked him up off the kitchen table and held him to her bosom.

Her Aunt May was the first to speak. "Niniane. Put that chicken down."

Niniane frowned. "Why?" She demanded.

"Because you're about to smother it, for one thing."

Niniane kissed the top of Charlie's head, and set him back down on the table. His heart sank within him, but Niniane did not move from where she stood beside the table, facing the aunts, whom Charlie couldn't regard without nervousness. But the two older women were not looking at him at all, but at Niniane. Suddenly it struck Charlie that there was something about them, something about the sunlight and the wood paneling of the kitchen walls and cabinets, about the smell of eggs and bacon and coffee that was hauntingly familiar. Something about being where he was at the moment . . . in this house, among these women, on this table, even though he had no idea what was going to happen even within the next few minutes, felt right to him. Proper. For the first time since Niniane had run away from the coop that first time he had written to her, Charlie began to relax. Niniane would protect him.

"I know you're gonna think I'm up to some stunt," Niniane said, her voice still high and breathless. "But I'm not, and I can prove it. All you have to do is take this chicken—he really does like to be called Charlie, by the way—out into the chicken yard and ask him to write something in the gravel for you, and he'll do it. Believe me, I didn't even know myself that he could write, and god knows I wasn't trying to teach him. I just happened to be out there writing a letter to Dillis and thinking out loud, and wondering what to say when Charlie started writing in the dirt! Come on . . . I'll show you." She made a motion to scoop up Charlie, but May reached over to stop her.

"Hold it." May said. "Niniane . . . let me see that chicken."

"No!" said Niniane, surprising even herself by shouting. "You'll hurt him!" And as a matter of fact she would not in that moment have handed her precious Charlie over to Mercedes Hernandez herself. Charlie was *her* discovery!

"Niniane." May said firmly. "I want to have a look at this chicken—this chicken that hatched on *my* farm in the coop that *Irene* built with her bare hands—that you have taken—asking no one—out of that coop where it belongs and brought into my house. I don't care if this chicken wrote Gone With the Wind–it could still have mites. Let me see it. Trust me, I'm not gonna hurt 'Charlie.'"

Irene snorted.

"Stop it, Irene," said May. She had taken Charlie and was holding him now up over her face in the sunlight. "Well, it's definitely a cockerel."

"I *told* you that," Niniane said. "I knew it was a boy, I didn't have to look. He acts just like a boy . . . he even asked me *out.*"

Irene howled, which caused Charlie to squawk and flap his wings wildly enough to cause May to let him drop back down onto the table, and he hid his head once again under Irene's napkin.

Irene stopped laughing.

After a moment, Niniane lifted the napkin and peeped underneath it. "Charlie, I'm sorry. I embarrassed you, didn't I? I shouldn't have said that. "

May whispered. "She's actually *apologizing*! What is going on here?"

Niniane picked up Charlie and went out the screen door and walked with him toward the coop.

The aunts followed.

↬

They all watched, holding themselves still as statues as Charlie meticulously scratched his greeting to the two aunts into the gravel of the chicken yard.

I'm Charlie. He wrote. *I know this is your farm and it's very nice. Niniane has been taking good care of me. I'm glad to meet you both.*

The two women stared down at the gravel, openmouthed and silent until Irene breathed a long low whistle.

"Jesus H. Christ!" Said May.

"I told you!" Gloated Niniane.

May shook her head, then bent her knees and squatted down on the gravel. She looked up at Niniane. "If this *is* some animal rights stunt, you better tell me now, or I swear I'll wring your neck," she said. She looked back at the chicken, who really did seem to have an air of intelligence.

"Uh . . . Charlie?" Her voice was unusually high. "Can the other chickens . . . well, are they like you? If we asked them to, would they write something for us like you just did?"

Charlie stood still. He cast his mind back to his first day or so out of the shell, when he came to recognize that he was one of many others like himself, and that his every need was not going to be provided for. He remembered seeing the seeds and kernels of corn scattered about the floor of the coop, and he remembered feeling instinctively his need to consume as many of them as he could manage to find in order to have something inside of him to keep him from . . . from what . . . disappearing? He remembered the sense of panic, the sense of all consuming desperation that arose within him when he realized that all of the other creatures like him in the coop needed exactly the same little grains that he needed. But there was only so much to go around, and due to his late hatching and smaller size and general inadequacy in the face of competition, he sensed that, left to himself, he probably would never manage to have all that he needed to stay alive. Back then he had known of no way to communicate his need to anyone, even to his mother. Watching the others, it was clear to him that the language of the chicken coop was not much more than silence and a number of peeps and rapid, frantic gestures that meant, vaguely, "Get out of my way."

I don't think so. Charlie scratched his reply. *I'm unique. I'm fashion forward.*

May read the chicken's reply aloud, twice, and stood up. She regarded Niniane with real bewilderment.

"*Fashion forward*?" May shuddered in the heat of the July afternoon. "Where the hell did he pick *that* up . . . ? I can't believe this . . . What do you think, Irene?"

Irene said nothing.

Niniane twirled with excitement. "See! I *told* you! Now maybe you'll listen to me when I tell you that animals have feelings! And Charlie's the proof! And he's going to change the world! No more animal captivity, no more animal slavery, no more suffering! Charlie, you're the Messiah!"

Charlie bobbed his head. He wanted to share Niniane's excitement, but he didn't quite understand what she was excited about. He was about to put his beak to the ground and ask Niniane what a messiah was, but before he had the chance, there was a low rumbling noise that turned out to be coming from May.

"Wait one minute." May crossed her arms against her chest. "Niniane! Quit that scuffling. You're raising dust, and it's getting up my nose . . . now listen to me. This is my farm, and this is my livestock, and I don't care if this chicken can write War and Peace, I don't appreciate your attitude, miss. There's nothing wrong with how we treat our animals here and you know it."

"May!"

"Don't interrupt. And before you start calling me a carnivore and a murderer, just *listen*. Beyond the fact that this is my farm, this chicken is not yours to decide his fate. Now, here we both agree. If this chicken has intelligence—and it looks as if he does—then he has a mind of his own, just like you and me. Who are you to tell him how he should feel! A chicken messiah! Get a hold of yourself, Niniane!"

"May, he can write! He can tell the world firsthand what it's like to be an animal in captivity!"

"Niniane, this chicken is not an animal in captivity. You act like I'm running a concentration camp here! What do want from me? I keep these animals clean and fed, they have a vet come in every few weeks, they're comfortable, not overcrowded, well treated . . . and yes, a lot of them get sold to producers, and some of them *we* eat. That doesn't mean we're going to eat Charlie—and to be honest, I'll probably never be able to eat . . . poultry ever again. But you know as well as I do animals in the wild have it a lot rougher. In fact, I'll bet you that the animals on this farm have on average a longer life span than on any farm in the south! Maybe *you* think this place is a pit of hell . . . " May put her hands on her hips, "But why don't we just ask Charlie?"

With not a little effort, she knelt down again in front of Charlie. "Now. Charlie. Is this such a bad place to be? Do you feel like you haven't been treated well by us?"

Charlie remembered how afraid he was of his own brothers and sisters before he made the acquaintance of the human race. *Not at all.* He scratched, quickly.

May rose, triumphant. "There! Right there in black and white. You see!"

Niniane was gripped by a sudden, unendurable impulse to pick up Charlie and spike him like a ball against the dusty ground. "Fine!" She shouted. "I'll just shut up, then. Forever. You all and Charlie can do all the talking, you just figure everything out, since you know everything!"

Niniane turned away and her shoulders slumped forward and heaved. Charlie stood now with the aunts, and gazed at her. He wished he knew what she wanted him to say.

May sighed. "Come on, Ninny," she said. "We know you mean well. You know more about how animals are treated on a large scale, I'll give you that. But right now, baby, we need to think about Charlie. You heard . . . saw what he said. He likes his little life here. He's perfectly content. Niniane, if you make a big deal of this, someone will come in here and take him away. Now, is that what you want?"

Niniane shook her head.

May put an arm around her niece's shoulders. "There you go. You're excited. I am too! But what Charlie needs right now is for all of us to take it easy. This is no time to make big moves that we might regret . . . "

"But what are we going to do now?"

"I don't know, baby." Said May. "What do you want to do now, Charlie?" She asked the chicken.

Charlie only knew he didn't want to be left behind in the chicken yard. He wanted to go wherever his beloved went and never see another chicken again. He wondered how best to get this across to the women, and in the end he decided upon a phrase from one of Niniane's magazines that had stuck with him. *I'm ready to move on to the next chapter in my life.* He wrote.

∽

Charlie's first free act upon entering forever into the human world was to relieve himself on the living room floor.

Niniane was the first to realize what he'd done.

"Charlie." She walked over, bent down, and whispered to him. "I hate to tell you this, but you can't do what you just did in front of people. I don't want to embarrass you, but . . . well, you've kind of disgraced yourself. I guess it's different for birds. For us when we . . . when nature calls . . . it's supposed to be private. Do you understand what I mean?"

Charlie blinked. He bent his head and began scratching with his beak on the hardwood floor. He stopped and looked up at her, apparently unaware that he had made no mark.

"Oh!" Niniane turned to her aunts, who were standing in the doorway. "How's he going to say anything without any dirt in here?"

"Good question," said May. She was staring at the small puddle of chicken do on her living room floor. "Maybe having him in here with us isn't such a good idea . . . "

"May!"

May held her hand up. "All right, never mind. But I won't have him scratching all over my hardwood floors with his beak. He's made enough of a mess already."

"Maybe if we could spread just a little bit of gravel . . . over in that corner, he could . . . "

"No." said May.

Niniane turned desperately to Charlie, who could only stand and blink. As the moments passed without a sound from anybody, and no movement from Charlie, Niniane grew panicked. "May, he doesn't know what to do!" She said finally. "And even if he did, he couldn't tell us! Look, he's paralyzed!"

"Wait." Said Irene. Everybody looked at her. She walked over and held her hand, palm up, underneath Charlie's beak.

Charlie bent his head and traced the letters gingerly at first, then firmly and distinctly into Irene's palm. *Hi Irene.* He said.

Irene repeated the chicken's greeting and then smiled.

"Just like Helen Keller!" said May. "Of course!"

Irene stood and stared at her palm, then shrugged and cracked her knuckles. Niniane and May sat cross-legged on the floor in front of Charlie, and he traced their names into their hands.

"This is great," said May finally. "But how are we going to deal with his pooping?"

What is pooping? Spelled Charlie.

Irene indicated the chicken's dropping.

People don't poop?

"Not where everyone can see," said Niniane.

"Or smell it," said Irene.

"Never mind that." said May. "What you have to learn, Charlie, is that there is a time and a place for everything. And the time and the place for that type of thing is definitely not on our living room floor."

Charlie took this in. He had become accustomed, in his short life, to the ease with which he had formerly relieved himself in the coop, where his productions were nothing compared to those of his more vigorous and well fed brothers and sisters. It had, in fact, seemed to him that depositing some waste was a good way to establish that this was where he felt at home.

Niniane sensed his confusion. "It's nothing personal, Charlie. It's just the way people are. I guess it's just another one of those ways that we're different. If we don't keep our waste products away from us . . . we get sick. I guess, in a way, we're not as strong as chickens. "

"It's not a big deal, hon." May tentatively patted the chicken's head. "None of us are born knowing these things. We all have to learn."

ᔦ

After that was settled, Niniane took Charlie on a tour of the entire farmhouse, the first stop being the bathroom on the ground floor. "That's where we relieve ourselves, Charlie," she explained. "That thing's called a toilet. We poo into that, and then we flush it—we just flip that little knob here— and it all gets whooshed away."

Where does it go then? Asked Charlie, after Niniane explained to him what the word 'whooshed' meant.

"I don't know," said Niniane, not a little testily, for she as if she should know. For the rest of the tour Charlie did not ask many more questions, although he did ask her if he could sleep on the gigantic, upraised, soft plane that she told him she slept on.

"I don't think so," she said. "I toss and turn a lot and I'd crush you."

It was decided that a corner of the downstairs living room would be made into a sleeping/living area for Charlie. He liked the view afforded by the sliding glass door that opened out onto the back porch of the farmhouse. Niniane tapped on the glass with her finger. "Glass," she said. "You can see through it, but you can't go through it. It's one of the most useful things that the human race has come up with."

Charlie stretched out his neck and tapped the glass door with the tip of his beak. Its cool solidity reminded him of his eggshell. *It's hard.* He said into Niniane's hand.

"Yes," she said. "So that nothing can get in that we don't want in here." *Like what?*

Niniane gazed out the window for a moment. "All the things that humans can't live with. It's hard for us to cope with extremes, Charlie. We can't take the heat, we can't take the cold. We can't take too much sun, we can't take too much rain. We think we're the most superior creatures on earth, Charlie, but really, we're not. We're just the best—or the first—to come up with so many different ways to keep ourselves safe. When you think about it, everything in this house was invented just to keep us safe from everything that we didn't invent . . . "Niniane paused, and for a moment seemed troubled. "What I was thinking, Charlie, was that I can pull out one of the drawers from that old dresser in the garage, and put some straw in it, and you could sleep in that. We'll put you over in the corner next to the fire-place, where it's nice and cool, and . . . "

Niniane was pointing to the corner with her free hand, so it was awhile before Charlie could get his beak close enough to her hand to indicate that he wanted to say something.

Can I sleep by the glass?

Niniane's eyebrows rose. "By the door? Well, I guess so. Why, Charlie? Do you want to be able to look out at night?"

Yes.

"But, Charlie, you'll be asleep, won't you? And, actually, we keep the curtains closed at night so that no one can see in."

What are curtains?

Niniane pulled the cord and demonstrated the curtains for Charlie. They were very old curtains, from Niniane's grandmother's day, and she thought them tacky, their pattern consisting of tiny, fading cornucopias against a cream background. Charlie was mesmerized by the sway of the fabric as it fell into stillness after meeting in the middle. Niniane set him on the floor.

Charlie stuck his head underneath the hem of the curtain and found himself looking out across the deck into the backyard of the farmhouse. To the left, far away, he could see his brothers and sisters scrabbling about the chicken yard. He looked out for a long time, then backed out from under the curtain into what was now a very dim living room. Niniane, who was standing behind him with a fingernail between her teeth, sat on the carpet and held out her hand.

"I guess you won't feel so far away from home if you can see it . . . is that it, Charlie?"

What exactly is home? He asked.

Niniane chewed on the end of a lock of her hair before answering. "It's . . . I guess it's where you want to be when you're somewhere that you don't want to be . . . it's where you're . . . it's where you know you are safe and loved, I guess . . . "

Then that isn't home. Wrote Charlie.

꒰

That evening, all four inhabitants of the farmhouse dined together at the round kitchen table. A place to the left of Niniane and opposite May had been set for Charlie; the chair being too low, he simply sat on the placemat and ate from a saucer of chicken feed, while Niniane (and also May and

Irene; to avoid an argument on this first night) ate a vegetable casserole that Niniane had prepared and frozen earlier in the week. The conversation, of necessity, excluded Charlie, for whom it really was impossible to talk and eat at the same time. But Charlie ate hardly anything, so absorbed was he in following the debate between Niniane and May about how he should be educated.

"Online." said Niniane. "It's obvious. You two need to accept reality and let me use the computer."

"Nope." Said May. "Farm business only. You know that, Niniane."

"May, for God's sake! This is important! I'm not going to just play around, I'm going to show Charlie the world!"

"I'm not going to argue with you, kid. You know how we feel." May wiped her mouth. "Now, my suggestion is that you simply read together . . . "

"That's what we've *been* doing!"

May peered at her. "You know, as a matter of fact, I've been wondering . . . How is it that you happened to be out in the chicken yard *reading?* And what *were* you reading, anyway?"

Niniane blushed and looked down at her plate. She hated to lie, but she would if she had to. "Different things," she said. "And I wrote letters . . . since you won't let me even check my email . . . "

"Give it up." Said May cheerfully. "Anyway, as I was saying, I think the encyclopedia would be the best thing. Our set is old, but . . . "

"It's more than old! It's from 1973! And it's missing D, and R, and . . . "

"LIKE I WAS SAYING, our set is old, and now that they have all those fancy computer ones these days, we can get a new set fairly cheap. I heard one advertised on the radio swap meet the other day, and for some reason I thought about getting it, and now that Charlie's with us, I think I will. Consider it your welcome gift, Charlie . . . "

Niniane seethed. There was so much on the web that Charlie needed to see! She was going to take him to the PETA website, and the site for the Humane Society, and Greenpeace, and . . . there was so much she wanted him to know, so much that he could do to stop all of the terrible things that were happening to animals all over the world as soon as he knew enough and was ready enough and *angry* enough to *speak out* . . . And yet once again, May and Irene in their stubborn complacency and paranoia about technology were standing in the way . . . it was infuriating. An encyclopedia for god's sake! No other source of information that she could imagine even approached it for conventionality. It would be up to her to *really* explain the world to Charlie.

As if she were reading Niniane's mind, May spoke into her thoughts. "Niniane, baby, if you would just think about it, you'd realize it's the best way. The encyclopedia isn't perfect, but it's comprehensive, and it's fairly unbiased, these days, and you know as well as I do that any idiot can put whatever they want on the internet. It's too easy to just see what you want to see on there . . . "

"How would *you* know?!"

"Niniane, you know what? I think you need to give me some credit for having some idea of how to help people . . . or chickens, for that matter . . . help themselves. Maybe I never taught a chicken to read, but I haven't been on this farm all my life, you know. I started the first battered woman's hotline in this state, remember that. And I've made mistakes, and I've learned from them. And most of the mistakes I've made had a lot to do with thinking that I knew best. I was seventeen once myself, Niniane. And I thought I knew everything. Believe me. You can ask your mother sometime."

"Maybe I'm not like you." Niniane's said. "Maybe I don't think I know everything. I don't . . . but I do know right from wrong, and . . . "

"That's what you think," said May. "But you'll learn. In the meantime, think about what's best for Charlie."

"What's best for Charlie is that he doesn't get slaughtered. Like he would have if he hadn't started talking to me!"

May put down her fork. "Niniane, do you want to help this chicken learn, or do you want to indoctrinate him?"

"You know the answer to that, May!"

"Well, can you think of any other way to let him learn at his own pace than giving him a set of encyclopedias?"

There was a long silence. "No," said Niniane finally.

"I'll be happy to buy him that set I heard about, then. It's the latest edition, and it's not missing anything."

"All right," said Niniane.

May looked at her niece with exasperated fondness. "I'll call about it in the morning. In the meantime, why don't the three of you go watch some TV. That should be interesting for Charlie, as if today hasn't been interesting enough. I'll clean up."

Irene and Niniane and Charlie went into the living room and sat themselves in front of the television for the next three hours. Charlie had many questions about what he saw, and much to think about as he lay in his hay-filled dresser drawer in front of the sliding glass door.

⤚

That first night in the farmhouse was a long and mostly sleepless one for Charlie. He spent much of it staring out of the sliding glass door at the darkness beyond, wondering what his mother and his brothers and sisters in the coop were doing. He wondered if they even noticed that he was missing, if they felt anything. It seemed to him that they wouldn't, for none of them, not even his mother, had ever expressed any emotion towards him other than irritation. In the chicken coop, except for those warm, eternal moments in Niniane's hand or lap, Charlie had always felt like he was in the way.

Here in the farmhouse, things were different . . . better even, but now that it was dark and he was left to himself, he felt lonesome. As he stared out the window he lifted his gaze to the distant stars and to the sickle moon that hung just above the dark line of the treetops. He had never had trouble sleeping in the coop. As fraught as his life had been with a sense of alienation and defeat, he had never experienced such absolute solitude as this. It was so still and hushed behind this sliding glass door. Even the sounds familiar to him that reached him from the outside; the shrill chirping of the crickets and the infrequent moan of the owl seemed muted and ghostly on account of the barrier. He could hear nothing from the part of the house above his head, where the three women were sleeping. Had he expected that Niniane would be with him even in the night? He supposed he had. But she was upstairs in her massive bed, unreachable.

He left the glass door and returned to his dresser drawer with this sense of separation from Niniane like a raw spot in his mind. He remembered her soft hands reaching into the coop and lifting him out into the sun as gently and naturally as if they were his own wings. He remembered resting in her lap, breathing in her scent, feeling the warmth of her body. Sometimes he would peer up at her face while she wrote her letters or read her magazine, (always out loud; for his edification, or so he came to believe) and at such times it seemed to him that she was the living essence of all beauty and warmth. Had he known what a goddess was, he would have considered her to be one, a being of infinite generosity that had chosen him, alone of all his brood, to be her devotee. But seeing her now, in what he knew to be her element, the farmhouse, among those Beings Much Like Herself whom she called May and Irene, was very unsettling. In their company, aspects of his beloved were revealed to him that were far from her usual gentleness and generosity. In the context of their household, he saw that she was relatively without much influence; he saw that somehow at the same time she felt superior to them. Just as he'd been when in the coop, with his brothers and sisters, Niniane with her aunts seemed incapable of expressing what was deepest within her. He recalled how she had fought against the encyclopedias, which, for his part, he could hardly wait to see! They sounded a lot like the magazines she read, but better; according to May, these 'encyclopedias' would tell him *everything*. Even in the early days, earlier that week, he had sensed that the magazines had limited relevance to his life. He wondered if Niniane had been hoping to continue his education with those magazines. But she had mentioned something called the 'internet,' something that the aunt called May clearly disapproved of. It bothered him that his beloved and her aunt did not agree.

Charlie sat awake in his makeshift bed and opened and closed his beak nervously. An old fear from earlier that afternoon was resurfacing in the dark. Had he, by speaking up, ruined everything? He could tell that some of the things he asked made Niniane unhappy. Would he, in the end, lose his savior and his beloved by gaining knowledge? He resolved that this would not be so. Surely there was a way for him to delve into the magnificent world that had admitted him into itself through his acquisition of language without hurting anyone. If he could learn how to read and write, surely he could learn how to please Niniane.

He closed his eyes; and to his mind came an image of Niniane, lying in her great bed upstairs, blissfully asleep. He felt almost as he was in the room with her, sharing her tranquility and beauty. Consoled by this fantasy, Charlie drifted off to sleep.

⌣

Upstairs Niniane tossed and turned, unable to relax in her great, queen sized four-poster bed. The events of the day had simply been too over-whelming. More than once she had to swallow the urge to tiptoe downstairs and look at Charlie just to make sure that he was real, that it was all true. And yet, each time the temptation to reassure herself got too strong to re-sist, it would fade. She would sit up in bed and run her hands up and down her stubbly legs to ease their restlessness. Of course it was all real, and in the end, given her convictions, why should it surprise her that a chicken could express feelings? And who better for an intelligent chicken to reveal himself to than a person committed to animal rights? Despite her doubts about there being any sort of design to the Universe, the whole thing felt providential. 'Whatever's out there, thank you." She whispered in the darkness, as her mind's eye—half dreaming—perceived, seated upon a cloudy throne, a twinkling-eyed and distressingly male and old and bearded Deity.

Chapter Six

Old Mortality

LATER ON THAT WEEK Charlie and Niniane sat on the front porch swing reading the 'C' volume of the Encyclopedia together.

"I never realized," Niniane shut the heavy book on her knees and looked down at Charlie, who was sitting on her lap. "How many important things begin with the letter 'C'. China. Communism. Cancer. Churchill. Corn. And, of course, Chickens."

And Christianity. Spelled Charlie into her hand. *That one was interesting.*

"I suppose so," said Niniane. "If you like that kind of thing. I, for one, don't."

Why not? Spelled Charlie.

"Religion," Niniane squared her shoulders. "Is one of those things that makes people get angry with each other for no reason."

Why?

"Because," said Niniane after some thought. "You just naturally want other people to believe what you believe."

Charlie gazed down the sloping driveway. All week now, Niniane and he had spent at least an hour or so of every morning leafing through the Encyclopedia. Although she didn't say so, Niniane was surprised at just how much she herself was learning from reading straight through the encyclopedia with Charlie, and they had only gotten so far as the first volume of 'C'! Charlie enjoyed these too brief times alone with Niniane, who spent the afternoons swimming in the modest above ground pool that her grandfather had bought years ago specifically for her use during the summers.

Maybe, he spelled into her hand, after a period of silence in which the girl and the chicken watched a crow strut back and forth across the narrow gravel driveway, *Maybe I could look at that one a little more when you go swimming.*

"Look at that what?"

Charlie paused for a moment to recollect the exact spelling of the word. *That Christianity.*

Niniane scowled. "Charlie why would you want to read about *that?* It's depressing."

Why?

Niniane groaned. The word 'why,' especially since they had been reading the Encyclopedia, was cropping up in Charlie's conversation with wearying regularity.

"Oh, Charlie, I don't know." Niniane lifted Charlie from her lap, put him beside her on the porch swing, and stood up, leaving the C volume, open to the three and 1/2 page article on Christianity. "Go ahead and read it, then. I need a break anyway."

Charlie couldn't begin to read until the porch swing, which Niniane had so abruptly slipped out of, stopped swaying, but soon enough he was quite absorbed in the Encyclopedia's description of the fundamental forms and tenets of a system of beliefs and rituals called Christianity.

⤸

One afternoon, following a dramatic thunderstorm that broke the heat wave, Niniane decided to take Charlie out across the east meadow to the tiny fenced in graveyard where many of her Blattery ancestors were buried. The little square of sparsely grassed, sandy soil was irregularly studded with grave markers of differing sizes and shades of brown and gray. Those grave markers had always appealed to Niniane, poking out of the soil at slight angles like curious little animals poking out of their burrows. In previous summers, whenever she felt she needed to be alone, but not too alone, she would steal away to the graveyard and wander among the headstones like a restless spirit, familiarizing herself with the names and dates of her mother's forebears. Three summers ago, driven by instinct, she had come to the graveyard alone just an hour or so after her first period started. The presence of those headstones, some of them moss covered and illegible, seemed somehow to be an appropriate witness to this inevitable, yet nonetheless jarring and not altogether unpleasant new aspect of her life. Now she wanted Charlie to know who and what came before him.

The afternoon was warm and clear, with that rare, pungent freshness of air that follows a summer thunderstorm. Niniane walked among the stones with Charlie held snugly between her crooked elbow and side and told him what she knew of the people lying there.

"That tall headstone back there . . . " She pointed towards the back of the graveyard with her free hand. " . . . we'll go over close so you can see. That's my grandfather. Can you read his name?" She leaned forward so that the chicken could have a closer look at the carved letters, and placed her hand, open palm up, near his beak.

Chester Elwood Blattery . . . spelled Charlie . . . *1918–1995 Devoted Husband and Father.*

Niniane nodded "Uh Huh."

What's that other letter . . . He inquired after a moment. *I've never seen that before?*

"What other letter, Charlie?"

That one . . . The chicken stretched out his neck to try to indicate the odd engraving. *It looks sort of like a 'G' inside an 'A' . . . ?*

"Oh, that!" Niniane shrugged. "It's some Masonic thing. Grandaddy was a Mason."

What's a Mason? Charlie asked, inevitably.

"To tell you the truth, Charlie, I honest to God don't know. It's something they only let men into. It's some kind of secret society."

Charlie said nothing, though he was intrigued.

"Grandaddy was a tyrant." Niniane said, "He and May never got along. They were always fighting about something, even when May and Mama were little, Mama says Grandaddy always had a hard time getting May to do anything the way he wanted. May says that Grandaddy always hated her because he was a male chauvinist and wanted a son, but Mama says it wasn't really that simple. She says that the reason May and Grandaddy never got along was because they were too much alike. But I don't think May and Granddaddy are much alike at all, except for being opinionated. But May's not as grouchy as Grandaddy was . . . of course, he was sick most of the time I knew him . . . "

You knew this Grandaddy?

Niniane laughed. "Sure I did!" She lifted Charlie and set him to perch on the old man's tombstone and flexed her elbow. "Let me rest my arm a little. Yes, Charlie, I knew Grandaddy. He didn't die until I was about eight. He was a grouchy old man. I didn't understand, back then, how unfair it was that they wouldn't let May come home to the farm if she brought Irene. Of course, he wasn't much nicer to my mother, but at least Daddy was allowed to come here. Granddaddy's problem was that he thought all women should be just like Grandma Mattie . . . " Niniane, with a jerk of her head, indicated the smaller stone beside the one Charlie was perched upon that read, within a border of graven lilies "Mattie Anna Jacobs Blattery Wife of Chester Blattery, born Aug. 31, 1923–Died May 1, 1990"

"That's Gramma Mattie, Charlie. You know, I never realized this before . . . but Gramma Mattie died on May's birthday!"

Did you know her, too?

Niniane took Charlie up again and bent him over to see her Grandmother's marker. "Yeah . . . I knew her a little. She died when I was little, so I don't remember her as well as I remember Grandaddy. She was nice, though." Niniane sighed. "She always called me Sugar Pie. I remember one time she bought me a little sunhat to wear that had Grandma's little Sugar Pie stitched on it. I wonder what happened to that sunhat . . . "

Charlie held himself still as Niniane spoke. He could not understand at all what she was talking about. What was a sunhat? Why didn't Grandma call Niniane Niniane like everyone else did? But he did not want to spoil the moment by asking anything. He felt as if he were being handed something as delicate as an egg in this story of Niniane's about her grandmother. At the moment, it did not seem to matter that he didn't know every word's exact meaning.

When Niniane spoke again her voice was more like her usual voice, and her expression was more determined than ever. "But she never stood up for herself, and Grandaddy treated her just like a child. It was disgusting. And then he had that stroke after she died. That's what bad karma will do to you, Charlie."

Charlie, again, did not know precisely what she meant by this last statement, but he kept his beak to himself. Niniane picked him up and they made their way towards the middle of the cemetery, to a waist high, rather unsteady looking headstone made of a kind of slatey looking rock that was dappled with some dry, whitish chalky substance. The wiggly letters engraved upon it were pale and shallow and difficult for Niniane and impossible for Charlie to read. But Niniane knew it by heart. She recited it for Charlie.

"Here lieth Nimrod Blattery, Welshman." That's all it says. No one knows when he was born, or when he died. All we know was that he came from Wales, and that his name was Blattery, and that he cheated some Tuscarora Indians out of this land. So he's my mother's oldest ancestor in this country."

Where is Wales? Ventured Charlie.

"Oh, it's all the way across the ocean. It's in England, or near it, I think."

This Charlie understood, having come just that morning to the 'G' volume of the Encyclopedia and reading all about 'Great Britain' a land across the ocean (whatever that was) from whence a number of poets came.

Did you know him?

Niniane snorted. "God, no, Charlie, he's been dead forever! For a long time, I mean. For about two hundred years, I think. You know, people only live to be about seventy years old. Well, Grandaddy lived to be about eighty-five or something. But no one gets much older than that, definitely."

How long do chickens live?

Niniane's elbow tightened a little. It squeezed Charlie a bit, but her voice betrayed nothing. "You know, I'm not sure Charlie. But I think it's about the same." She walked over to the next gravestone. "Rosa Delphinia Blattery." She read. "Granddaddy's sister. Now that's a really sad story, Charlie."

Facing this marker was a long, flat, rectangular slab of stone which rose about a foot out of the ground, and Niniane sat on this and set Charlie in her lap and told him the story of Polly Oxendine Blattery, her great-grandmother, and it was a story that Charlie thought was very sad indeed, even though he did not understand many of the details, even though Niniane made an effort to explain those concepts that Charlie, in his innocence, would not yet have encountered in experience or in the Encyclopedia.

"She was just a little baby when she died." said Niniane. "See?" She pointed to the dates on the gravestone, then read them aloud. " Born December 12, 1929. Died September 23, 1930. Budded on Earth to Bloom In Heaven, it says under that." Niniane shook her head. "That's too young for anyone to die. She wasn't even a year old." She looked at Charlie, but did not offer her hand.

Charlie wouldn't have known what to say even if he had been able to say anything. Death to him was still a great enigma; from his reading in the Encyclopedia he had come across it enough to associate it with that feeling of impending, inescapable annihilation that had come over him in the coop those first few days of his life when he had realized, in that wordless, instinctual way he had of perceiving information before he had acquired human language, that he could not compete with his brothers and sisters for what he needed in order to survive. But it was still unclear to him whether or not death was the absolute end of everything. The attitude that human beings appeared to have toward it seemed to him much like the attitude they obviously had toward the deposition of their bodily wastes; it was something they never liked to speak about, except when confronted with its reality, and then their comments and the expressions of their enviably mobile features would range from grave seriousness to panic to calm sadness to hilarity. This was true, he was discovering, not only of the women of the farm, but of the people he saw every night on the device they called the TV.

"It's very sad," Niniane said again. "What happened was, this little baby was killed in a hurricane that came through here." She shaded her eyes and looked out over the horizon in the direction of the storm that had passed over them earlier. "A hurricane is a big storm. Like the one we had this afternoon, with lots of thunder and lightning and rain. But a hurricane is like a thousand times worse, because it's so windy. The wind can be strong enough to . . ." she looked all around her as if in search of an example. ". . . to blow a whole house to pieces. A hurricane can blow away anything."

Gripped by the precariousness of existence, Charlie blinked.

Niniane swallowed and continued. "Anyway, May says that Grandaddy and his brother and their father were in town for something when the storm hit . . . they didn't have weather reports then, so they didn't realize how bad a storm was on the way . . . and that Granddaddy's mother was by herself with the baby and got scared when the windows started rattling and things started falling down in the house, so she ran outside with the baby, and the winds snatched the baby right out of her arms and dashed it up against a big maple tree in the front yard. May said that one of the neighbors came by after the storm to check on things and found Granddaddy's mother trying to chop down that huge tree with a little axe. She had the baby set in a carriage right beside her just like it was asleep. That neighbor tried to stop her and she chopped him right in the shoulder with the axe. He almost died himself."

Niniane closed her eyes for a moment. From the first time she had heard of this grisly incident, one of many in the history of her mother's family, it fascinated and horrified her. Though she had no idea what it would be like to be in the middle of a hurricane, and even she had no idea what her grandfather's mother looked like, the scenes of the storm and its terrible aftermath were as vivid for her as any of her own personal memories.

She could easily see in her mind's eye the roiling dark clouds and buffet-ing winds, she heard the rattling of the windows and the clunk of falling objects, she felt the panic of the young woman left alone with a little baby in a house that must have seemed as if it were moments away from total collapse, she saw the screaming baby, soiled in its terror and glistening with rain, slipping out of her mother's grip like a too tightly held ball and flying to its death against the trunk of the maple tree. For some reason Niniane could picture, with a terrible clarity, the baby's brains clinging like gray lichen to the soggy brown bark of the maple. And she could feel her own great grandmother's shock and disbelief and confusion as she scrambled to pick up the still, silent, open eyed baby, wrap it in the apron she was wear-ing, then disappear into the farmhouse; then, when the storm had passed she saw her great grandmother stride out to the tree, pushing a stroller with one hand and shouldering an axe. And the furious, implacable face of her great-grandmother was always her own face, and she could never look at it with her mind's eye for long.

Niniane opened her eyes. "They took her away—Granddaddy's moth-er—after that. She died in the State Asylum in Raleigh." The sun was high in the sky above them now, even though it was late afternoon by the watch on Niniane's wrist, and Niniane's t-shirt and cotton skirt were clinging to her back and legs in the damp heat. "I think I need a good long swim." She said brightly. "Do you want to come along and watch me Charlie? Or do you want to go inside and read?

Charlie relaxed in her arms. They were walking out of the cemetery now, down the hill to the farmhouse. Once they were over the graveyard fence, Niniane stood still a moment so he could answer her.

I don't feel like going inside. He said. In truth, his beloved's unease over the tragic tale that she had told had transferred itself completely to Charlie, and he really didn't feel like being alone inside while the sun was shining so brilliantly after the storm.

Chapter Seven

Dillis

ON THE WAY BACK to the house from the little graveyard, Niniane pointed out a low, wide stump in the front lawn about a half dozen yards away from the driveway. "That was where that tree used to be." She said. Charlie did not reply, but waited for her to move on into the house. But she stood there, looking at that stump as if she could see a ghost sitting on it, for what seemed to Charlie to be a long time. The sun was high and fierce, and Charlie, clasped high off the ground between Niniane's warm arm and side was beginning to feel the need for shade. After a while Niniane averted her gaze from the remains of that fatal tree whose roots still reached deep into the earth and would until the end of days. They went inside and she released Charlie into the cool dark embrace of the farmhouse as she set him down in the living room to wait while she changed into her bathing suit.

Charlie could hear May humming tunelessly in the tiny office down the hallway as she tapped inconsistently on a keyboard. Irene, he supposed, was out in the fields, or in town, doing whatever it was she did in those mysterious places that seemed to be her world.

Charlie sat contentedly gazing out the sliding glass door. Life was so companionable and wonderful and peaceful now, as compared to the chicken coop. It was if he was being rewarded here for his suffering there, and he wondered if he could expect this happiness to last forever.

Just as he was pondering these things, Niniane came downstairs and scooped him up. She tugged at the handle of the sliding glass door and then the two of them outside in the heat. She strode across the deck, down the stairs and loped over the grass to the pool, then climbed the stairs onto its narrow circular deck. She laid out the towel she'd brought along and set Charlie on it, then jumped into the pool with first a squeal, then a shiver, then a moan.

"Hey, Charlie?" she swam over and said with an uncharacteristic wheedling note. "You know, it's been so amazing having you around that I totally forgot that I told Dillis he could come and visit. There was a letter from him on my dresser when I went upstairs. It must have just come today . . ." Niniane avoided looking at Charlie. "I don't know what I'm going to tell him."

She sighed. "No matter what I say, he's going to think something's wrong. I mean, before I got here, I made him promise to ask off work and everything . . . "

Niniane folded her arms on the rim of the pool and rested her cheek on them. She continued to speak to Charlie without looking at him or offering her palm so that he could answer. "I wish I could think of something to tell him so that he won't think . . . so that he won't get the wrong idea . . . "

Not for the last time, Charlie was glad that his facial features were not capable of any real range of expression. Without being conscious of it, he'd been hoping that in her excitement about him, Charlie, Niniane might have forgotten all about that creature Dillis, whom Charlie could only consider to be a rival. But of course she had not forgotten. And what was worse, the unfamiliar, unsure note in her voice and her reluctance to look at Charlie seemed to him to mean that she wanted his rival around! For the first time in his life, Charlie wanted to hurt someone. Back in the coop, he would rather have died than fight for what he needed, because he could only lose. This was different.

Niniane hazarded a glance at Charlie. It was so hard to tell what he was thinking! "Charlie?" she said.

He turned his head and looked at her out of his right eye. He opened and shut his beak. She held out her hand, palm up.

Tell him to come. The chicken scratched.

Niniane looked him in the eye. Was she imagining that his beak was scratching a bit harder than usual?

"Are you sure, Charlie? I promise you, you'll like him. He's a very decent person. I wouldn't let just anyone come here, you know."

I'm sure. Charlie scratched, a bit more gently.

Niniane was relieved, and yet she felt vaguely, guiltily troubled, as if she had inadvertently stepped on an ant. She reached up and put her damp hand on Charlie's smooth, feathered head. "I love you, Charlie. I hope you know that."

Charlie thought he should be happier to hear that than he was.

⤴

But in the next few days to come, life on the farm settled into a comfortable routine. Charlie rose with the sun, far earlier in the morning than any of the other inhabitants of the farmhouse, and usually spent that solitary portion of the day looking out the sliding glass door with all the absorption of a human being gazing upon a work of art. The view was, for him, at once exciting and soothing. He liked to watch as colorful flighted birds fluttered among the feeders that hung from the trees in the backyard, though it disturbed him a bit to see them pull worms from the ground. He marveled at the deftness of the squirrels who scampered up and down and across the backyard trees, and he often wondered what all these creatures of the yard who lived so close to the farmhouse and yet who seemed to be, unlike his own kind, free, thought about, if anything. Sometimes he would find himself watching the squirrels as they twitched and curled their agile tails so spasmodically, and he would wonder if perhaps those erratic, peculiar motions might have some squirrelly meaning.

Usually May was the first of the women to come downstairs, and she would always greet Charlie with a sing-song 'good morning!' He would follow her into the kitchen and perch on the counter to watch as she made breakfast. The Irene would come down, but she rarely spoke until she had her black coffee in front of her. Niniane was always the last to come downstairs. She liked to have a shower before starting the day.

After breakfast Charlie and Niniane read through the Encyclopedia volume for the day. Lunch was casual. Usually Niniane made a sandwich or salad for herself and fixed a bowl of seed for Charlie after they finished reading. Then Niniane would either go outside to be by herself for a while, or go into town with Irene on some errand. Later in the afternoon Niniane almost always went swimming. She claimed that the water and the exercise invigorated her and cleared her thinking, and after a while Charlie had to agree that the effect that the water had on her was salutary. She was generally more relaxed afterwards. He usually went with her to perch on the poolside as she swam. The sight of her moving herself with such pleasure in that expanse of water was enough to make Charlie dizzy with adoration and wistfulness. How he wished he were what they called a man! At these times he would ask himself whether or not he would make the change, if such an opportunity were offered, even if the price to pay would be his uniqueness. To be a human among humans, free from the bonds of a form that was a contradiction to his emotional needs! He had never seen a male human in person before, but he had seen many on TV, and for the most part they seemed to him to be creatures possessed of not only the freedom and energy and generosity of the three women of the farm, but also of a certain unconscious density which he, Charlie, felt lacking in himself. Men, it seemed to Charlie, were driven by an inner force that enabled them, like his brothers and sisters back in the coop, to succeed over and against one another, but without the bleak single-mindedness of the "normal" chicken. With the prospect of encountering, in Dillis, a real man, Charlie felt keenly his own perceived and familiar inferiority.

He had seen enough of the magazines to know that the word "boyfriend" implied a physical closeness he wished—however hopelessly—that Niniane would reserve for him. Niniane's having a male friend of her own species was understandable, even inevitable, but still, maddening and depressing.—Why,–He asked himself,—can't I be *him*?

On the whole, though, Charlie had to admit that he was very glad he was who he was. He took to words and their ability to express for and convey to him those ineffable and yet terribly vital things called ideas just as his brothers and sisters had taken to grubs and seeds, with an innate, rejuvenating appetite. He spent a good bit of time puzzling over questions that in time he would come to recognize as existential. Why was he here? Why was anybody? He knew he was unique among chickens in his ability to make himself understood to the humans, but what did it all mean? Niniane had made it clear that she believed he was supposed to speak out against the widespread human practice of eating other animals, but as much as Charlie wished to agree with his beloved about everything, her did not share her conviction that the eating of animal flesh was intrinsically evil. Didn't chickens eat grubs and seeds and other living things? Wouldn't anything, if it came down to a matter of continued existence or extinction, eat anything? That life was lived at the expense of life Charlie knew from his experience as the smallest, weakest hatchling. And, grateful as he was to Niniane for saving him and to the aunts for harboring him, what Charlie desired more than anything was to somehow be able to contribute to *their* well-being. In fact, the idea, which occurred to him more and more frequently during his long nights alone in the living room after the women had gone up to sleep, of being eaten by Niniane was mysteriously thrilling.

Niniane, he knew, would be horrified to imagine that he had such thoughts. But his endless questions regarding the nature and purpose of everything kept his mind occupied during those times—and they were frequent and lengthy—when there was no one to talk to or read with him. He knew the women had other concerns than him, and though this made him feel a bit sad, it forced him to think for himself. Ultimate questions as to the meaning of life became his concern, and these questions kept him busy and eager to learn more about those aspects of life that humans had always claimed a monopoly upon. His attention became more and more drawn to those articles in the Encyclopedia that touched upon religious or philosophical matters, and while he knew that Niniane was sure to become impatient with his interest in these issues, he sometimes felt he had an ally in Irene, who, while she never said much, had an air of brusque serenity that drew Charlie to her. One night after supper, while she and he were sitting together at the table while Niniane removed their plates and May did the cleaning, he'd asked Irene what a soul was. She had replied, with uncharacteristic promptness.

"It's what makes you you and me me."

After that helpful explanation, in spite what came later, Charlie never questioned whether or not he had a soul.

After swimming, Niniane would towel herself dry, then, with her towel wrapped tight enough around her long brown hair to pull the corners of her eyes up into a fetching slant, she would come out and sit beside Charlie, dangling her feet into the water, her damp, slim hand set palm upward at her side in case Charlie wanted to chat. Often they would just sit together silently for a while, absorbing the sunlight and the warmth and the gentle, lively sounds and smells of the countryside. At such times Charlie was reluctant to bring up any subject that he knew would irritate Niniane . . . particularly the subject of religion.

He did want answers, though. Because when it came to religion, or more specifically Christianity, much of what he read under that subject heading in the Encyclopedia did not make sense to him. The article was full of vocabulary that seemed specialized and remote and purposefully puzzling, such as the term 'incarnation' and the never clearly explained notion of the 'trinity.' But the story of the young man who had performed miracles, the last but not least among them being his own return from the dead, had an appeal for Charlie that he could not put his claw on. Something about the whole story was charming, yet at the same time rather alarming. One afternoon at the poolside he'd asked Niniane if she was familiar with this Jesus person, but she only rolled her eyes back in her head and disappeared under the chlorinated water for quite a while. Charlie realized that name of Jesus in particular aroused in her a contempt that she couldn't suppress; and that to find out more about this Christ business he would have to get hold of a book called a "bible" to read, and go to a place called a "church." There had also been mentioned, in the article, some activities called "sacraments" that he would have to participate in, but those, evidently were secondary to a knowledge and acceptance of the factuality of the original story of Jesus' unusual birth, dramatic life, gory death and miraculous return. Charlie tried to put the subject out of his mind altogether, as it's incompatibility with his separate and equal desire to make Niniane happy in all things was distressing, but the images and questions continued to preoccupy him. It seemed there were longings within his tiny (but rapidly expanding) chicken breast that even his love for Niniane could not fulfill. Charlie spent many hours at night speculating in his drawer, at times not falling asleep until the wee hours of the morning when he would awaken, before all the women in the house, to the raucous sound of a rooster—who may well have been his biological father—crowing.

Traditionally, the three women were accustomed to spending their summer nights leisurely, reminiscing or debating and often playing cards on the kitchen table until bedtime. The arrival of Charlie didn't change that. Since it was impossible for Charlie to hold his own cards, he did not play. But he liked to perch at his place at the table and watch and listen as the ladies played their game of rummy. In this way his knowledge of them grew without his having to ask a lot of questions.

Dillis arrived late one Friday afternoon, when May was setting the table for supper. Charlie, who was feeling too apprehensive to be by himself, sat on the countertop and watched her cook.

"I guess that's him," sighed May as the sound of a car crunching up the gravel driveway reached them in the kitchen. "He better be as quiet as she promised he is . . . "

Almost immediately, Niniane came running in, breathless, her hair still damp from her swim that day. "It's him!" She yelled. "Charlie, May, come out there with me to meet him!"

She swept Charlie up with a swiftness that made him dizzy.

With her free hand Niniane grabbed her aunt as well. "You too, May. We should all be together. Where's Irene?" She did not wait for an answer, but ran outdoors, squeezing Charlie too tightly.

⌐

Dillis climbed out of a small, dirty olive green car. He held an overstuffed rucksack in both hands, and his thin face was flushed. He faced the three inhabitants of the farm, his lips parted and raised over small, irregular teeth. He was squinting as if he was staring into the sun; and in fact, the sun shone directly in his eyes, as it was low and he was facing west. Facing Dillis from the porch, Charlie could see the setting sun reflected by the boy's round spectacle lenses as two identical shimmering orange yolks.

"I'm here." The unimpressive young man said, which Charlie thought was a pointless thing to say.

Niniane handed Charlie to May, and ran over to where Dillis stood, blindly beholding them, and embraced him with such vigor that they fell against the side of the dusty car. They kissed one another. Charlie looked at the gravel on the ground.

⌐

At supper that night, Charlie found it hard not to stare at Dillis, even though he was determined not to like him, and even more determined not to let on. Dillis looked nothing like Charlie had imagined him, nothing like the human males he had seen on TV. Dillis seemed, in comparison to the three women, to be underdeveloped. His frame was very slight and he was tall. His glasses gave him an air of intelligence, but his vocabulary was poor. For the first time Charlie felt he was in the presence of a human being less intelligent than himself.

By suppertime, Dillis' dramatic introduction to Charlie had already taken place. Just after the boy arrived, he'd been shown to the living room, which was to serve him, as it did Charlie, as his bedroom. They all sat down and waited for Irene to come in from the fields. When she arrived, she greeted Dillis with a grunt and a brief, strong handshake, then left to take a shower, having spent the hot afternoon shoveling silage. May excused herself to start preparing their supper, and once they were out of the way Niniane asked Dillis to sit down on the sofa beside Charlie and hold open his hand, palm up.

"I've been meaning to ask why you're carrying a chicken around," he said. "Is it for supper?" He laughed at his own wit.

At this Niniane turned pale. "Dillis, don't even joke about that. You don't know what you're saying. Now, I'm going to ask you to do something," she said, stroking the small chicken's head with one finger, "and I need for you to trust me. What you're about to witness, Dillis, is something truly amazing. This is going to blow your mind. Are you ready?"

There being no answer to such a question in such circumstances, Dillis nodded, bewildered.

"Okay," Niniane took a deep breath. " Dillis, this chicken is called Charlie. Now, I want you to ask Charlie a question."

Dillis blinked and looked up at Niniane whose expression was watchful. This was some kind of test. She wanted to see how he was going to react. He wondered for a moment what he was supposed to say or do in order to please her. Was he supposed to go along, or was he supposed to object? It seemed to him that Niniane would be against teaching animals to do tricks. Even though she'd had a dog all her life until its death of old age the year before, Dillis knew she now even questioned the morality of keeping animals as pets. But maybe, he thought, being here has mellowed her out . . . Her letters, though, hadn't indicated any change in her way of seeing things.

"You want me to ask him a question? What is he, psychic?" He slapped his own knee.

"I'm serious," said Niniane. "Ask him a question. Remember, his name is Charlie. Introduce yourself. And ask him a question. Anything."

"*Charlie!?*"

"Go on." said Niniane softly, setting Charlie on the cushion beside him. "I'll explain everything, don't worry. Just ask him a question."

Dillis couldn't hold her gaze, her expression was so solemn and patient and unlike her. "All right." he said, after a long moment.

"Charlie . . . " he said. "Why did the chicken cross the road?"

Charlie did not know what to say. He looked up at Niniane, who scowled at Dillis. "Be serious." She said. "Ask him a real question, and then hold your hand out in front of him, like this . . ." She demonstrated, and then took Dillis' hand and set it palm up in front of Charlie's beak

"Oh, just go ahead, Charlie," she said. "Just say anything."

Charlie lowered his beak and scratched, *Hi,* rather tersely.

It took a while. Charlie had to repeat his performance three times before the boy's brow wrinkled, and his jaw slackened and he gaped at Niniane. "Wow!" he said. "He spelled 'Hi.'! That's neat!"

Niniane smiled. She could tell he didn't get it, not yet. "Go on, Charlie," she said. "Keep your hand still," she said to Dillis.

Charlie suddenly felt terribly weary. Gathering all the moral and physical strength his little self-possessed, he lowered his head and pressed his beak into the boy's rather sweaty palm. *Niniane loves you very much*, he scratched.

This time Dillis' lips moved as the letters formed in his palm, and as comprehension dawned, he looked up from the chicken to Niniane, his eyes wide. This was not something that Niniane would ever say to him, much less go to the trouble of teach a chicken to say. What this chicken was saying, he was saying on his own. He looked back down at the chicken, and snatched his palm away from the reach of its beak.

I'm glad you're here, Charlie was about to say, however insincerely, but there was no chance, as Dillis, at that point, began waving his arms in the air, all the while staring at Niniane. His teeth were chattering. Niniane took the boy's hands, held them still between her own, then drew him toward her and held him close, making soothing sounds. Charlie had never seen Niniane like this, so maternal. It was as if was more important to her in that moment than reassuring Dillis.

⏝

That night, wide awake in his drawer, Charlie waited impatiently for sleep while the young man breathed heavily, stretched out on the longer section of the L-shaped sofa which faced the television. He was out of Charlie's view, but Charlie could not tune out the sound of his deep, irregular breathing and the occasional little snores and groans that issued from the boy. Eventually Charlie rose and trotted across the room and around the couch to look at him.

Dillis lay there, covered up to his chest with a light, pale blue bed sheet. His mouth was slightly open and his eyes loosely shut, giving the impression of that most profound relaxation that follows upon and in a certain sense compliments, extreme agitation. Charlie thought he looked different without his glasses on; he looked more like a man than a boy.

Charlie stretched his neck and inspected Dillis' glasses, which lay, unfolded, lenses down, on the wooden coffee table. Charlie understood that the glasses helped the boy to see. May had a pair that she wore on a chain around her neck and placed in front of her eyes during card games or when reading the newspaper.

Charlie suddenly became possessed by an urge to snatch those glasses up off the table with his beak and hide them somewhere, or better yet break them into a million pieces. The prospect of his somehow incapacitating Dillis suddenly seemed so possible and so inviting that Charlie was in that moment stunned by the sensation of power that welled up in his tiny chest. If I told her, Charlie thought, thinking of Niniane, that I didn't like him . . . or if I told her that he did or said something mean to me, she'd make him go away.

Charlie stepped back from within reach of the boy's glasses and closed his own eyes. Before his mind's eye a scene played out in which Niniane, with the expression and righteous might of an enraged Amazon, threw Dillis' flailing body from the front stoop of the farmhouse onto the hood of his vehicle.

Charlie felt a chill in the air, and on the couch the boy's body twitched, then stilled. He licked his lips, wrinkled his forehead, moaned. Charlie recalled the unseemly excitement and disbelief and outright panic with which Dillis had reacted to the evidence of Charlie's writing ability. It had taken the boy a full half hour before he could bring himself again to offer his palm to Charlie. Even through supper and the card game afterwards he had persisted in periodically staring at Charlie through those rather smudged spectacles and shuddering.

Niniane and May and Irene were shocked by me, Charlie realized. But he's different. He's –Charlie looked at the floor and searched for the word. He's *stunned*. He can't believe me even though he's seen me. He's afraid he's going crazy.

Charlie trotted back to his own cushion, then rose and looked out the glass door at night on the farm. In truth, the boy's panic and his lingering astonishment had made the chicken himself feel rather unreal. It was, as he'd known since the first time he'd written to Niniane, no fun when someone can't believe you're real.

Chapter Eight

Spiritual Cramp

DILLIS JOINED NINIANE AND Charlie at their regular encyclopedia reading the next morning after breakfast. He still seemed shaken. He was not able to keep from staring at Charlie over the breakfast table as Charlie ingested his feed the only way he could, with his head thrown back and with his throat expanding and contracting in subcutaneous motion. It irritated Charlie to be stared at while he was eating, but he put up with it.

However, with Niniane sitting between them on the back porch glider, Charlie felt that at least some things were back to normal. That morning they were well into the 'J' volume of the encyclopedia, which Charlie found to be one of the more interesting. The article entitled Japan, read the day before, started Niniane on a tangent in which she recounted for Charlie the U.S. policy of detaining American citizens of Japanese heritage in internment camps during the Second World War. This led to a further discussion in which Charlie was made aware of the practice of chattel slavery on the very farm upon which the two of them presently sat. From there a discussion of the categorization of humans into phenotypic groups called 'races' followed, until Niniane's throat had gone dry.

She opened the encyclopedia volume on her thighs and turned to Dillis. "Now." She said. "We're already up to the letter 'J'. Yesterday, we read the article on Japan, and I told Charlie all about the internment camps during World War Two."

"Okay," Dillis said. He still could not get over the fact that the chicken could read and write. But having slept a deep and dreamless sleep the night before, he felt a bit steadier. Niniane's familiar bossiness helped, too.

Chickens might read and write, the sun could fall from the sky, but Niniane would always be in charge.

"So," he peered across her at the chicken. "This is how you learned to read? From Niniane reading to you?"

Sort of. Charlie scratched. He noted again the curious smell that Dillis' skin had, a slightly sour, sharp, not unpleasant odor utterly different from the women's' fresher, less overpowering one. *I didn't know what I was doing, though. Niniane would read out loud, and somewhere along the way it just all started to make sense.*

"Why don't the rest of the chickens read? Would they, if we read out loud to them?"

Both Niniane and Dillis looked at Charlie. Dillis' hand was steady, waiting.

No. Scratched Charlie.

"Why not?" asked Dillis.

Without a pause, Charlie scratched. *They're not the same as me.*

Dillis repeated aloud what the chicken had scratched into his palm.

"Charlie!" Niniane cried. "How can you say that? They haven't had your opportunities!"

Charlie drooped.

Niniane placed her little finger under his beak and lifted his little head. "Charlie," she said. "You can't be the only chicken . . . out of God knows many in the world . . . who can communicate. If one chicken can do it, every chicken can do it, under the right, humane conditions . . . don't you think so?" Niniane remembered that when she'd introduced Charlie to May and Irene he'd been under the same impression that he was unique among his species . . . "fashion forward," he'd called it, with his limited vocabulary, but she thought that since then he should have gained some perspective. Charlie was unique, yes, but he was also privileged.

Dillis stretched out his hand. "Maybe Charlie's a savant. Is that what you are, Charlie?"

What's a savant?

Dillis considered. He replied that he wasn't exactly sure. But he had heard the word applied to people on television who had inexplicable abilities. Most of them were in some way autistic, which made their talents seem all the more remarkable.

That's it! Scratched Charlie. *That's what I am. A savant!*

Dillis repeated this.

"That is the most conceited thing I've ever heard you say, Charlie!" gasped Niniane.

Charlie was instantly distraught. Niniane had been annoyed with him before, but never so blatantly critical. He wondered what he could say to take back what he said, even though he felt, deep down, that he was right. Still, how *did* he know that the others couldn't learn to read if they were taught? In theory Niniane was right, there was no reason why the other chickens shouldn't have the capacity to learn, but he had a feeling that that no chicken, including himself, was capable of acquiring any ability upon which its personal survival did not depend. Charlie's survival had depended upon his being able to communicate with that Being which had delivered him from a world in which he could not survive. The others *could* survive, so why should they need to communicate with any other kind of being? Their advantage and their stupidity were intimately related. But he wasn't sure how to explain this to Niniane. *I don't know.* He scratched.

She pursed her mouth and repeated his words to Dillis. "He's not usually so hung up on himself." She said.

Dillis reached over and stroked Charlie's neck. "Aw, give him a break. He's not saying he's any *better* than the rest of them . . . he's just different. Right Charlie?"

Charlie nodded.

Dillis smiled. "See?" he said. He leaned back in the glider, laced his hands behind his head and stretched his long legs with the air with what seemed to Niniane to be insufferable smugness. She slammed the encyclopedia closed. She stood up, clenched her teeth, then took a deep breath, turned, and regarded Dillis and Charlie coolly. "Since you *guys* know so much," she said. "I guess you don't need me here."

With that she tossed the 'J' volume of the encyclopedia to Dillis, who caught it just before it would have landed, pointedly, between his legs. Struggling to open the sticky sliding glass door, Niniane disappeared into the farmhouse, leaving the boy and the chicken alone on the back porch glider. Dillis, his grin faded but remaining, placed the encyclopedia on the floor and lifted the chicken onto his lap. "Oy." he said.

Charlie looked through the sliding glass door through which his beloved had passed, but could only see the reflection of himself and Dillis on the glider. Dillis patted his little head. "She'll be all right," he assured his anxious new friend. "She gets huffy like that sometimes."

For a moment Charlie felt disloyal, then he felt betrayed. What if Niniane went back to the coop, found another chicken, (most likely one of his own stupid siblings) and succeeded in teaching *it* how to read! Even though something in him was sure every other chicken would only ignore her, the mere idea of her reading with another chicken was more painful than he could bear. He wilted onto Dillis lap and his head rested against the skinny young man's bony chest. Dillis, he saw clearly now, did not mean to be his rival, and would be sorry to know that he was. In the midst of this dread, Charlie's affection for Dillis came to life. His only real rival for the love of Niniane was her own indomitability, which he would not, for his own happiness, exchange. It occurred to him that his life was doomed to futile, hopeless devotion. Beneath him, Dillis' thin body shifted.

"Sorry, man," the boy said. "My leg's going to sleep." He set Charlie on the glider beside him, then picked up the encyclopedia. "Well," he said. "Who needs her anyway, right? I can read just as good as she can. Let's keep going . . . "

Charlie pumped his neck gratefully. Dillis opened the book to a random page in the middle, and began to read aloud, hesitating often, and mispronouncing many words.

⌇

Niniane spent the next hour or so in her room alternately lying down on her bed and sitting up on it, and trying unsuccessfully not to dwell on the morning's disagreement with Charlie and Dillis. It wasn't that she was convinced that any other chicken could read and write–and if she were honest, she knew she would not really want another chicken to be as special as Charlie–but the interference from Dillis was infuriating. She was used to Dillis contradicting her all the time, but it was not the kind of attitude she wanted Charlie to pick up.

Sitting lotus-style on her bed, Niniane closed her eyes and tried not to mind so much. But her feelings were shadowed by a familiar, bitter emotion she could not name.

When the name emerged she suppressed it, but it surfaced again like a belch. Excluded. It made her feel excluded when both Charlie and Dillis would not agree with her. And after she had been the one to save Charlie!

And yet, she knew that she really had done no such thing. She'd read aloud to amuse herself and to keep herself company. It really had nothing to do with Charlie. And Charlie's ability had very little to do with her. What he had learned, he had learned on his own, through her, but by some mysterious agency completely beyond Niniane's understanding.

Niniane at that point decided that if she stayed in her room by herself one minute longer, she would go crazy. She didn't want to go downstairs where she might have to run into Dillis or Charlie, so she grabbed her secret stash of magazines from under the bed and dashed down the hallway to the bathroom, where she immersed herself in a scented bath until she heard Irene's truck crunch into the driveway. While in the tub she allowed herself to cry a bit, and with the tears came the reassurance (she knew not from where) that a prophet is often despised in her own country. That afternoon she joined Dillis and Charlie at the pool with her sense of purpose, as well as her nerves, rejuvenated; and, what's more, her skin and hair were clean and fragrant.

⤶

That evening, while the four humans played rummy, Dillis, who was losing, informed them that, in the course of the afternoon, he and Charlie had gone through all of the worthwhile articles in the 'J-K' volume of the Encyclopedia.

"At this rate," he said, watching as Irene masterfully shuffled the cards for the next hand, 'He'll be through the whole set in two weeks. Then you'll have to get him something else to read!"

May, Irene and Charlie looked over at Niniane. She knew they expected her to make some politically charged suggestion. So she denied them the satisfaction of anticipating her by remaining silent. In fact, she was hoping to get Charlie interested in her well-marked, paperback copy of Peter Singer's *Animal Liberation*, which had been a gift from Mercedes Hernandez. But that could wait until Dillis went back home. She shrugged and gathered the cards that had been laid before her and appeared to study them as if her life depended on the hand she was about to play.

Dillis held his hand out to Charlie, who was perched near the edge of the table between himself and Niniane. "Charlie, what do you want to read after you finish the encyclopedias?"

I don't know. Scratched Charlie. Dillis repeated this for the group.

"What do you suggest he reads, Romeo?" May said to Dillis.

"I don't know." Dillis eyed May cautiously. He couldn't tell, by the bantering way she always addressed him, if she liked him or not. "I'm not a big reader. What do you think, Niniane?"

Niniane raised an eyebrow. "Don't look at me." she said. "It's up to Charlie. It's his life, not mine . . . "

Charlie gazed warily at his beloved. He knew very well that it wasn't like her not to have an opinion. He opened and shut his beak, and she stretched out her hand to him desultorily.

But I can't decide all by myself! He scratched. *I don't know enough about the world.*

Niniane shrugged and rearranged her cards. "Some people think I don't either." she said, flicking a glance over her cards at the other human beings. "Read whatever you want to, Charlie."

Are you still going to read with me?

Something in the pressure of the chicken's beak on her palm communicated a sincere wish to share his experience with her. Niniane softened. She was letting everyone's attitude make her cynical when it was natural that they didn't understand her unique mentoring relationship with Charlie, and natural that they should be concerned that she was too much of an influence. But she knew, and obviously Charlie knew that she knew, what was best for Charlie.

"Of course I will, Charlie." she stroked his neck.

Even if you don't like it?

"I don't exactly love the encyclopedia, but I still read it with you, don't I? It's all a part of the important task of educating you, Charlie, and I love being a part of that. So, read what you want us to read, as long as it's something that will help you to understand the world better" she said this last emphatically.

I want to read the Bible, then.

Niniane threw her cards down on the table and covered her face with her hands.

"What did he say?" the others shouted.

Niniane just moaned.

Dillis held out his palm and Charlie repeated his request.

"He wants to read the Bible!" Dillis said wonderingly. "What for, Charlie?"

I want to know more about Jesus. Charlie scratched.

Dillis repeated this, wide-eyed. "Jesus Christ!" Shouted May.

Yes, that one. Wrote Charlie.

ᔕ

"Y'know, Charlie." Dillis said that night, as the two of them sat on the sofa chatting, too keyed up to sleep, "I think it's interesting that you believe in God. I really do. Now, I'm not sure I *agree* with you, but, I have to admit, it's interesting." He paused, scratching his stomach thoughtfully. "But Niniane thinks you're nuts. And those butch aunts do too."

Charlie strode over to the head of the couch, and Dillis held down his palm so that they could communicate.

I don't want them to be upset with me.

"Well, you have to admit, it's odd." Dillis shrugged. "But then again, you're odd, Charlie. If you can read and write, why shouldn't you believe in God?"

Charlie wondered what was so extraordinary about believing in God. The Encyclopedia, after all had seemed to take for granted the existence of such a being. God had been mentioned in many articles throughout, and even had one of His own. There had been, he remembered, a small article he and Niniane had read together at the very beginning of his education entitled 'Atheism;' this, in fact, had been his introduction to the very concept of 'God;' upon reading it he had asked himself immediately if he disbelieved in a being conceived as the perfect, omniscient, omnipotent originator and ruler of the universe, the object of faith and worship. Niniane had explained to him that those words meant, essentially that Atheists did not believe that there was a Person who made things the way they are and who is responsible for the existence of everything. Charlie remembered feeling very shocked that there were people who would argue that there was not a maker responsible for what has been made. His impression was that those 'Atheists' who were his first encounter with the articulation of 'God' were a peculiar minority, aberrations among humans just as he was an aberration among his own species. He could not imagine, at that early point in his life, the degree of distraction that might lead to such a commonplace repudiation of the unseen yet obvious. As he had gone further in the encyclopedia, it became clear that even those who did recognize a creator disagreed as to the nature of this mysterious Being. The very humans he had come to live among did not like the idea, at least, of Christianity. He had heard May and Irene mention a 'Goddess' here and again, and it made sense to him that Niniane, who had such a horror of violence, would be repelled by the idea of a young man nailed to a cross being an object of worship. But Charlie never dreamed that she simply dismissed the idea that there was a creative force. He thought perhaps she believed in a Goddess, like her aunts, a deity with whom she could identify as a capable, dynamic female.

Are you an atheist? Charlie asked Dillis.

Dillis had always assumed that he was. As he had always assumed that poultry could not speak English. He considered his answer, hoping to not offend or upset Charlie. Finally he blurted out, "I just don't know, Charlie. I guess I don't see how anyone can know for sure. But I don't think anybody should have to believe in God if they don't want to."

Charlie took this in. Under what circumstances would one 'have' to believe, in anything? It seemed to him that things did not require belief. Things existed independent of belief. When he was in the shell, he believed in nothing beyond the shell, not even his mother, who had made the shell, but his mother, and everything in the world had been in existence regardless of his lack of belief or knowledge of them. He had not believed in Niniane before she presented herself to him, yet, she had existed, otherwise none of this would be happening. He had not believed, in fact he had denied to himself, that he and Dillis would be anything other than enemies, yet, here they were, Charlie perched in Dillis' lap, discussing, amicably, the most profound of topics. Charlie had no experience of God, but he had experienced enough in his singular journey to realize that experiences were, if not deceiving, maddeningly incomplete.

Why would anyone <u>have</u> to believe in God?

Dillis sighed. "People are funny, Charlie. They want everyone to believe exactly what they believe, do exactly like they do. People don't like anyone that's different."

Neither do chickens, Charlie thought wryly.

That's what Niniane said once. He thought for a while. *I guess I better not read the bible if Niniane thinks it's not good.*

Dillis rolled his eyes. "Charlie," he whispered, "she's just mad because she wants you to spend all your time reading about lab rats and slaughterhouses. Don't pay any attention to her. Read what you want to read. It's *your* education, after all. It won't kill Niniane to read the bible. It's not like you're telling her she has to believe it? Are you?"

No. Said Charlie. *But I don't want her to hate reading with me.*

At this Dillis found himself close to tears. He'd snuck off into the woods to smoke a joint right after the card game, and because of that he was becoming sentimental.

"She'll never hate reading with you Charlie," he said, awkwardly embracing the chicken in his lap. "Believe me. She loves you like you were her baby. She'd do anything for you. She just gets snotty about things sometimes. It's how she is. She'll get over all this . . . this . . . messiah complex she has when it comes to you. She just doesn't want you to go too far and become a fanatic. That's all. Just don't become a fanatic, and everything'll be okay. Trust me."

Charlie lay his head gratefully against Dillis' ribs, then he craned his neck around to tap the boy's hand. Dillis opened his palm.

Will you read the Bible with me?

Dillis' eyes widened behind his glasses. "Sure," he said, "At least until Sunday. You know I'm going back home on Sunday."

Charlie had forgotten that. He didn't know what to say. *Why?* Was what he finally scratched into the palm of his friend's hand.

"I have to." Dillis said, but as he said it he knew he would not leave the farm, not now. He would figure out some way to stay, if for no other reason than to help Charlie and Niniane from freaking one another out.

⏤

Dillis went swimming the following afternoon with Niniane. This did not bother Charlie as much as he would have thought it would. Dillis, after splashing around awhile, got bored with exerting himself and leaned against the side of the pool next to where Charlie perched, and they both watched Niniane as she swam her even, swift laps past them.

"I guess . . . " said Dillis as he was doused his generally smudgy glasses into the chlorinated water, "you're gonna want to be baptized."

Baptized? Charlie recalled the word from his reading of the encyclopedia, but for the moment, absorbed by his view of Niniane's graceful, hypnotic swimming, he could not connect it with its meaning.

"You know." said Dillis. "Dunked under water. That thing that Christians do."

Christians have to be dunked under water?

"Well, yeah, I think so. They make a big deal about it, don't they? I thought you knew."

No. Scratched Charlie. He tilted his head and looked down at his quivering reflection in the chlorinated water. There was so much, so much that was important that he did not know! Every day it seemed clearer that there was information he needed that no one on the farm could offer. Niniane did not like Christianity, and May, speaking for herself and Irene had told him that they, being witches, did not so much dislike the Christian religion as they felt it was awfully limiting.

Can you baptize me, then? Right now?

Dillis laughed. "I can't do that Charlie! You can't just let anybody baptize you. It has to be done by a priest, I think. Besides, I'm a Jew."

Charlie remembered reading in the 'J' volume of the Encyclopedia about that form of religion called Judaism with Dillis, but Dillis had not mentioned then that he was a Jew.

You are?

"Sure I am. Don't I look like a Jew?" said Dillis, making a grotesque sneering expression to emphasize his nose.

Charlie couldn't answer that, as he was unaware that a Jew was supposed to have a particular appearance, but he remembered a photograph from the Encyclopedia article on Judaism. It didn't look much like Dillis, though. It was a tiny picture of a gaunt, white bearded man with a small black cap pressed down over his long white hair who stood bent low over a table that had candles at all four corners. The man was peering and pointing with a stick at what the caption called a 'torah scroll.' That image stuck with Charlie. Charlie remembered thinking when he saw that picture that this old man was someone who would understand why he wanted to learn more about this Jesus and God business.

Niniane passed behind Dillis on what must have been her twentieth lap. Charlie noticed that her skin was becoming nearly as brown as Irene's. With her long, sun bleached brown hair, the effect was breathtaking. Suddenly, she submerged, and Charlie brought his attention back to his conversation with Dillis.

Maybe I should be a Jew!

Dillis smiled at Charlie. "Well, you've sure got the beak for it." He threw his head back and stood in the water for a full half minute, his skinny shoulders shaking with mirth while Charlie looked on, totally perplexed. Finally Dillis composed himself. "Seriously, though. I don't think so, Charlie. You pretty much have to be born a Jew."

You do?

Dillis considered this. He remembered being told once that one of his great-aunts, upon her marriage had had to become a Jew, converting, at least officially, from the Catholicism in which she'd been raised. "I went to some classes, took a bath," She'd said, the manicured tips of her gnarled, arthritic fingers brushing invisible lint from the bosom of her blouse, "and boom! I'm a Jew! My father didn't speak to me for years . . . "

"Well, you can convert." said Dillis. "If that's what you want to do. But . . . " here Dillis blushed and grinned. "Since you're a boy, they'll probably want to circumcise you." He gave Charlie's underside a quick glance. "If they can find it . . . " Dillis grinned.

Find what?

"Never mind . . . " said Dillis, still grinning "I'm sorry Charlie. Do you really want to be a Jew? I'm sure you can, if you really want to. It's not all a bed of roses, though . . . "

Charlie remembered the picture of the man with the scroll. That image had impressed him, but in an entirely different way than the article about Christianity, which had at once uplifted and troubled him. Yes, he wanted to be as serene and focused as that old man in the picture, he wanted to be as easygoing and affable as Dillis; it would be nice to be a Jew like them, just as it would be nice to be a human instead of being a freak of a chicken. But, he perceived, as he watched Niniane kick off against the edge of the pool for another lap, these things called religions seem to choose you, rather than the other way around. As do these things called women.

I guess not. He scratched into Dillis' palm.

Dillis nodded. His parents being hippies, he had never practiced Judaism to any significant degree himself, and could not imagine why anyone would want to keep kosher or go to temple.

"What do you want to be, then?" He inquired of Charlie. "There are all kinds of Christians. Hundreds of different kinds, I think."

Charlie had gathered that from the encyclopedia article. *What's the best kind?* He inquired.

"Don't ask me!" Said Dillis. "I wouldn't know. I think deep down they're all the same, anyway."

Then why are there so many different kinds?

"That's a good question," said Dillis. "What did the Encyclopedia say about that?"

Charlie cast his mind back to the Encyclopedia article on Christianity. There had been a mention of something called the 'filioque' over which there had been some early disagreement, then the selling of some things called 'indulgences' which had led to a major upheaval called the Protestant Reformation. After that point it seemed to Charlie that the once all-encompassing body called the Christian church had broken like a shell into a thousand jagged pieces. He couldn't even remember all the different denominations that had been cross referenced at the end of the article on Christianity, but a few that stuck in his mind on account of the sheer poetry or strangeness of their names were the Jehovah's Witnesses, the Christadelphians, the Swedenborgians, and the Church of the Nazarene. *They don't like each other,* was his reply to Dillis. *So they can't be all the same.*

"I don't know about that," said Dillis. "They all seem the same to me. They just argue about details. Stuff that isn't important. Don't worry about it too much, Charlie."

Dillis slipped off the edge of the pool into the water, leaving Charlie to think. It was easy enough for Dillis to tell him not to worry too much, about what kind of Christian to be, since he didn't have to worry about what *he* was, he already was something, apparently. He was a Jew, and what's more, a human being. His identity would never be at issue the way that Charlie's constantly seemed to be. Dillis' place in the world was settled so that he could go on to think about other things. But Charlie, having wandered into the labyrinth of Christian identity, felt a responsibility to discern a path to the heart of the matter. The figure of Jesus, himself a welter of contradictions, was compelling, and for some reason Charlie felt an ineffable sense of intimacy with him. But there was more to Christianity than Jesus, wasn't there? He wished there was someone who could tell him what to do.

Oh, thought Charlie. He felt a familiar constriction in his little heart, a keen, painful consciousness of his aloneness. I can write on Niniane and Dillis and May and Irene's palms all I want, but none of them, no matter how much I love them and they love me, will understand what I mean, or what I need. I guess if I get baptized, like Dillis says, that'll help. I'll be a Christian, then, and the other Christians will be my friends too.

But the questioned remained as to what sort of Christian was the right kind to be. Obviously no one on the farm was going to be any help to him on that front. With a start, Charlie realized that he was going to be the one, in the end, to initiate his journey out of the only sanctuary he'd ever known.

⌒

When they finished swimming, Niniane and Dillis and Charlie went inside, and while Niniane was upstairs changing her clothes before supper, Charlie got Dillis' attention and asked him if he would take him to where there were some Christians.

Dillis turned pale and withdrew his hand from under Charlie's beak. "I can't do that, Charlie!" he half whispered, half squeaked, "Niniane would kill us both! And listen, Charlie, you've got to be careful . . . I was being nice before, but you gotta understand . . . Christians . . . well . . . at least out here in the country, especially in the South . . . a lot of them are crazy. I mean *really* whacko. They hate everybody. And a chicken that reads and writes . . . I don't know, Charlie. Even if you do like Jesus . . . they still might think you're possessed by the Devil or something."

The Devil was another figure from the Encyclopedia that intrigued Charlie, and he thought he wouldn't mind learning more about him from these crazy Christians who knew him, but he could see that Dillis was too disturbed to say more about that. He reached for the boy's hand. *But didn't you say I need to be baptized by a Priest?* He scratched.

"Not right this minute," said Dillis. "What's the rush, Charlie?"

I don't know. Charlie scratched miserably.

Dillis patted the chicken's head awkwardly. He was sitting cross legged on the floor in front of the sliding glass door with Charlie perched on his thigh. "Is it really that important to you, Charlie?"

Charlie detected a note of sadness in his friend's voice. It was a moment before he scratched his reply.

Yes.

Dillis sighed. He felt the way he imagined a mother bird must feel pushing a fledgling out of the nest for the very first time. I'll never have kids, he told himself.

"All right, Charlie. Whatever you need to do, I'll help you. But not right away. Don't you want to know more about these people before you . . . reveal yourself?"

Yes . . . but how?

Dillis hugged Charlie. It was more important than ever, now, that he figure out some way to stay on the farm for as long as Charlie needed his support on this weird spiritual journey. I'll stay in the barn if I have to, he told himself. It won't be the first time a Jew hid out in a barn.

⌣

The following afternoon, Dillis drove into town. After some effort he was able to locate a branch of the county Public Library. He was shocked by the meager selection of books on religion and philosophy available in that inadequate and underfunded small town branch, but at least that made choosing books easy. Using May's library card, he checked out the entire collection of books within the 100–299 Dewey classification system. He returned to the farm with about thirty books of varying length.

And so, for the next couple of weeks, except during meals, Charlie did little else but read, forgoing the card games and even those pleasant afternoons spent poolside watching Niniane swim. In addition to getting the books for him, Dillis came up with a method by which Charlie could read on his own by having the top edge of the book secured underneath one of the heavy cushions from the living room sofa. With some effort, Charlie could turn the pages with his beak, and very soon he found that reading on his own went much faster than reading while his friends turned the pages for him and voiced their own opinions.

At first all this reading made him feel even more confused. Dillis put the books in front of him in no particular order, and so, working from thinnest to fattest, Charlie began with a slim paperback with a portrait profile of a glaring, mustachioed human male on the cover. This book was called *The Anti-Christ* by Freidrich Nietzsche. That afternoon Niniane, upon peering down over Charlie at what he was reading, shrieked and said, "Charlie! What are you reading that for! That's not even Christian! It's worse! Nietzsche was a total Nazi!"

Charlie did not fully understand what a Nazi was, but he knew it was bad. In a way he was relieved. Although he thought the prose style of *the Anti-Christ* was captivating, particularly in those passages such as the one entitled '*The Psychology of the Redeemer,*' there was something histrionic about it. It was a book to enjoy, but not to take all that seriously. He found himself wondering if there were people who took what the book was saying absolutely seriously, and decided there could not be. Such people would no doubt behave in ways so thoroughly bestial that they would lose all sense of what it is to be a human, or even a sentient being.

From there Charlie went on to skim through a half dozen or so books about astrology. The prose style of these, compared to the Encyclopedia and The Anti-Christ, was friendly and simple and refreshing, but he didn't understand very much of what they were saying. At one point he asked Niniane what his sun sign was, and after some thought she told him that, having hatched on the 21st day of June, he was on the cusp of Gemini and Cancer. He then asked her what her sign was.

"Aries. Why?"

I'm reading about astrology.

Niniane had kissed him on the top of his head and said, "I'm glad you're being open-minded, Charlie. But take it all with a grain of salt, okay?"

Charlie wasn't sure what she meant by that, but when he looked up his signs and her sign in the glossy purple and gold paperback entitled *Linda Payne's Love Signs* and found that he and Niniane, being water and fire, were rarely compatible, he lost interest. From astrology he went onto a colorful paperback with large type, titled, rather alarmingly, *Chicken Soup for the Christian Soul* which, not surprisingly, he found at intervals nourishing and nauseating. None of these books, however, were bringing him any closer to a sense of where, within the world of Christendom, he might find his place. Towards the end of the week, he began to lose patience, and he regarded the stack of unread books beside the sliding glass door hopelessly. This is no good, he told himself. What I'm looking for isn't in a book. It was precisely at that point that his glance hit upon the title on top of the stack that was to set in motion a chain of events that would lead him to where he would never have dreamed of going. It was a rather small book, bound in lavender buckram, with the simple, succinct, and very promising title *On Certainty*.

⤳

In the trials to come, Charlie was to discover that, no matter how confused he might become, he could restore himself to a degree of assurance regarding his own existence by recalling the words of item 239 in Ludwig Wittgenstein's posthumously published collection of aphorisms entitled *On Certainty*. Just when he had given up hope of finding, at least within a book, some sign to guide his way, he encountered, in Item 239, a confirmation of that conviction that was deepest in him but which he had not before had the words to say. "Catholics believe . . . " Item 239 said, in part, " . . . that in certain circumstances a wafer completely changes its nature and at the same time all evidence proves the contrary."

At the time of this seminal moment, Charlie was alone in the house. May had gone with Irene into town for some reason, and Niniane and Dillis were swimming. No one heard him crow, or saw the burgeoning, blood red comb on the crown of his head stiffen. He'd been flipping through the pages of *On Certainty*, which was printed on the left in German and on the right in English, without much attention, when the phrase "Catholics believe" caught his eye and led him to discover what, in fact, or at least in the view of this Wittgenstein character, Catholics believe. At first, in finding no word about God, or about Jesus, or even the woman Mary, about whom, Charlie already had gathered, Catholics believed more than any other religion, he was disappointed. What was this about a wafer? Charlie read it again, wishing—not for the first time—that he could sound out what he was reading, the way his friends could. "Catholics believe . . . that a wafer completely changes its nature . . . when all evidence proves the contrary."

Through the sliding glass door the summer sun, invisible to Charlie at its zenith, bathed the world in transforming light. He could hear the muffled but not so distant sounds of Niniane and Dillis in the swimming pool, splashing and chatting. Charlie crowed again, aware that no one would hear him, but it seemed to him to be important to make a joyful noise. I'm not alone! He crowed. Catholics believe what *I* believe! They believe in the unbelievable! They'll believe I belong no matter what I look like!

Thus Charlie made up his mind to be baptized into the Roman Catholic Church.

⌒

Dillis was the first one he told. Charlie told him that night after the card game, after the women had gone upstairs to bed.

"Catholic!" Exclaimed Dillis. "Wow. That's hard core. How come, Charlie?"

Charlie hesitated before answering. How could he put it so that his friend would understand? Should he scratch out the passage from Wittgenstein? Was it even necessary or wise or possible to explain? In the hours that had passed since his epiphany, Charlie's mind had been pleasantly overcome with an otherworldly calm. He hadn't said much to anybody about anything, so wonderfully at peace did he feel with himself and his decision to dedicate himself to something that he could be sure would mirror his deepest convictions. He'd spent the afternoon reading as much as he could find among his collection of library books about the Roman Catholic Church, and while some of what he found out was disturbing, such as the fact that that church would only admit male human beings to their mysterious priesthood, for the most part what he read only served to strengthen him in his new allegiance. One book in particular had charmed him, and he read it voraciously, in one uninterrupted two hour sitting. It was titled *Letters to a Niece*, and its author was one Baron Freidrich Von Hugel, whose photograph was printed on the frontispiece. The Baron, whose shaggy white hair and beard and pale, intense gaze made him look, Charlie thought, like a bearded Irene, was not a Catholic priest, but simply a well to do old man who spent his time advising many people, among them one of his nieces called Gwendolyn, as to how they might best live as Christians. The artless rhetoric of these letters to a niece charmed Charlie. Each one began with "My Dearest, Lovable Sweet Little Gwen-Child," or some other such saccharine phrase and then went on to elucidate, using an odd mélange of sophisticated theological terms and mundane imagery, the peculiar logic of Catholicism. One passage in particular had struck Charlie with a sense of a mind very near his own, and he wished this Von Hugel was still alive for him to talk to. "You see, My Gwen . . . " the Baron wrote:

> . . . how vulgar, lumpy, material, appear great lumps of camphor in a drawer: and how ethereal seems the camphor smell all about in the drawer. How delicious, too, is the sense of bounding health, as one races along some down on a balmy spring morning; and how utterly vulgar, rather improper indeed, is the solid breakfast, are the processes of digestion that went before! Yet the camphor lumps, and the porridge, and its digestion, they had their share, had they not? in the ethereal camphor scent, in the bounding along upon that sunlit down? And a person who would both enjoy camphor scent and disdain camphor lumps; a person who would revel in that liberal open air and contemn porridge and digestion: such a person would be ungrateful, would she not?–would have an unreal, a superfine refinement? The institutional, the Church is, in religion, especially in Christianity, the camphor lump, the porridge, etc.; and the "detached" believers would have no camphor scent, no open air, bounding liberty, had there not been, from ancient times, those concrete, "heavy," "clumsy," "oppressive" things—lumps, porridge, Church.

Surely, felt Charlie, his friend would see the wisdom in that. But when Charlie considered asking Dillis to take up that book of letters to a niece and read that passage for himself, it made him feel funny. He wanted to keep it to himself. And there was no need, really, to convince Dillis of anything, because Dillis was not standing in the way of anything, in fact, quite the contrary. And, if he's not against me, Charlie thought reasonably, he's with me.

"Charlie?" said Dillis, while Charlie, who seemed frozen, beak lowered about a centimeter or so above the boy's palm was pondering these things. "You there, Charlie? Why the Catholic Church, I said?"

Charlie considered for another moment, then lowered his beak. *Isn't it the biggest one?* He scratched.

"I guess it is." said Dillis. "But that doesn't mean it's the best. Although, it's not the worst, either. But I'll tell you one thing; Niniane's not going to like it. May and Irene won't either. They'll say its sexist, you mark my words."

Charlie hadn't thought of that. He lifted his head. The implications of his decision rose up in his mind like some ominous roiling cloudbank. Niniane would indeed be unhappy, that was for sure. Charlie knew enough to realize that the refusal of the Catholic Church to allow women to be priests was at best insulting and at worst dangerous. And yet, the words of Wittgenstein and Von Hugel had had an impact upon him that he could not deny. It was to the Roman Catholic Church that his encounter with them referred him, and it was to the Roman Catholic Church that his spirit inclined. The sprouting comb on Charlie's head flushed and stiffened with sorrow and shame and not a little excitement. He turned away from Dillis' palm and thought about what to say. *She'll get over it,* he scratched in Dillis' palm, and he didn't even realize how much he sounded just like Dillis himself.

Chapter Nine

Campaigning

THE NEXT MORNING, CHARLIE found that he didn't want to share his new identity with Niniane and the aunts right away. He mentioned this to Dillis before breakfast, and Dillis readily agreed to keep mum. In the meantime, they campaigned separately with the women to allow Dillis to stay at the farm for as long as possible.

Niniane wasn't hard to convince. "You'll lose your job, you know." She said to Dillis when he approached her with a request for her to speak to her aunts about letting him stay and help with Charlie.

"I know." Dillis said. "I don't care. This . . . this is more important than a job."

They were walking along the tree line that bordered the east pasture where the cows grazed, and Niniane leaned against Dillis' shoulder. She was glad he was staying, glad he realized that what was happening here was more important than any dead end deli job. But she could not deny that she was a bit jealous that it took Charlie and not her to lead Dillis to the light.

Charlie took on the aunts. After breakfast, the chicken appealed to May's low key yet steadfast irritation with Niniane's vegan stridency. *I'm going to miss Dillis*, he scratched into May's palm as he sat perched on the counter next to the sink while she washed the breakfast dishes. *I wish he didn't have to leave.*

"That's nice." Said May with a knowing look at Charlie. "I thought at first there might be some friction between you guys. But it's worked out okay, hasn't it?"

Charlie's comb burned and tingled, and he ducked his head. On top of everything else that these human females could do, could they read minds as well? He had practically forgotten, himself, how jealous he had been of Dillis before the boy had even arrived. Had it been that obvious?

He waited until May finished scrubbing bacon grease from the bottom of a cast iron pan and signaled for her palm. *I guess now that he's going home, Niniane will be the one to pick out books and stuff for me. You and Irene are always so busy.*

May turned and regarded the chicken. "I guess that's true, Charlie. How do you feel about that?"

Okay, said Charlie. *The stuff she likes me to read is pretty interesting. Even if it is scary.*

May's eyes narrowed. "What do you mean, scary!"

Charlie's wings ruffled for a moment. It was his version of what the humans called a shrug. *You know,* he scratched, *kind of scary . . . the things they can do to chickens . . . in other places. She showed me this magazine article about a processing plant in some place near here called Smithfield, and it had all these chickens without their feathers hanging by their feet from this pole . . .*

Charlie broke off here to rest his beak for a minute—he wasn't used to writing at such length, and it was hard on the neck, as well. The picture he was describing was something that Niniane had actually shown him one day before Dillis' arrival, and it *had* been awfully disturbing. To see even a dated black and white image of such a number of his kind, lifeless, stripped of their feathers, waiting passively to be processed into chunks of meat for anonymous humans to eat . . . it had stayed with him. Even now, recalling the grim, blank expressions of the men in the picture as they stood wearing white caps and smocks over a conveyer belt loaded with yet more limp, naked dead chickens, Charlie wanted to shake the image out of his head. He would rather not ever think about such things, but sometimes it was necessary, and mentioning it to May was having the desired effect. Her free hand was on her hip now, and her mouth was set in a thin line before she spoke.

"That little sneak!" she said. "I'll process her! To show you something like that! I swear to Goddess, sometimes I think she needs a good old fashioned spanking. No wonder you're going Christian on us!"

Charlie wasn't sure what May meant by that, so he let it pass. *Dillis doesn't like it when we look at stuff like that, either. He says it's propa . . . propa . . .* Charlie raised his head and waited.

"Propaganda," finished May. "Dillis said that?"

Charlie nodded.

"In front of Niniane?"

Charlie nodded again.

"And what did she do?"

She called him a complacent capitalist meathead.

May snickered. "Well I'll be. Good for him." She laughed. "Wait'll I tell Irene."

Charlie would have smiled, too, if he was able. He waited while May chuckled and shook her head, then reached for her palm. *I wish he didn't have to go home.*

May stopped laughing and bent close to Charlie and winked. "Maybe he doesn't have to . . . at least not right away. I'll have a little chat with him this afternoon. He's a good kid. And the more the merrier, right?"

Charlie nodded.

⏩

And so the summer days passed. Dillis eased effortlessly into the routine. When Charlie finished the entire Encyclopedia, Dillis mentioned that they might as well start on the bible.

They had just come to the end of the W-X-Y-Z volume of the Encyclopedia. Dillis closed it with a bang.

"Well, I hope you guys enjoy your bible study," said Niniane, standing up.

Dillis looked at her wide-eyed. "You said you'd read with us!"

Niniane crossed her arms over her chest. "That was before Charlie said he wanted to read the bible! Dillis, has it ever occurred to you that this might be difficult for me? Charlie may have strong feelings, but so do I. My grandfather was a religious nut, and when I was little we had to go with him to church—to a Southern Baptist Church, Dillis—every weekend every summer! I've had enough bible to last forever."

"Aww, come on, Niniane, that was a million years ago!"

"That doesn't matter, Dillis! In case you forgot, we live in a patriarchal society that privileges the Christian religion. You of all people ought to realize that!"

Charlie ducked his head.

Dillis was silent for a moment, and when he spoke it was in a voice lower and steadier than any Charlie or even Niniane had ever heard him use before. "Niniane, give me a break. This is a chicken we're talking about. We could take him right now, wring his neck and eat him for dinner if we wanted to and he couldn't do a thing to stop us, and all you can do is complain about having to go to church when you were a kid."

There was a long silence. Charlie felt dazed. He had never before heard the brutal truth about his unique situation put so plainly. His very life completely depended upon these humans being well disposed toward him. If he had not tried to talk to Niniane, he realized, it was conceivable that he would not be alive today. And if he really upset her–or May or Irene or Dillis—made them angry, if they withdrew from him their presence, their protection, what then?

It was Niniane who broke the silence. "That's not fair, Dillis. I would never do anything to hurt Charlie. Never. And I'm not comparing my situation with his, either."

Charlie felt ashamed for having doubted her. He wanted to tell her that he understood, and that she didn't have to read with them, but her arms were still crossed.

After a moment, Charlie reached for Dillis' hand.

Niniane couldn't help herself. She waited a minute, and then when Dillis didn't say anything back, but nodded to Charlie, she glared at him. "Care to let me in on your conversation? Or am I too unreasonable?"

Dillis looked at her calmly. "He said that he doesn't mind if you don't read with us. And he just asked me if I've read the bible."

"And you nodded? Dillis, when did you ever read the bible?"

"In Hebrew school. A long time ago."

"Oh that." She said. "But you couldn't have read the whole thing."

"No one reads the whole thing," said Dillis. "Except maybe rabbis and priests."

Charlie wrote again into Dillis' hand. Niniane touched Charlie lightly on the head. "Charlie," she said. "I'm sorry. You know how I am. I'm just concerned. This is all so strange to me. But Charlie, I want you to know you can talk to me about anything. Go ahead." She opened her palm.

Well, I do have a question.

"What, honey?"

Well, I was wondering if you know any priests.

Niniane shrieked. "Of course I don't know any *priests*! Why?"

"He wants to be baptized." said Dillis.

"*What*?!"

"He wants to be *baptized*, Niniane. He's decided to be a Catholic."

Niniane covered her eyes with her forearm.

"I keep seeing a big church with a statue of Mary in the yard not too far down the highway." said Dillis.

Niniane flared. "Dillis, we can't take Charlie to a Catholic *church*! They'd think we were crazy! And as soon as they figured out that Charlie really can write . . . oh, I don't even want to think about what they'd do. They'd say he was a demon or something."

"Niniane, no they won't . . . the Pentecostals would, but not the Catholics . . . they don't do that anymore . . . this isn't the old days . . . "

"I am not taking Charlie to a Catholic Church, Dillis!"

Dillis stood up. "Well, what are you gonna do, Niniane? He wants to be baptized and go to church, for Christ's sake! You don't have any right to keep him from doing that if he wants to!"

Niniane's fists clenched. If she had known, in the beginning, that Dillis would ever speak to her this way, she never would have invited him to the farm. He was clearly too sentimental, too eager to cater to Charlie's naïve whims. "Dillis, you know it's too dangerous."

"I don't know that, Niniane."

"Well, I do."

"*How!?*"

"Dillis, don't shout at me. You know as well as I do that the Catholic Church is not progressive when it comes to animal rights."

Dillis stood up and leaned into Niniane's personal space. "That's what this is all about, then. You don't trust *anybody* who doesn't think exactly like you. Especially when it comes to Charlie. My God, you don't even trust Charlie! Can't you see . . . he's a spiritual cat!"

Niniane gritted her teeth. "Can't *you* see that if Charlie just goes out and does whatever he wants he'll end up on a grill! He's only a month old, for God's sake, Dillis! Maybe he's a chicken genius because he can read and write, but he doesn't know *anything* about the real world!"

"No one is going to grill Charlie, Niniane. Especially not some Catholic priest."

Niniane drew a deep breath. When she spoke, her voice was so whisperey that Charlie could barely hear her. "But they might take him away."

Dillis sat down. The two humans looked down at Charlie, still perched on the glider seat, taking in everything. Dillis spoke first.

"Yeah, they might do that. Charlie, maybe it's too soon. If word gets out about you, someone might try to take you away."

Charlie opened and closed his beak. Dillis held out his palm.

Why would anyone try to take me away?

"Because you're one of a kind, Charlie. To the rest of the world, you'd be a freak. People would never leave you alone. They would keep trying to figure out how you can do the things you do. They might not care about you, Charlie, the way that we do."

Why wouldn't they?

A swift, sorrowful look passed between Dillis and Niniane before Dillis answered. "Niniane's right about one thing, Charlie. People are usually pretty dangerous. They're only out to please themselves. Even if they didn't want to eat you, they would try to . . . what's the word . . . *exploit* you one way or another. They'd probably try to figure out some way to make money off you, I bet."

Charlie noted the re-occurrence of that word 'exploited.' He had not seen it in the Encyclopedia, and he still did not know exactly what it meant, since Niniane had run away screaming as soon as he'd asked her that question in the very beginning. He decided that now was not the time to ask again. Whatever it was, it couldn't be as bad as the coop had been. He opened and closed his beak.

Dillis held out his palm.

Are you sure you can't baptize me?

"I'm sure Charlie."

And Niniane can't either, or May, or Irene?

"I don't think so."

Then I guess I need a priest.

When Dillis repeated this, Niniane began to cry. Sitting down on the glider beside the resolute chicken, sandwiching Charlie between herself and Dillis, she stroked the feathers on his back and tried to compose herself. "I'm sorry, Charlie. I know this is important to you. I just feel like . . . I guess I'm just afraid of what's going to happen. One priest knows, then the whole church knows, the next think you know they'll be calling the *papers*, then probably the government will want to run tests on you or something and . . . God, I don't even want to think about it. If there was just some way we could keep it a *secret* . . . " she broke off and sighed, a long, shuddering, hopeless sigh.

Dillis snapped his fingers. "Wait a minute!" He grinned. "We'll take him into one of those . . . whadayacallem . . . confessionals! We'll *confess* that we've got a miracle chicken! That way they can't tell anybody!"

Niniane groaned. "Dillis, that won't work."

"Why not?!"

"They can't keep everything secret, for one thing. That's unethical. What if a murderer came in there, and . . . "

Dillis sat down on the glider and waved her words away. "It is secret, Niniane, even if you admit to murder. I'm telling you. It's perfect!"

"Dillis, what makes you think you know how the Catholic Church handles things? You're Jewish! I bet you've never even been inside a Catholic Church."

"Niniane, I grew up in east Boston for fifteen years. All my friends went to Confession. I'm telling you, they can't rat you out, those priests."

Charlie reached for Dillis' palm. *No matter what you say, they can't tell anybody else?*

"That's right."

You can tell them anything?

"Yep. That's what they're there for."

Charlie turned to Niniane and opened and shut his beak. She held out her soft, damp, fragrant palm.

Don't worry, he scratched. It gave him such joy to reassure his beloved that it was all he could do to keep from crowing.

Chapter Ten

Disturbing the Priest

"Here." Said Dillis, pointing to the display on May's computer screen. "Our Lady of Pity, Rt.32 six miles out of Maxton, Fr. Carl Frank, Parochial Vicar."

What's a parochial vicar?

"I have no idea."

Charlie couldn't stand the glare of the computer screen. It hurt his eyes and made him feel nervous. He backed up to the edge of the desk, turned around, perched, and waited for Dillis to finish scrolling up and down the screen. Finally Dillis logged off, leaned back, and regarded Charlie.

"So. Ready to give them a call? Father Carl Frank. Sounds like an nice guy." Dillis held out his hand.

Charlie shook his head slowly back and forth. A bit of wattle was beginning to sprout under his beak, and he sometimes shook his head like this to relax himself, to feel the new and somehow comforting weight of his own development.

I have to think.

Charlie thought a lot, lately, before doing anything. The conversation on the glider just a few days before had thrust upon him a very uncomfortable sense of his own mortality. He now recalled, with a chilling clarity, images from the encyclopedia that he'd dismissed before. One image in particular haunted him this morning, it was of a row of chicken carcasses, plucked and beheaded, one following the next like a gruesome shish kebab on a stainless steel pole that penetrated their body cavities from esophagus to anus. Reflecting upon that image, Charlie now shared, to some degree, Niniane's concern about strangers, even Catholic priests.

We have to be careful.

☙

The next morning Fr. Carl Frank arrived at his tiny office in the rectory of Our Lady of Pity and found a number of sticky notes left by his secretary, who had taken all calls while he had been on his Monday Sabbatical. He stared for a moment, uncomprehending at a curious one near the bottom of the pile. He had a terrible hangover.

"3:51 p.m. Monday. Please call 555-5362 ASAP. A theological question to be answered. Ask to speak to Ninny Ann or Phyllis.?"

☙

The priest from Our Lady of Pity called near lunchtime, and Niniane, who answered the phone, made him hold until she found Dillis and Charlie, who were on the porch plodding through Genesis.

"Come inside," she said. She had not yet brushed her hair, and this, along with her lowered brow, made her look unhinged. "There's a priest on the phone, and I can't handle it."

Dillis nudged Charlie, grinned, and gathered him up. "It's for you, Snoopy!"

They followed Niniane inside, and Dillis took the receiver, still holding Charlie in the crook of his arm.

"Hello," he said. "This is Dillis."

Charlie strained to understand what the voice on the other end was saying, but all he could hear was garble.

"Well," began Dillis, in a voice unusually high and plaintive. "I was wondering if you might have some time to talk this week. You see, I'm interested in joining the Catholic Church, and I heard the first thing you need to do is talk to a priest."

More garble.

"Oh, I'm not anything. I mean, my family's Jewish, but we don't believe . . . I mean . . . "

Silence. More garble.

"No sir, I haven't. I mean, Father. They wouldn't be interested. This is just . . . "

Dillis was interrupted in mid-sentence. Then—"I'm seventeen."

A lengthy garbling.

Dillis grimaced. Charlie pecked him, alarmed, but Dillis waved his hand and mouthed the words "It's okay."

"I wouldn't do anything against their wishes, Sir. They're really . . . open-minded. Old flower children, you know . . . "

A long silence. A garbled question.

"Oh I could come by anytime." Dillis said. "I'm on vacation."

Some more garbling, then Dillis hung up the phone with repeated thanks. He set Charlie down on the counter and faced him. "Boy, was he a grouch! But we have an appointment, Charlie. Thursday afternoon at two thirty."

Charlie looked at Niniane, who bit her lip and ran upstairs.

"Oh, Jeez." Dillis said. "Don't pay any attention to her, Charlie." Charlie opened his beak. *I'm scared. I need something to eat.*

Dillis and Charlie sat at the kitchen table, and though they had recently had breakfast, they shared a piece of well-done, liberally buttered toast and ice tea. At one point Dillis turned to Charlie and said, with a conspiratorial wink, "I decided not to say anything right away about confession, because he asked me so many questions that I forgot. Anyway, I figured that it would be better to tell him I'm not catholic, but that I *want* to be, then tell him I have to confess, and *then* hit him with you. And then . . . well, you'll take it from there. What do you want to say to him first? What do you want to know?"

Charlie had not thought about that. What would he say? What did he have to say? Ultimately, he wanted to be baptized, to become a Roman Catholic, but should he come right out and say so? In his experience, humans were always so stunned by the fact that he could communicate at all that it took quite a while for them to even pay attention to *what* he was saying. He wondered what he could say to bypass all that drama.

I'll tell him I believe in transubstantiation.

Niniane woke up that night in the wee hours, whimpering. She'd felt thoroughly uneasy, in her body as well as in her mind, ever since the priest had introduced himself to her over the telephone. She went to bed right after supper. She was upset by May and Irene's' noncommittal reaction to the news that Dillis was planning to take Charlie into town to visit, of all things, a catholic priest. She'd expected them, if only in the interest of their own privacy, to put up more resistance. But when Dillis told them, the aunts simply glanced at one another and nodded as if they'd seen it coming. When Niniane interjected that she had tried to talk the two males out of this pointless and perilous adventure, everyone, even Charlie, ignored her. She left the table without another word, on the verge of some very embarrassing and angry tears.

She'd fallen to sleep almost instantly. Her clothes, still damp from the heat of the day, were still on her, and the curtains were left drawn. She dreamed of many things, but the final dream woke her up with a start that left her sitting upright in bed facing her own dim image in the mirror above her grandmother's antique vanity. Within that dream, she was in some garish, unfamiliar fast-food restaurant with Dillis, eating what she thought was a perfectly vegan soybean burger, but which was actually, she realized with a sickening jolt that woke her up, none other than Charlie. For a brief but interminable moment upon waking, she could not clear her mind of the final image from the dream, the image of the smooth, shiny, unmistakably familiar tip of Charlie's beak poking almost imperceptibly out of the ground up mealy mass which made up the patty she was lifting to her gaping mouth.

After the immediate horror of the dream receded and her breathing became normal, she lay back down and gazed wide eyed at the ceiling. The room looked strange and dimly haunted with the curtains left open; there was a new moon out which lent the darkness inside and outside an eerie crystalline quality.—It was just a bad dream—she told herself.

She turned her head to see the bedside alarm clock. It was exactly five minutes past midnight. There was nothing for her to do but wait to fall back to sleep.

But that fall was a long time coming. The dream and its final image nagged at her like a speck in her eye; nagged at her to admit its existence and to respond to it, to allow it its meaning.

It's just a dream, she told herself, but telling herself this did not bring sleep or peace any nearer. She sat up again in bed and remembered something May had once told her about something Irene had told *her* about Irene's five-year stint in Women's Prison in West Virginia for aggravated assault upon a police officer. Irene had said that the hardest thing about leaving something awful behind was the prevalence of that something in your dreams. You never stop having prison dreams after you've been in prison, said Irene, because a part of you never leaves, no matter how hard you try. It's become a part of you, because you've been there.

—Will a part of me always eat meat?—Wondered Niniane.—Does a part of me want to eat Charlie?

She stood up. She walked across the room and leaned over the glass covered surface of the old vanity. She gazed at her own face in the mirror and sighed. Her tan face looked ghastly in the moonlight. A few strands of long brown hair stuck to her damp cheek.—I look and feel like hell—She thought. Into the mirror she mouthed the words—It was just a dream.

But it was no good. The horror the dream evoked in her made the questions it raised impossible for her awakened mind to ignore. I'm asking too much of Charlie, she admitted to herself. He's never going to want to speak out against the meat industry. He may do it, but he won't want to do it. It won't mean anything to him, even if it means the world to me.

Niniane turned away from the mirror and lay back on her bed, her arms and legs spread against the rumpled sheets.—He wants to be like Dillis—she thought.—He doesn't love me anymore. I'm not the one he listens to now.

Niniane sighed. This was not exactly the truth, she knew, but it was close. For the first time she felt like she was beginning to understand Charlie; and that what she understood was light years away from what she had always believed about him. She reiterated in her mind a phrase that summed it up for her.—I'm not the one he listens to now . . .

—Why doesn't he?—

Because he has a mind of his own. He may be a chicken, I might have taught him how to read and write, but the way he thinks has nothing to do with me. It's just that I can't imagine not wanting to do something to stand up for yourself. He doesn't have any rights in this society, but he's more worried about his soul, whatever that is.

What good, Niniane thought, is a soul without a body? Your body is your self!

Lying in the dark, Niniane's hands moved up and down and across her own body. Her upper arms, her breasts, her stomach, her thighs, she reached for them all as if to reassure herself that she did indeed possess them. The thought of being without this healthy young flesh, a disembodied soul without any tangible boundaries, made her shudder.

It occurred to her, finally, that Charlie might feel trapped within his. Poor Charlie, she thought.

She pictured him in her mind, a fast growing, if slightly scrawny chicken who, like his comb and wattle, was just beginning to come into his own. She remembered the first words she had ever understood him to say to her those few short weeks ago that felt now like a lifetime.

Kick him to the curb, girl!

Niniane smiled in the darkness. He does love me, she thought. Even with all this Catholic stuff. Dillis says that when I'm swimming, he can barely take his little eyes off me.

She turned over and drew her pillow to her chest. So I can't be that bad, she thought.

Not long after this she drifted off to sleep.

⌒

The next morning, Niniane was up and showered and dressed even before May and Irene woke up. She went downstairs to see if Charlie was awake yet.

He was, of course. Charlie was always up before sunrise, and as the days passed it took more and more effort to suppress the crow that filled his throat as the first pale rays of morning sunlight crept underneath the curtains into the living room.

Niniane tiptoed over to his drawer by the sliding glass door and squatted. "Morning, Charlie." she said, and held out her hand.

Good morning. He answered. *Why are you up so early?*

"Oh, I've been up for a while. It's a big day," she said. "Aren't you excited?"

Charlie lifted his beak from her palm and looked at her. She'd been so mad the evening before! She'd left them at dinner, and without her the rest of the humans didn't seem to have much to say. May and Irene had gone to bed far earlier than usual, and Dillis just watched the television. Sensing the real tension that everyone was feeling on his account, Charlie had been dreading the preliminaries of his excursion to see the priest, but now here was Niniane, up with the sun, apparently in a good mood! He lowered his beak.

Yes, he scratched. *I'm excited. But I'm a little scared, too.*

"I don't blame you," she said. "You've never been away from home before. But everything's going to be okay Charlie, don't worry. We won't let you out of our sight."

Charlie blinked. We? Niniane was coming? Charlie squawked.

"What is it, Charlie? Listen, don't be scared. We're not going to let anything bad happen."

Charlie's heart sank. Now that he thought about it, it made perfect sense that she would insist on coming along. After all, she was his savior, at least in a literal sense, and her protective, if not to say controlling nature would demand that she be with him every step of the way, even on a pilgrimage of which she disapproved. He trotted over to where the two curtains that covered the sliding glass door met.

"Do you want me to open up the drapes, Charlie?" said Niniane.

He nodded.

She opened the drapes, and as she did so Charlie thought fast. Now that he knew that Niniane wanted to go with him, it became clear to him that she must not. Her presence, he realized, would dominate the encounter no matter how hard she tried not to interfere. And he knew that if she were along he would be unable to allow himself to speak (or scratch) freely. It was one thing for Dillis to be along, for Charlie's friendship with Dillis had no element of possession, and thus no excitement or anything else that might compromise a direct and unmediated apprehension of the will of God. But Niniane was a different matter. He couldn't imagine Niniane and God in the same room.

"Charlie?" she sat down beside him and held out her palm.

You can't come with me, he scratched, before he could chicken out.

"What!?" She snatched away her hand. "Charlie, what are you talking about? Of *course* I'm going with you! If you think I'm going to let you go all the way into the town to see some Catholic *priest* with only *Dillis* to keep an eye on you, you've got to be out of your mind . . ."

In that manner her earlier and totally uncharacteristic solicitude lifted like the morning fog. Charlie waited for her to remember that he needed her hand, close by and steady if they were to communicate.

Eventually she remembered. "Are you even listening to me?" she demanded, and held her palm down in front of him.

Yes, he scratched. *But please don't be mad. I just don't think you would be very comfortable if you went with us.*

"I don't *care* about being comfortable," she said. "But somebody has to be along to make sure you don't do anything . . . " She sputtered, blushed, and was silent.

Charlie knew what she was going to say. Stupid. To her, this affair of the soul was nothing more than a fool's errand. Charlie was not offended. In the days and weeks to come he all too often found himself feeling the same way.

I really wish you didn't want to come.

"*Why,* Charlie? You're going to need support. And guidance. How are you going to know what and what not to say to this priest? You have to be *careful,* Charlie."

93

Careful was what he knew he must resist the temptation to be. He took what was, for a chicken, a deep breath. If he was going to take a stand, he would have to start now.

I have to do this without you, he scratched gently into his beloved's palm. She withdrew her hand and looked at it for a long time as if his words were visible. Once again she doubted the goodness of her own heart—a terrible feeling. She was as lost and frustrated as she had been the night before after waking up from that awful dream.

"How about if I stay in the car?" She said finally.

Charlie shook his head. Even that, he knew, would be affect him. *I want you to stay here and wait for me,* he scratched.

Niniane kept her palm out, expecting Charlie to say more, to explain further, but there was nothing more he could say. "All right." She said finally. "I'll be here."

⌒

The rest of the morning was taken up with the business of fine-tuning their plans. Dillis had driven into town the evening before to fill his tank with gas to make sure there was little chance that they would have to stop at any point along the way. In the end the trip, at least to and from the church, went smoothly.

For Charlie the drive was a treat in itself. It was suggested that Charlie should ride in the trunk, but Niniane refused to hear of it. She found a yellow milk crate that Dillis strapped into the passenger seat of the old Plymouth. From there Charlie could see the sky through the passenger window. But as they began their journey, the young chicken was too overwhelmed, too entranced by the new experience of moving at such high speed to do much more than squawk.

Dillis couldn't help laughing. At times like these, unlike others, it was easy to see that Charlie was still a chicken, for all of his intelligence.

Dillis held out his hand. "Are you scared, Charlie?"

Being spoken to brought Charlie back to his senses, somewhat. *No.* He scratched. *For a minute I thought I might pass out, though.*

"Oh!" said Dillis. "Why didn't you tell me?" He eased on the brake until the car was crawling. "Once we get closer to town, I'll have to pick up the speed again. If we go too slow, we might get stopped by a policeman, but if that happens just stay cool . . . I've got it all worked out, I'll just tell him you're sick and that I have to get you to the vet. But it would be better not to get pulled over at all, though. You think you'll be okay?"

Yes. Said Charlie. He looked out the window of the passenger seat at the trees they were passing on the country highway. A moment ago it had all been just a greenish-brown blur, but having slowed down, Dillis had restored the scenery to a recognizable reality for Charlie. He wished he could see what Dillis called the street.

He turned his head to observe Dillis in the act of driving. It was soon clear that Dillis was obliged to keep his eyes on the road and his hands either on the steering wheel or on a stick with a knob that stuck up between their seats, and so could not really communicate with Charlie. Seen through the open sides of his spectacles, the boy's eyes were more intensely focused than Charlie had ever known them to be. Music was playing loud, very loud, all around them. While they were still near the farm Dillis had turned the volume down for a moment to apologize for this. "I can't stand not to have music on when I'm driving. When I'm driving, I don't like to think."

There was something else that Dillis had done once he turned the car off of the long gravel drive at the farm onto the country highway. He reached into the small opening in front of Charlie ("that glove compartment door broke off a long time ago," he'd said, obscurely) and withdrew a small square package out of which he shook, awkwardly, with one free hand, a white paper stick which he then set fire to and sucked as it slowly turned to ash.

"Cigarette." He'd said to Charlie. "Don't tell Niniane. She'll probably smell it on me anyway. They *are* bad for you, she's not wrong about that. That's why I don't smoke all the time. But I let myself have a few when I'm driving. I like to feel free."

Charlie sat in the passenger seat of Dillis' car throughout the slow, steady ride to the church, and felt free, himself.

Dillis pulled into the parking lot of Our Lady of Pity and pointed out the statue on the treeless, sunburned lawn to Charlie. "That's how I knew there was a Catholic Church nearby," he said. "I remembered seeing that statue of Mary when I was on the way to the farm."

Charlie gazed at the statue for a moment. He could see it quite well through the holes in the side of the milk crate he was still hidden in. It seemed to him that the stone lady on the lawn with her hands cupped, palms out, to either side of her rippling gown, was preoccupied with the flowers around her feet.

"Ready?" Said Dillis, peering into the crate.

Charlie nodded, though his comb and wattle had suddenly grown cold. He supposed he was as ready as he ever would be.

⌣

It was a modest church, as Catholic churches go, with little of the ornate décor that Charlie had come to associate with Catholicism from the color pictures in The Encyclopedia. Dillis, holding the milk crate against his chest like a Wise Man bearing a gift to the Christ Child, walked through the front door of the smaller building, which the priest had told him was the Rectory, and blinked in the sudden absence of sunlight. "Hello?" he called, into what he thought was the emptiness of the dim front room.

"Can I help you?" said a female voice jarringly close by.

Dillis jumped. Just ten feet in front of him a rather bloodless looking woman dressed in a pink blouse and a red cardigan sat dwarfed behind a large wooden desk. She was peering at him suspiciously and her pale, freckled hand was inching toward the phone on her desk.

"Yes . . . " Dillis squeaked. "I'm sorry I yelled . . . I couldn't see. Umm . . . my name is Dillis Walksi, and I had an appointment to see Father Frank?"

The woman behind the desk's eyes widened for a second, then the corners of her lips curved upward in an officious smile. "Oh yes," she said. "Have a seat, please. I'll let Father know you're here."

She pushed a button on her telephone, snatched up the receiver, and spoke into it with a voice all sweetness and light. "Father Carl, your two thirty, Mr. Walksi has arrived." She paused, her smile growing wider and revealing a line of small, too regular teeth. "Yes, Father," she said, and hung up.

She pointed out a chair to Dillis, who still had not sat down. "Please have a seat," she said. "Father will be with you in just a minute."

Dillis nodded nervously, and perched on the edge of a chair set against the wall by the door, propping Charlie's milk crate on his knees. He looked around the room at a number of small, antique looking wooden tables upon which were set unlit lamps, decorative boxes with Byzantine looking portraits on the lids, and thin, cheap looking magazines with titles like St. Anthony's Messenger and The Franciscan Herald. There were windows on either side of him, but the Venetian blinds admitted only a dim, corrugated shadow of light into the room. He wanted to ask the woman why it was so dark in there, but her face was glowing in the light of the computer screen that she was staring primly into.

Dillis looked down at Charlie and tried to communicate, by raising his eyebrows, that everything was okay. The chicken held his gaze as if it were a lifeline.

After what seemed a long time, the dark wooden door to the left of the receptionist's desk opened and the priest walked out. He was a stocky, swarthy man of medium height and a wide, smooth, and yet pinched looking face above his roman collar. "Mr. Walski?" he said. "I'm Father Carl Frank. Please come in."

Dillis stood and entered the priest's office, which was lit as brightly as the world outside. The large windows behind the priest's enormous and cluttered desk were unblinded, with a view of the meager and deserted playground behind the church. Dillis stood in front of the desk, holding his milk crate, until the priest closed the door behind them and motioned for him to sit down.

"Please have a seat, Mr. Walksi. What's that you have in your crate?" The priest peered into Charlie's conveyance as he passed Dillis on his way to his desk. "Is that a chicken?" He said. "Well, of course it is," he answered himself. "Is there some reason you've brought your chicken along with you, Mr. Walski?"

"It's not my chicken," said Dillis, sitting down and balancing the crate on his knees. "It's my girlfriend's chicken. I told her I'd take him to the vet after I got through here."

The priest raised one thick eyebrow. "Nothing serious, I hope," he said smiling.

"No, just a routine checkup," said Dillis, and looked down at Charlie. He felt already as if the conversation were getting out of hand. He cleared his throat several times.

"Uhh, I guess, I guess I better start by saying that I want what I tell you today to be just between us. I mean . . . I guess what I'm trying to say is that I have a confession to make." He looked up at the priest and pulled his lips in between his teeth.

The priest leaned back in his swivel chair and looked at Dillis the way one might look at a total stranger that has walked up to one and proposed marriage. "Confess?" the priest said. "But you said on the phone that you aren't Catholic. That you're of Jewish heritage, in fact, if I remember right. Why would you feel the need to make a confession?"

Dillis gripped the handles of Charlie's milk crate. "Does that matter? If I'm Jewish, I mean? If I have a confession to make? Does it only count if I'm a Christian already?"

"I wouldn't say it doesn't *count*," said the priest. "But I don't think you understand what Confession—in the context of the Church—really means. These days we call it the Sacrament of Reconciliation, which mean that we confess in order to be reconciled to God, and to our neighbor, and to the Church. And if you aren't a member of the Church, then . . . " he spread out his hands above his desk. "Well, it's not the way we do things. You're jumping the gun, to use an old expression. In order to be reconciled to a community, you first have to be a part of that community. Do you see what I mean?"

Dillis' leg, underneath the milk crate, began to jiggle uncontrollably. He searched his mind for another tack to take. "Well what if . . . " he said. "What if I have something I need to get off my chest before I do something like join the Church? What if I want my conscience clean before I do something like that? Can you hear my confession then?" He looked up at the priest hopefully.

The priest looked across the desk at the clearly rattled young man before him. After sixteen years of ordained ministry and four excruciating years in this godforsaken rural parish smack in the middle of the state's most xenophobic fundamentalist protestant stronghold, Father Carl Frank had been forced to deal with many off the wall situations, but a chicken toting, nervous teenaged Jew was, even for Our Lady of Pity, unusual, if not fishy. He began to get suspicious.

"Mr. Walksi," he said, leaning forward and lowering his heavy eyebrows. "The Sacrament of Reconciliation is one of a number of the Sacraments of the Church, and they are all interlinked. They can't be taken in isolation. I'm afraid you cannot just demand the Sacrament out of some sense of personal guilt. Your desire must grow out of your commitment to the Catholic faith. We take this very seriously, Mr. Walski. Confession is not a game."

"I know that! I know!" said Dillis. "I don't think it's a game, really! You've got to believe me! I know it's serious. I just thought, that maybe there was some way . . . I mean, I have something that I need to confess, and it's urgent . . . " Dillis began to feel frantic, and the milk crate began to shake violently with the motion of his jiggling knees. "I'm screwing this whole thing up . . . " He said, half to the priest and half to Charlie.

The priest held up his hand. "Mr. Walski, wait a minute. I'm just trying to impress upon you the seriousness of what you're proposing. If you are truly sincere about exploring the possibility of reception into the Catholic Church, I'll be more than willing to listen to what you have to say . . . "

"I am!" Dillis said. "I totally am serious!"

"As I was saying . . . " the priest overrode him, "I am willing to listen to what you have to say, and you may consider out conversation to be within the scope of a pastoral counseling session. That's not the same as the seal of Confession, which is inviolable, but it will ensure that whatever you wish to divulge to me will remain between us unless it involves the threat of harm to yourself or any other person. Will that be all right?"

"I don't know." said Dillis. He looked down into the milk crate. "I honestly don't know. Can I have a minute alone to think about it?"

The priest rolled his eyes. "Of course," he said. "Why don't I just . . . "

Inside the crate, Charlie motioned to Dillis by opening and closing his beak. As the priest watched, Dillis stuck his hand into the crate and seemed to lapse into a kind of fugue state, staring blankly into space, and moving his lips slowly as if he were Daniel puzzling over some writing on the wall that none other could behold.

"All right." he said, after a minute of this. He looked the puzzled priest straight in the eye. "That's all right, then. If you can promise me what I'm about to tell you will stay between us until I tell you different."

"You have my word," said Father Frank. "So long as you are clear about the limits of confidentiality . . . "

"You bet." said the boy. He took a deep breath. "All right then. Father, get ready, because this is going to blow your mind. I guess the best way to put it is that there has been a miracle, and I have the proof of it right here. There's been a miracle on my girlfriend's farm, and it involves this chicken." He lifted Charlie out of the box and smiled at him, then turned him to face the incredulous priest. "Father, this is Charlie. Umm . . . can I set him on your desk?"

The priest nodded.

Dillis set Charlie on a clear space near the corner of the priests cluttered desk, next to a square stone paperweight with the letters 'K of C' embossed into a gold medallion set into its center. "Now, I know you're not going to believe this, because I didn't either, at first, so just try not to jump to conclusions. Just try and think of this as a miracle, and then maybe, for you, it'll be easier to believe than it was for me. Father, I need you to hold out your hand . . . palm up, like this, and put it over here where Charlie can reach it."

Father began to stand up. "Mr. Walski, I told you that I'm not interested in playing games . . . "

"Please!" Dillis begged. "Just give me a chance! Don't you believe in miracles?"

"Yes," the priest growled. "But I also believe in not wasting my time with foolish adolescent pranks. You may think you're original, Mr. Walski, but I was a young man myself once, and believe me . . . "

"Please!" Dillis held his hands clasped together in front of his face like a condemned witch begging for mercy. "You've got to believe me!"

The priest's cheeks inflated, and his swarthy skin deepened in color. He reached for the phone, and then, a glance into Dillis' eyes that was meant to further intimidate the boy detected in them the unmistakable blaze of real, panicked desperation. Father Frank sighed and his hand left the phone. "All right, Mr. Walksi. What is it you want from me?"

Dillis stroked Charlie's head and back. "If you just hold your hand out . . . like this . . . yes. All right, go ahead Charlie."

Charlie bent over and touched his beak to the large, fleshy palm of the priest. He hesitated. For some reason, this point of contact impressed him with a sense of its enormity. Once he scratched a message onto the palm of this human being, his life would change irrevocably. He had no idea how this stranger would react to him, and there was none of the sense that he had had before with Dillis and the aunts, that no matter what, Niniane was in control. Charlie wished, now, that he had let her come along, but it was too late. He gritted his beak and said a silent prayer, than began tracing letters onto the palm of the priest.

"What is it doing?" The priest looked at Charlie, then Dillis. "Tickling me?"

"That's how he talks," said Dillis. "Father, he can write. And he can read. Just like any human being. My girlfriend taught him how. Now, if that's not a miracle, I don't know what is!"

The priest turned red and reached for the phone again.

"No!" Dillis stood up so fast that the milk crate tumbled to the floor with a clatter! "You *promised*! You gave us your *word*! You can't tell *anybody*!"

"Mr. Walski! Calm down!" The priest was alarmed. The boy in front of him was absolutely, genuinely terrified. The pupils of his eyes, behind those smudgy lenses, were dilated with panic. And, the priest realized, he had said 'us.' He had actually referred, without even thinking, to himself and the chicken as 'us.' As if he had a relationship with the chicken that was as vital and intimate as that between two human beings. This young man, Father Frank thought, may be psychotic, but he is not joking. For him, if for no one else, the chicken was another person. Father Frank put his hand on the boys shoulder to calm him. "All right," he said slowly, calmly. "You're right. I promised. I won't say anything. Sit down, Mr. Walski. Don't worry. Let's see what Charlie has to say."

And the priest lay his hand down, palm up, in front of Charlie, who scratched his greeting. *Hello. My name is Charlie. I believe in transubstantiation.*

⌒

When they got home, Niniane, having heard the car crunching into the long driveway, perched on the square of concrete stoop in front of the front door to intercept them. She held out her arms and Dillis transferred the chicken into them.

I'm going to bed. Charlie scratched into her palm.

Niniane looked at Dillis, who shook his head slowly. "He says he wants to go to bed." Said Niniane. "What's wrong? What happened?"

"Let's just go inside," Dillis said, very carefully. "Niniane, there's nothing to get upset about. Everything's all right. Charlie's just exhausted. And so am I, to tell you the truth."

They walked around the house and went in through the sliding glass door, avoiding May and Irene, who were in the kitchen. Niniane lay Charlie in his dresser drawer and looked down at him anxiously. He had never sat in her arms so stiffly before. She stood and Dillis motioned her over to him. He put his arm around her shoulder.

She turned to face him. "Tell me what happened, Dillis! He's upset!"

"He's just tired, I told you . . ." Dillis guided her towards the sofa he slept on every night. "It was a heavy meeting . . .."

"What do you mean heavy!?" Niniane hated more than ever Dillis' vague, hippieish way of speaking. She leaned back out of his reach. "Was the priest mean to him? Is he going to run his mouth? What happened!?"

"Calm down! Niniane, I told you, I had that covered. Don't you ever listen to me? Jesus, if that priest was going make trouble, do you think we would have just come right back here? Give me some credit! Look, it's going to be okay. It just wasn't what Charlie was expecting, that's all."

Niniane slumped and held her face in her hands for a moment. She wanted all at once to embrace Dillis and break every bone in his body. What he said made sense. If Charlie was in any danger from this priest, then Dillis would not have brought him back to the most obvious place he would be. Still, Charlie was upset—very upset—about *something*. He wasn't just 'worn out.' He was catatonic.

"What do you mean it wasn't what he expected?" Niniane waved one slim brown arm over the back of the sofa at Charlie. "What's wrong with him? I've never seen him so . . . so . . . *cold* . . . " She found she was on the verge of tears.

Dillis reached for her hand and held it for as long as she would let him. "Just let him have some time . . . " he said. "Come on in the kitchen, and I'll tell you what happened . . . "

⌒

Charlie lay awake in the dim living room, listening to the murmur of voices from the kitchen. He knew they were talking about him. He couldn't make it all out, but he could basically guess what was being said. Dillis was telling the women what happened at Our Lady of Pity.

After a long time the lights went off in the kitchen, and everybody went to bed; the three women padding in their bare feet through the living room to the stairs so as not to wake Charlie. Dillis, stripped to his shorts and a T-shirt and then lay, snoring and uncovered, on the couch. Charlie left his drawer and stuck his head between the curtains to gaze through the sliding glass door.

The night was overcast, and a blurred sickle mood hung overhead. Charlie thought it looked like it was under water; it seemed to shimmer like Niniane when she was swimming. He stared at it awhile, his mind stilled. The effect of the moon and the familiar sounds of the farm were calming, and he could reflect upon the events of the afternoon without feeling too lost.

⌒

Father Frank sat there with his palm outstretched and his forehead wrinkled.

Dillis was standing over Charlie now, his hand lightly touching the chicken's back. "One letter at a time. Go slow, Charlie, like you did with me at first."

Charlie repeated his statement, but the Priest only shrugged. "I don't know . . . " he said.

"Try all caps, Charlie."

Charlie repeated himself once again, this time in large capital letters, each one taking up the entire width and length of the priest's palm. By the time Charlie began to spell the word 'transubstantiation,' the palm began to tense up underneath the pressure of his beak, and he knew the priest finally understood. He looked up to see the priest staring at him with his mouth and eyes wide open.

Suddenly the priest jerked his palm away, collapsed into his swivel chair, and backed up in it against the window behind his desk. Charlie watched, dumfounded as the priest bent over and began to make a horrible, heaving noise that was followed by the sound of thick liquid splashing on the hardwood floor.

"Holy Shit!" Dillis yelled. "He's puking!"

Dillis grabbed Charlie and bolted for the door. Then he remembered the milk crate. He ran back, picked it up, and glanced at the priest, who was still retching behind his desk. "Father Frank . . . are you okay? I'll get your secretary . . . just let me put Charlie back in his box."

The priest only retched and groaned, and Dillis stood paralyzed with Charlie in one arm and the milk crate in the other. Finally Father Frank raised his and his face was pale and running with sweat.

"Go . . . " he said, between tiny moans and heavy gasps. "Go to the church . . . wait for me in there . . . " he retched again " . . . just leave me alone a minute . . . and . . . and tell Mrs. O'Connor to find the mop and bucket, leave it outside my door, and then go home for the rest of the day."

Dillis nodded, put Charlie in his crate, and gave the priest's instructions to his secretary, who spluttered questions at the back of the boy as he and Charlie exited the dark foyer of the rectory. Dillis ran across the stretch of gravel and grass that separated the church building from the rectory and struggled with the heavy wooden door that opened into a dim and aromatic sanctuary. As the door inched to a close behind him, Dillis took a deep breath. It had been a long time since he'd been inside a church or synagogue, and it amazed him how much the same they all seemed, no matter how different they were. They all had a smell, not a uniform odor, but a smell peculiar to themselves, and they all looked nicer when no one was in them. Dillis lifted Charlie out of the crate so he could look around.

It was difficult for Charlie to see much in the darkness, but the sweet, powdery incense smell affected him. At first it was somewhat overpowering, and for the second time that afternoon, he thought he might pass out. But Dillis' grip around and beneath him was steadying, and by the time

Dillis slipped into one of the wooden pews near the front of the church and set Charlie down beside him, Charlie was so at ease that he trotted all the way down the length of the pew and back in order to get a closer look at the stained glass window that overlooked them.

It's quiet in here. He scratched into Dillis' palm. *But too dark. It's a little scary.*

Dillis nodded. He looked over at the stained glass window that Charlie had gone over to investigate; it depicted a white bearded man with golden skin dressed in what looked like a white toga. The man's long, tapered, slim fingered hands were cupped against one another in front of his chest, and underneath his long, slim bare feet a purple banner with yellow letters unfurled.

"Athanasius Contra Mundi," Dillis read. "Whatever that means."

There was a brief flash of light behind them, and they turned. The priest had arrived and was walking slowly down the center aisle toward them. Dillis stood up.

The priest grunted and waved him back down. "Move down," he said, edging into the pew. "And put that chicken between us."

"He's called Charlie . . . "

The priest sighed. "Yes. Set him right here . . . if he doesn't mind. I'd like him to scratch . . . once again, and slowly, please . . . what he was scratching into my hand before I . . . was indisposed."

Once again, Charlie spelled out, slowly and carefully, his announcement about transubstantiation. As he did so, the shook his head slowly in disbelief, but he held his hand steady. When Charlie had finished, the priest lifted his hand to his face and gazed at his palm as if he had never seen it before.

"Unbelievable." He whispered, his head still shaking from side to side on his short, thick neck. "Just unbelievable. This has got to be a dream."

"It's not." Said Dillis quickly. "Believe me, I know how you feel, though." He gulped. "But Father Frank," he said, his voice ringing throughout the sanctuary, "That's not the main thing. The main thing is, Charlie wants to be a Catholic, and I think you need to do whatever it is you have to do to make that happen. I know it's strange and all, but stranger things have happened, haven't they? I mean, look at Jesus! Walking on water, casting demons into pigs, parting the Red Sea . . . next to all that, Charlie's not such a big deal, is he? And in Brockton, near where I grew up, there was a statue of Mary in a lady's house that could cry real tears like a baby doll . . . "

Father Frank covered his face again. "Please . . . " he said. "Oh, God, you've got to tell me this is a joke . . . If this chicken . . . if this chicken really can communicate . . . I mean, communicate out of its own experience, of its own free will . . . well, that changes everything! If this chicken, by some bizarre twist of fate, really believes in God, do you know what that means? It means this chicken had a *soul*, for Goodness' sake!"

"Well, of course he has a soul!" said Dillis. "That's the whole point, isn't it?! And he wants it baptized, so he can be a Catholic. Can you do it right now? That would be great."

"Right now!" Father Frank sounded horrified. "Right now! Are you out of your mind?! This is a chicken we're talking about here! We don't even baptize a human *being* until after at least six months of catechesis! I'd have to speak to the Bishop before I'd even *think* about enrolling this bird into RCIA! And *then*, my God, what a scene *that* would be!" The priest stared past them at some scene in his mind and after a moment began to shake his head again. "Oh, this can't be happening. It just can't be happening."

Charlie, who had been perched between the priest and Dillis but unable to put a word in because the two of them were too busy talking at each other to notice him, suddenly stood, stretched out his wings, and crowed. That singular noise reverberated through the sanctuary like the blast of a trumpet, and both Dillis and the priest looked down at him with expressions of absolute astonishment, the priest because he still could not imagine that Charlie could really be listening, and Dillis because such self-assertion was so unlike the Charlie he knew.

"What is it, Charlie?" said Dillis, holding out his palm.

Charlie shook his head and turned to the priest. "He wants to talk to you," said Dillis.

The priest gulped and extended his palm.

All I want, he wrote. *Is to be a Catholic. I don't want to make any trouble.* He lifted his head and looked up at the troubled face of the priest.

Father Frank softened. "I believe you," he said quietly. "But it's not that simple. I can't just baptize anybody who asks . . . unless, of course, it's an emergency. But under normal circumstances, the Church has very definite procedures . . . "

So these are normal circumstances? Scratched Charlie hopefully.

"No," the priest smiled a nervous smile. "But it's not an emergency, either. You're not dying, are you?"

No! Said Charlie.

"God forbid." Said Dillis.

Father Frank drummed his fingers on the pew. "May I ask you something, Charlie?"

Charlie nodded.

"Why here? You know, don't you, that there are many churches, many denominations. Why did you choose the Catholic Church?"

Transubstantiation, Charlie scratched promptly.

My God, Father Frank thought, there he goes again! Not only can he communicate, but he can even spell correctly! Half the yokels in this diocese probably can't spell communion, much less transubstantiation!

"What about transubstantiation, Charlie?" he said.

I think it explains a lot.

"What do you mean?"

Charlie thought, suddenly, unexpectedly of his mother. Would she really have left him to starve? Or had she, through some wordless animal instinct, known that Niniane would come along to take care of him and deliver him unto a world in which he could not merely survive? Had all this, had all the fear and pain and uncertainly he'd known in the past been foreordained? He wondered if he would ever know.

Things are not always what they seem to be.

"I've never thought of it that way," said Father Frank. "But you're right. I'm not sure, though, that it implies a Christian understanding of the doctrine. It is the body and blood of Christ that are offered in the Mass. Do you know what that means?"

That a wafer changes its nature when all evidence proves the contrary.

There was a long silence during which Father Frank rubbed both of his temples as if to ward off a migraine. Beside them, Dillis sat, vigilant, transfixed. He didn't know what Charlie was saying, but he felt proud of Charlie anyway.

Father Frank stood up and walked over into the aisle and looked at the altar. "Charlie," he said. "I'm glad you've come to see me. I wish I could give you what you want without reserve, but you must understand that there are many things . . . many other factors to consider. I know that I have promised you pastoral confidentiality, but I really feel that I should consult with one of my colleagues about this matter. I promise you that I'll do everything in my power to make sure your privacy and safety aren't compromised. Can I have your permission to speak with the Bishop about you?"

Charlie looked at Dillis, who drew his lips between his teeth and widened his eyes. Charlie regarded the priest, whose dark face seemed to glow with emotion, and nodded.

Whatever you have to do to baptize me, he scratched, *do it.*

The priest sat back down beside the chicken. He lifted his hand and briefly touched the growing comb on Charlie's head. "I'll be in touch," he said, "Thank you for coming."

Dillis picked up Charlie and placed him back in the crate. "Listen . . . " He gripped the priest by the wrist and squeezed it. Never in his life had he ever felt so determined and aggressive. "I hope you know what you're doing. Because if this chicken gets hurt, or taken away from us, there'll be hell to pay. You understand?"

The priest nodded.

Dillis softened his grip. "He trusts you." He said in a softer voice. "I can tell. So I guess I can trust you too. Just don't do anything stupid, okay? I . . . I love this chicken, man . . . " His voice broke.

"I can see that you do." The priest remarked.

⮌

As far as Dillis was concerned, the meeting was a success, but Charlie, though he did not say so, felt the lack of an assurance he had vaguely expected to receive. The priest's phrase "This will change everything!" made Charlie feel frustrated. All he wanted was to be baptized . . . it was that simple. The priest was making things more difficult than they needed to be.

Charlie rested his comb against the cool glass of the door. He stood in this dejected position for a long time, feeling only that somehow he had once again upset an equilibrium that he did not know existed. Was this his fate? To forever want the impossible, and to want desperately, as if not only his life, but something far more consequential than that depended upon his having what he could not have? He heard again in his mind's ear, Father Frank's complaint. "This will change *everything!*"

He lifted his head from the cool glass pane and looked directly at his own reflection. It does not! He thought. I'm not that different, I have a soul just like anybody else. If I'm baptized, it won't change *everything.* Charlie returned to his drawer. It was a shame, he thought, that the very first Christian to meet him had to be so narrow-minded.

⮌

Back in his rectory apartment, Fr. Frank lay in a very warm bath with a very dirty martini. He must relax deeply, he told himself, in order to have any hope of getting some sleep after such an encounter with—there was no other word for it—the paranormal. It had all been very disturbing. After Mrs. O'Connor had barged into his office with the mop, Father Frank thought fast and told her he must have had food poisoning. She called the sexton to take care of the mess and led Father Frank into one of the conference rooms where there was a row of six plush chairs upon which he lay for a good twenty minutes, trying to pray.

Providentially, in times of extreme stress, it was Father Frank's gift to be equipped with a tentative but sure sense of the presence, within the painful and contradictory, of God. He felt that this gift was necessary in his situation as a basically urbane priest in the most backwards of rural parishes, and without it, he would have long ago taken to drinking even more than the one binge a week he normally allowed himself. As it was, the consolations of prayer had been wearing thin lately, but he turned to them now in desperation. His head throbbed and his bowels felt as if they had turned to lard. What, he'd implored his sense of the numinous as he lay flat on his back on the row of chairs in the darkened conference room, was going on with this chicken?

He'd gone through it all, then, in short order, all the possibilities. The kid was a psychotic savant with a knack for animal training. This was a case of demonic infestation. The end result, no matter what, was bound to be humiliating. It was a nightmare. What was he supposed to do with a sentient, theologically astute chicken? Miracle or not, I don't want to deal with it. Joke or not, it isn't funny. This is just too much, he said, make it go away. I swear I'll stop drinking. I hate you God, he'd said, I hate this church, I hate *the* church, I hate life. I hate everything.

Thus he struggled with God. And as is the case with all honest struggle with the omnipotence, there came in the end a sense of surrender, and with that understanding, and with that the strength to struggle with the self. He sat up and heard the voice of his own convictions with absolute clarity. Get up, go to the church, talk to the boy, to his bird if necessary. This is why you are a priest; this is your responsibility. No matter what. No matter what this turns out be in the long run, it is waiting, in the sanctuary of your church, for you.

And so he'd made his way over to the sanctuary, where he'd learned from Charlie all about his amateur theological investigations. The chicken

spoke, (or, rather, wrote) as others he'd met in his life who, despite significant odds, achieved a remarkable degree of spiritual maturity that contra-
dicted lifestyles and personalities that seemed on the surface to be ungodly.
He remembered a woman he'd visited several times during his internship as
a hospital chaplain in Washington D.C.; a casualty of American hardheart-
edness in the face of poverty and disadvantage; she was dying of advanced
untreated hepatitis, addicted to crack, petty, paranoid and demanding. She
had been, on top of, and in spite of all that, a staunch Pentecostal. She'd
been suspicious of him as a Roman Catholic Priest, but somehow seemed
to appreciate his visits. The nurses in the ward had requested that he see
her in the hopes that his company would distract her enough to keep her
from harassing them for more pain medication than she needed. In this,
he'd been unsuccessful, but she'd been perfectly happy to have him in the
room while she pestered and berated the medical team, and they'd spent
one afternoon amusing themselves with a child's book of bible puzzles that
had been left by a candy striper. She'd looked at him that day, while he'd
been encircling, with unconscious and childlike pleasure in a small accom-
plishment, the name of the prophet Elijah in a word find, and she'd said, in
a voice at once like and unlike her usual ravaged, plaintive whine, that even
though it looked like she was going to die, God was still looking out for her.

He set his glass on the porcelain edge of the tub, closed his eyes, sank a
bit lower in the now lukewarm water, submerging that body of his that was
becoming, as the years flew past, distressingly meaty and cumbersome. He
was tired, and he had too much experience of the stubborn nature of human folly to harbor any romantic religious illusions. For all of her reckless,
if beautiful 'faith', chances were that woman in D.C. had died as wretch-
edly as she had lived, without any respect. God's ways are not our ways,
he reminded himself. You have no reason to think you have the answers.
"Tomorrow," he said, aloud, "I'll call the Bishop. He'll handle it."

With that, Father Frank finished off his martini, drained the bath and
went to bed.

Chapter Eleven

Catechumenate

LIFE ON THE FARM accelerated in pace as Charlie prepared himself for further encounters with officials of the Roman Catholic Church. He thought it would help him feel more competent as a potential Christian if he read the bible from cover to cover, but it was taking forever and so many passages of it were long and boring and incomprehensible. The only bible in the house was the black leather bound King James Bible that reminded Niniane of her grandfather, and which had, in fact, belonged to that disagreeable old man. The humans discussed it over cards one evening, and after a moment of staring into space with the flat expression of somebody who is struggling with the question of whether or not to tell some uncomfortable truth, May left the game without a word and marched up one flight of stairs to the second floor, then another flight to the attic. She returned holding a book about the size of a volume of the Encyclopedia and bound in a brightly illustrated cover. She sat down, laid the book flat, and pushed it across the table over to Charlie.

He read the title to himself. *The Bible Story.* Beneath the golden lettered title there was a brightly colored illustration of a bearded man in flowing violet robes standing near the summit of a mountain holding two curiously shaped plaques above his head. The expression of the man's face communicated an intense disapproval. Beneath him a congregation of hooded, turbaned, and bare human heads stared up at the man and his plaques as if he held them spellbound. It was a picture Charlie could look at, he thought, for hours.

May reached over and opened the book for him. "It's full of pictures," she said. "and the writing is very simple. Not that you can't read on a more advanced level, Charlie, but I think this would be the best way to get the basics before you try to read the real thing. These books . . . there's a whole set of them . . . are the closest I ever came to reading the bible." She looked at Niniane and smiled. "Your grandmother got them for me and your mom when we were little girls, and we used to look at them for hours. Even before we really knew how to read. The pictures . . . of course they're too Eurocentric . . . but they're marvelous anyway. They almost tell the story themselves. There's one in the last volume . . . I think it's a picture of the Good Samaritan . . . and even the Samaritan's donkey has a sad look on his face when they come across the Jew who was beaten and robbed. I think there's ten of them in all. I'll get the rest down tomorrow."

While May was explaining, Niniane and Dillis left their seats and went to stand on either side of Charlie, looking over his tiny head at Volume One of The Bible Story. Every few seconds Niniane reached over and turned a page. The pictures, she had to admit, were fascinating. In one of the first ones, a naked man, his privates strategically obscured by the position of his thigh, lay fast asleep on the ground while a disembodied hand traced a bloodless incision at the bottom of his ribcage. "Womb envy," Niniane sneered, but her hand lingered for a bit before she turned that page.

The next day May presented Charlie with the entire set of *The Bible Story* and by the end of the week he had skimmed through all of them. He found that he was particularly drawn to those stories, such as Jonah and the Whale, and Balaam's Ass, and Christ's casting of a legion of demons into a herd of swine, which involved animals as either direct or indirect agents of revelation. From the reaction of Father Frank to him, Charlie would never have thought that non-humans played any sort of speaking part in the bible, and when he mentioned this to Dillis, the boy told him that the priest probably hadn't read the whole bible, as Catholics tended to think the bible was less important than the Pope.

This concerned Charlie somewhat, but he decided not to worry about it. His conception of the papacy, garnered from the description of the dramatic history of that office in the Encyclopedia, was that through the centuries it was steadily becoming less presumptuous, and would soon gracefully retire itself in favor of a more democratic system of leadership.

⌒

For his part, Father Frank took up the question of Charlie's baptism with his immediate superior, the Rt. Rev. Bishop Vincent Serxner.

"Vinnie, has anything like this ever come up before?" asked Father Frank of the Bishop, who met him in the rectory of Our Lady of Pity.

"Are you serious, Carl? Of course not!" He rubbed his eyes wearily. "And of course it would have to happen in my diocese, of all places . . . Are you sure about this Carl? You really don't think it's some stunt?"

"As sure as I can be," said Father Frank. He sipped from his glass of iced tea. He'd offered one to the Bishop, but the Bishop had declined. Father Frank had not had a drop of alcohol since the day after meeting Charlie, and found that he was constantly and pleasantly thirsty for other liquids, particularly water with lemon. "You'll see what I mean when you meet him. When I'm not right there with him, I start to think I'm crazy, but when he was actually writing in my palm . . . well, it's like I could tell, somehow, that he could really understand what he was saying. And even talking to the boy . . . I don't know. It's just obvious that to him, this chicken is really another person. He treats it like–like a little brother, really. Not like a pet at all. And after a few moments, it seems perfectly natural . . . "

"Maybe to you . . . " said the Bishop. " . . . And you're sure they haven't told anyone else? Just you? No reporters? No neighbors? The girl's parents? Anybody?"

"As sure as I can be," said Father Frank. "Just the boy knows, and the girl, the lesbian aunts, and me, and now you. At least that's what the boy and the chicken told me. They're afraid something will happen to the bird if word gets out."

"They're right about that," said the Bishop. "The secular media would have a field day. A chicken who wants to be baptized Catholic! They'd be on us like . . . like vultures! Especially with all that molestation coming out of the woodwork. This is top secret, Carl. Until we know how to proceed with this, I don't want you to say anything to anybody . . . not Mrs. O'Connor, not your parents . . . no one." There was a moment of silence. "Except your confessor, of course."

Father Frank rolled his eyes and smiled, and gazed at the merrily sparkling ice in his glass of tea. Why did he feel so good? It was at once lovely and a little scary. "Don't worry," he said. "You can count on me. See you Friday at the farm."

"I'll never forgive you for sticking me with this." Said Bishop Serxner half seriously. He stood up and patted his white comb-over in place. "Just when I'm about to retire, you come up with a talking chicken. Why couldn't this have waited until next summer?"

"God doesn't want you to retire, I suppose." Said Father Frank. "And neither do I."

◡

When the Bishop called, May answered the phone. The Bishop introduced himself in his most pastoral manner and asked if he might call on Charlie at the farm. "That's up to Charlie," May told him. "We'll call you back."

She took his number and went outside to where Dillis, Niniane, and Charlie were all perched indolently of the back porch swing. They weren't even reading. It was a clear, terribly hot day and the sun, shimmering insouciantly above them in the blank blue sky seemed to draw all the life force on earth unto itself. May held the loose collar of her dress between thumb and forefinger and drew it away, then toward her chest in order to fan her face. She thrust her chin out at Charlie. "A Bishop just called," she said. "Name of Vincent. He wants to come here and talk to you."

Charlie's wings stirred. It had been nearly a week since his trip to Our Lady of Pity, so enough time had passed for the idea of another person knowing about his existence to seem alarming and risky. He opened his beak and May held her palm out. *He's coming here?* He scratched.

"That's what he wants." Said May.

Charlie nodded. He glanced at Niniane, whose face was turned sharply to the left, away from him, so that she appeared to be staring intently at the rather grimy white aluminum siding of the farmhouse. He could see, on either side of her thick ponytail, that the muscles of the back of her neck were tensed. Timidly, he reached over with his beak and lightly pecked her leg. She turned to look at him.

"What?"

Is that all right? He scratched into her palm.

"It isn't my decision, Charlie."

I want you to be there this time. He scratched. *I want him to meet you.*

Niniane was silent. A phrase came to her mind from some source she could not place, and she found it irritating. "Whither thou goest, I will go . . ."

She scowled. The remainder of the phrase dwindled off into the forgotten, but the first six words circled over the landscape of her memory like a bird of prey. "I don't like this, Charlie. It's getting out of hand. A stranger . . . a Bishop, for God's sake . . . coming *here* . . . I can't just sit there and pretend I agree with anything he represents . . . "

Charlie had her palm in front of him, but he could not bring himself to scratch his immediate thought: But he's not a stranger to *me* . . . he's a Catholic . . .

I don't want you to pretend. But you could help me. I'm getting scared too. I want to be baptized, but what if he's not as nice as Father Frank? I want you there with me. I want you all there. You and May and Irene and Dillis.

It took Charlie a long time to scratch all this, and as he did so, an image arose in Niniane's mind of Jesus, looking like a sinister, snickering, berobed, bearded hippie stealing away from the farm in the middle of the night with Charlie held captive in a pillowcase: Christ the kidnapper. She felt a hot surge of hatred for the Lord. She held her breath, then repeated Charlie's words to Dillis and her aunt.

"We'll be there, Charlie," Dillis assured him. "No one's going to dis you, not even a Bishop."

Niniane sighed. "It's not too late to call it off, Charlie," she pleaded, though deep down she knew it *was* too late. She felt the way her great grandmother must have felt in the moment between when the baby Rosa slipped out of her arms and the moment Rosa's skull smashed against the tree. Niniane shuddered.

Charlie nodded to May, who went back inside and called the Bishop. They made arrangements for him to come to the farm Friday afternoon— the very next day.

⤻

The Bishop parked his gray Mercedes behind Irene's muddy pickup and stepped out onto the gravel driveway. The farmhouse stood before him, its garage door open like a choking mouth, displaying a chaos of farm implements, old bicycles, lawn and garden bags, and cardboard boxes inside. While the Bishop stood, peering into that crowded darkness, a human figure began to move within and then proceed from it. It was a young man, the Bishop saw, tall, thin, with longish wavy brown hair and round eyeglasses. The Bishop stepped forward. "You must be Dillis," he said, offering his hand.

Dillis, noting the Bishop's large ring, wondered if he was supposed to kiss it. He shook the Bishops' hand.

"Yes, sir," said Dillis. "I'm Dillis Walksi. Charlie's inside. Just follow me."

The bishop looked back at the driveway. "Where's Father Frank? I don't see his car."

"I don't know, Your Honor. I guess he's running late."

The Bishop followed Dillis into the messy garage, then through a screen door in the right corner of it that opened into the kitchen of the farmhouse. Through the kitchen into the living room he could then see two middle-aged women sitting on a sofa, a young girl in a rather tattered brown recliner, and in her lap–even after all he'd heard, it still seemed unreal—a young male chicken.

Dillis preceded the Bishop into the living room. "The Bishop," said Dillis, ceremoniously. The two women on the sofa looked at one another, looked at the Bishop, smiled, and nodded. "Have a seat," said Irene, indicating a rocker across the coffee table. "I'm Irene."

The other, stouter woman stood and offered her hand. It was worn and yet delicate, with surprisingly soft, pale skin, like the hands of women who spend their lives tending children. "I'm May Blattery," she said. "Thank you for coming. Can I get you anything?"

"No thank you, Ms. Blattery." Said the Bishop. He shook her hand and sat down. He turned to the girl with the chicken in her lap. "And you must be Niniane."

Niniane swallowed, raised an eyebrow, nodded. "Hello." She managed to say. She had expected a minor pope type in flowing robes and a tall white hat. This man, in his sansabelt pants, loafers, and knit shirt looked like someone her father would play golf with. It was a little unnerving.

The Bishop nodded at the chicken in her lap. "And this is Charlie?"

Dillis had come around to stand beside the recliner. "Yes sir," he said.

"Well," said the Bishop, aware that his face was coloring as he addressed the chicken personally. "I've heard a lot about you Charlie."

To the Bishop, at least, it seemed as if the next moment was an eternity of extremely uncomfortable silence. Everyone in the room, including the chicken, was watching him intently.

"You have to hold your palm out." Niniane said flatly.

"Oh, my, yes!" Said the Bishop. "Father Frank told me about that; what am I thinking. He had hoped to come along, but I guess he's been held up." The Bishop closed his eyes briefly and prayed a brief prayer for forgiveness for this necessary white lie, the truth being that he had no idea where Father Frank was. As Bishop Serxner prayed, he allowed himself a split second fantasy of sending a drunken and repentant Father Frank to an even more remote rural parish for being so irresponsible. He held open his palm. "I understand you would like to become a Catholic, Charlie."

Yes.

The Bishop took his hand out from under Charlie's beak and stared at it for a moment. He stood up. He shook his head. "Excuse me," he said, and he went through the kitchen into the garage, then out into the driveway. Once at his car, he leaned against the driver's side door, and stared at his palm again.

Yes. The motion of the creature's beak seemed to repeat itself in the skin of his hand. It tickled. He saw again the bob and weave of the chicken's tiny head as he wrote the word 'yes.' It would be comical if it weren't so disturbing. The Bishop looked up at the sky. "Why God?" He whispered, his voice suddenly gravelly.

Forty years in ministry had taught him that the answer to this question was never immediately forthcoming. He looked toward the farmhouse. He couldn't be sure, but it looked like a small figure was standing on the windowsill gazing out at him. I mustn't worry him unnecessarily, he thought. I've got to pull myself together. So he took a deep breath and headed to the front door, but not before he took one last look down the long gravel driveway in the hope of seeing Father Carl Frank's car approaching.

⌐

Later, Niniane stood alone at the front of the garage as the Bishop's car backed out of that gravel driveway. She stood there long after the car had disappeared.

The others were all inside. The Bishop had asked Niniane to see him to his car after he concluded his meeting with Charlie. She's been surprised when he'd asked her to do that, because she had not said more than five words to him since his arrival. Everyone, even her dreams, seemed to be implore her to allow Charlie's to pursue this foolhardy catholic lunacy without question. It's not, she'd thought, while she watched Charlie's beak scratching the Bishop's palm, that I don't think it's important for Charlie. I know it is. I just don't trust these *men.*

At one point, while the Bishop was talking to Charlie, basically repeating to him what he'd told Father Frank, Dillis had put his hand on her shoulder. Subtly, with as little movement as possible, she twitched, and he took his hand away. Not long after that the Bishop looked right at her and said he was afraid he's have to be going, but that he would appreciate it if she would see him to his car. The old man rose then, bent over, placed his right hand upon Charlie's comb, mumbled for a moment with his eyes closed, then shook hands with Dillis and May and Irene. He followed Niniane out through the garage, and spoke to her as they stood beside his car.

"Do you have a minute or two to talk, Ms. Westvane?" He said.

She shrugged again. "I guess."

The Bishop's bushy eyebrows crooked and rose with professional sympathy. "You aren't very happy about me being here."

Niniane shrugged again. "It's what Charlie wants. He has a mind of his own—" she winced internally as she heard herself repeat what everyone was so fond of telling her, "—and I—" here she looked into the Bishop's face—"I support him, no matter what choice he makes. Even if I don't agree with it."

"You don't agree with Charlie's becoming a Christian?"

"I don't agree with Christianity." She said.

"Then why does Charlie?" Said the Bishop.

Niniane was startled. She looked up into the Bishop's face with real amazement. "How should I know?"

"You can't know . . . unless he's told you. But I suspect these are not comfortable matters for you to talk about, with anyone. Your convictions."

"You're wrong about that. Everyone knows what my convictions are. Animals should not be slaughtered and subject to the needs of humans. All life is precious. Humans aren't the only animals that feel fear and pain. Charlie's proof of that. But I knew all this long before Charlie came along."

"How did you know?"

Niniane scowled. That was none of this old man's concern. "I just did."

"You sound like a young woman with a strong sense that we human beings are subject to a dangerous pride."

"That's for damn sure."

The Bishop smiled. "Some would say that those who acknowledge the limits of human reasoning are on the threshold of faith."

Niniane glared at him. "Maybe," she said. "And maybe some others would say that its obvious from the mess the world is in that humans aren't—and shouldn't be—in charge of everything. That doesn't mean we have to give our hearts to Jesus. It just means we see what's going on, and we want to stop it."

The Bishop was quiet a moment. "All right, Ms. Westvane. I'm not trying to convert you. I'm just trying to understand more . . . about the nature of Charlie's abilities . . . and his faith. His desire to be baptized is so extraordinary, and to me really quite moving. But I'm concerned about you, too, Ms. Westvane."

Why? This isn't about me."

"It's about someone you love. None of this would be happening if you didn't truly love Charlie."

Niniane stepped back. She shoved her hands in the back pockets of her cut-offs. It was a very warm day. She suddenly felt very conscious of how much of her legs were showing.

"What do you want from me?"

The Bishop looked down the driveway for a second. To the right, to the left, and in the distance, there seemed to be nothing inhabited but this farm. Back in the living room, this girl's distress, made palpable in her neglecting to suggest, despite the length of the meeting, that the Bishop hold Charlie rather than she, seemed to dominate the entire atmosphere in the room. She was acting, he realized, like a person holding a massive grief at bay.

"Ms. Westvane, this is more about you than you realize."

"What do you mean?"

"I mean that you are a major factor in this undertaking. If Charlie is baptized, you need to think about what that is going to mean for you and your friends and family. What I'm saying, Ms. Westvane–"

"Oh, for God's sake, call me by my first name."

"For God's sake, then, what I'm saying, Niniane, is that Charlie will make history. And by virtue of that, so will you. Nothing like this has happened before in the entire history of Christianity. Now, from talking to Charlie, I can see that he doesn't quite realize what all this means. And also from talking to Charlie, I can see that the one person he really loves, more, maybe than his own soul, is you. And frankly Niniane, I need you to help him to see that he implicates you all in what he is doing."

"Me!"

"You. And your aunts. And your . . . young man."

"But . . . I don't want to have anything to do with all this church stuff. And Charlie knows that! He wouldn't drag me into it."

"He wouldn't . . . but the world will, Ms . . . Niniane. You are going to be involved in spite of . . . and because of . . . Charlie's naiveté. Unless someone . . . perhaps you . . . can help him to see that there is more at stake here than just his sense of religious affiliation . . . " The Bishop looked meaningfully at Niniane.

There was a silence. "You want me to talk him out of it." She said. "You want me to get him off your back."

The Bishop looked away. Of course she was right. She was no fool. "I suppose so." He admitted. "This is not going to be pretty. The Roman Catholic Church is very resistant to change. And Charlie's desire for baptism represents a change so fundamental it could turn the Church upside down . . . not to mention our lives . . . you could explain to him that the implications are enormous . . . you could save yourself . . . and Charlie . . . and the Church . . . a great deal of controversy . . . "

Niniane peered at the Bishop. "I'm not going to do your church's dirty work." She said. "Sorry."

The Bishop smiled. "I won't either." He said. "I'm going to refer the matter to the Archbishop. Tell Charlie that we'll be in touch soon." He raised his hand in a reflexive gesture of blessing, got in his car and drove away, leaving a long low cloud of dust to settle. Niniane went inside to report to the others that the Bishop was kicking Charlie's baptism upstairs.

What does that mean? Scratched Charlie onto Niniane's palm.

"I think it means he doesn't want to say no, Charlie."

Then why doesn't he say yes?

"He's a fraidy-cat, Charlie." Said Niniane, reverting, in her indignation, to a forgotten childhood term.

What's that?

Niniane was going to simply say that it was another word for coward, but suddenly and surprisingly her heart softened towards the Bishop, who had at least spoken to her as if she were an adult. "He's just trying to be careful." She said. "Don't worry too much, Charlie."

Chapter Twelve

Fractures

THE ACCIDENT HAPPENED THE very next morning. Enjoying a rare moment to himself without his beak in a book, Charlie was walking along the perimeter of the wooden railing that encircled the raised back patio when he was frightened by the sudden presence of a large orange, uncivilized looking cat on the railing less than ten feet in front of him. Providentially, Niniane was walking into the living room at that exact moment. She saw through the glass door what was happening, screamed and struggled with the heavy sliding glass doorway which tended to stick in its runner, scrambled outside, but by then the damage was done. Charlie had fallen nearly ten feet to the ground below, and the cat was getting ready to pounce when Niniane, shrieking, pushed the cat off the porch railing, then hoisted herself over the railing onto the grass to where Charlie lay motionless.

"Charlie! Are you all right?!" she screamed, but of course, there was no audible answer from Charlie. His beak opened and closed several times, so she knew he was alive, but she did not think to hold out her hand so he could speak. She started to pick him up, but as soon as she did he emitted a strangled squawk and his left wing beat the air.

"Oh my god," Niniane moaned. "Oh my god, Charlie." She stood up and screamed. "DILLIS! MAY! IRENE! GET OUT HERE, QUICK! IT'S CHARLIE!" Her voice broke on the final syllable. She cupped herself like a shell over the injured bird.

Dillis was in the shower, having slept late, but May came running. "What is it?!" She shouted, scrambling down the stairs of the patio, but before Niniane could answer May saw Charlie lying not completely motionless underneath her niece.

"Did he fall?" She said. Niniane raised herself to a kneeling position with her hands over her mouth and nodded.

"From up there? Oh dear . . . " May bent down over the fallen chicken and touched his head gently. "Charlie?" She said. The beak opened once again, feebly.

"He can't move!" Niniane bent down beside her aunt. "I tried to pick him up, but it hurt him, he screamed and beat his wings, but he didn't get up–oh *Jesus*, May!"

May ran her hand along the length of Charlie's body. Niniane gasped. "Don't *hurt* him, May!"

"Niniane, be quiet." Said May. She took a deep breath. Niniane stood up, took a step back, then took a step forward and leaned over Charlie again.

"Is he gonna be okay?"

"I said be *quiet.*" May's voice roughened the final word, and Niniane took a step back and stayed back. She looked around for the cat, which had landed, despite Niniane's shove, on its feet, and stalked away into the woods from whence it had come.

With excruciating slowness, May lifted the chicken. Again, he beat his left wing, but not as frantically as when Niniane had tried to lift him. May ran her hand lightly over the wing and it stilled. She lifted Charlie to the level of her face and peered at his right side. She ran her hand over him, this time on his right side, and once again Charlie emitted a high pitched, gurgling squawk.

May set him down. "It's his wing. He's broken it."

Niniane moaned.

May stood up. "Niniane, go inside and get that milk crate. And a pillow from the sofa. Hurry!"

"What are you gonna do?! Is he all right?"

"We're taking him to the vet, Niniane. What else can we do?"

⌐〜

It took a full forty-five minutes to get to the veterinarian's office, which was located in a small town 25 miles to the north. They took Dillis' car, rather than Irene's truck, which could only seat three. The vet confirmed May's diagnosis without even a second glance at Charlie.

"Broken wing," she said abruptly after prodding Charlie briefly very much in the same way May had. "How'd it happen?"

"A *&%$•~@ cat was about to get him and he fell off the porch railing." Said Niniane, tearfully.

The vet raised an eyebrow and looked at Irene. "You had a chicken out on your porch?" She said.

"It's a long story, Nancy." Said May.

May set the milk crate on the chrome exam table and the vet leaned over him. "He's a nice size. Good color in his comb, and his eyes are bright. Shame he had to get hurt. The hens won't have much to do with him now . . . " She said. "Tsk. What do you want me to do?"

"Can't you help him?" Niniane's voice was a helpless squeal.

"Hush, Niniane," said May. "Nancy, our niece has been raising this rooster for herself as a pet. He's not really livestock. Whatever you can do to set his wing, do it. We're all attached to him. We don't want him . . . " She glanced warningly at Niniane. "E-U-T-H-A-N-I-Z-E-D."

The veterinarian nodded. "Gotcha." She'd seen it a million times. Every once in a while, even the most unsentimental farmers got attached to one of their animals and just couldn't treat it like the others. Something, she guessed, just made the animal seem special, and when that happened, no matter what, that animal got royal treatment. She knew a pig farmer in the next county, a huge, burly, no-nonsense redneck named Pittman who actually had a Christmas stocking for one of his sows whom he called, interestingly, Big Mama.

"Well, he'll never play piano," said the veterinarian. "But I'll fix him up." Seeing that her joke had little effect on the chicken's owners, the doctor sighed and then in a flat voice directed the human beings into the waiting room so that she could treat the patient in peace. It got on her nerves when the owners huddled.

⤸

The vet told them it would be best for their chicken to stay at the animal hospital overnight; just on the slim chance that he might reinjure his splinted wing back on the farm, but his owners insisted that they take him home. "He'll be still," said the young girl. "We keep him in the house, anyway. He's very well trained."

"Whatever you say." Said the doctor, and handed the prescription for painkillers to May. She watched as the little group walked out into the parking lot with the groggy chicken in a yellow milk crate. She turned to her receptionist, who was straightening up the magazines that Dillis had left open and in disorder on the waiting room table and said, "Poor chicken. At least he didn't put up a fuss when I wrapped his wing. He really was pretty easy, but I still think it's a shame . . . "

"Why's that?" Said the receptionist, since she knew she was expected to.

The veterinarian sighed and ran her fingers through her hair. "I don't know why, but it makes me sad. It's one thing to get attached to an animal, but it's another thing treat it like it's something it isn't. If that girl keeps that chicken inside all the time, he'll be miserable. Chickens are not humans. That bird needs sunlight and exercise and pretty soon he's going to want to mate, but with that bad wing I doubt he'll have any luck."

The receptionist grunted. She was a temp, and did not plan on staying at this job after the end of the week, primarily because she didn't approve of her boss's occasional use of profanity. As a member of the Cornerstone Christian Assembly, she did not approve of women in positions of authority other than the sacred office of motherhood, and she would not be working at all had her husband not told her to in order to save up money for the mission trip to Mexico they were planning as soon as their youngest son completed his long distance transport training course, got a job and was out of the house. She also did not approve of those two strange women who lived on the old Blattery place, and she was disgusted to see that there were a boy and a girl who were obviously too young to be dating with them and glommed onto each other without an ounce of respect for anyone else around them. And crying, at least that girl was, like the world was ending over a chicken with a broken wing. It just goes to show, she told herself, how lost and misguided people are when they don't have Jesus in their lives.

The receptionist's terse grunt and pinched expression were not lost on the veterinarian. "Why don't you go on home, Ms. Matthews." She sighed. "I'll lock up."

"Thanks." Said the receptionist, and without meeting her boss's eyes, she moved past her to the reception room, took her purse and Good News Bible in its custom embroidered zippered case, and left the building.

༄

Niniane, Dillis and May were so preoccupied with checking in on Charlie to see if he felt okay that not one of them noticed, as they all peered into the milk crate that Niniane was holding, that the receptionist was walking right by them.

Dillis, having asked Charlie how he was doing, had his hand in the crate, and was waiting to feel the cool, gentle, firm scrape of Charlie's little beak.

"What did he say?!" The receptionist heard the teenage girl demand. "Dillis, did he say anything?"

"Hold on, Niniane!" Said the boy. He withdrew his hand "He said he feels better, but he's sleepy. He wonders if it's the shot they gave him."

"Of course it is! Tell him it's just the shot, that he's fine . . . "

"Well, what on earth . . . " the receptionist cried. She burst out laughing. With one motion, three heads turned in her direction, and the receptionist, who had seen miracles and who herself had experienced that anointing of the Holy Spirit which granted the gift of tongues, realized that she'd never seen three human beings at the exact same moment each turn so deathly pale.

↬

"Niniane." Said Dillis firmly, with all the manfulness he could muster. They were back at the farm, sitting on the back porch, and he was trying to look her in the eye. "She's not going to say anything."

"Then why did she just laugh at us and run away? And she pulled out her phone as soon as she got in her car, and started talking to someone. You saw it just like I did, Dillis!"

"Oh, she was probably just returning a call! She doesn't have the slightest clue about Charlie, Niniane, people talk to their pets all the time . . . "

Niniane dismissed this optimism with a click of her tongue. "She's still going to say something. I know it. She's going to go home and say to her husband, 'you know, I saw the funniest thing. Those two that have the farm out that way, Well, I always knew they were strange, but today they came to the office and tried to talk to this chicken of theirs that broke his wing.' And the husband's going to say, Well, that's it; they're on drugs out there on top of everything else. Go on and call the sheriff.'"

"Niniane, you're being paranoid."

"You're being naïve. You're from Boston, Dillis, you don't know what people are like out here. They don't like anything that's different. They've never liked May and Irene. One time, when I was little . . . well, when I was thirteen . . . a couple of the older boys who worked over on the Bracey's farm chased me all the way home from the lake, calling me a little lezzie. I'd been swimming, and I don't know what they might have done if they caught up with me . . . anyway, when I was little, when my grandparents were alive, the people out here used to be nice to me, but ever since May and Irene bought the place . . ." Niniane hung her head. She hated this. She wanted to think of the farm as a place out of the world, inviolable and protected. Her aunts and their confidence in themselves and the integrity of their way of life made that illusion a reality—most of the time. But things were changing. Fast.

Dillis stood up and walked around. Just inside the sliding glass door, Charlie was sleeping with the aid of the shot the vet had given him, free for the moment of pain and worry. Dillis wished, suddenly for his marijuana stash, the last of which he had smoked the night before. He shoved his hands in his pockets and walked back around and knelt in front of Niniane.

"Niniane, please don't worry, babe. It'll be okay."

Niniane still sat slumped in the porch swing, and Dillis took her hand, which remained limp and unresisting and warm in his own. He suddenly wanted, more than anything, to kiss her, to hold her close to him, silent and sad, in that swing, and to have her cling to him. He doubted that would happen. But her eyes were open, and looking, with something not unlike need, into his.

"I wish I thought so," she said. "I'm scared to death. Aren't you?"

Dillis sighed. "Yeah. I am."

"Even if she doesn't say anything . . . " Niniane squeezed her eyes shut. "And I know she will. I know it."

Dillis tightened his grip on her hand. Still she didn't resist. He took off his glasses with his other hand and rubbed the bridge of his nose. "I know. It doesn't matter. He's not safe with us anymore. I mean, we can't keep him safe."

"What's going to happen to him?" Niniane leaned forward and rested her soft, warm cheek against Dillis' neck.

"He's going to get baptized."

"Then what?"

"I don't know. "

Niniane said nothing, and Dillis' hand moved from her shoulder to her waist. He drew her body in towards his own and held his breath, waiting for her to pull away. But she didn't. They rested upon one another like this for a while, and Dillis was reminded of those first few weekend nights that they spent together in the backseat of his car. This was a Niniane he'd sometimes thought, especially since he'd made his decision not to return to high school, that he'd never see again. He took a deep breath, taking in with it the scent of her hair and her skin. This, he thought, is better than weed. Why can't she always be like this? He lifted her hair from her cheek to kiss her.

Niniane stiffened and pulled away. "Dillis?" she said abruptly, as if she was finding herself suddenly awakened in an unfamiliar place. "Listen. I know what to do. If that secretary makes trouble, we'll just take him home. To my house. My parent's house, I mean. We won't tell anyone, not even Irene or May. That way, he'll be safe, and he'll be with me, until we can figure out what to do. Don't you think that's a good plan?"

"Sure." Said Dillis. He sighed and hunched over, and looked down through the cracks in the planks of the wooden patio floor at the damp dark ground underneath. Taking Charlie to Niniane's parent's house probably would do any good, but Dillis was suddenly too tired to argue or even care.

Niniane stood up. She leaned over and kissed Dillis warmly and wetly—on the cheek. "I really do love you, Dillis," she said. "I'm so glad you're here with me through all of this. A lot of guys wouldn't be able to handle it. But I knew you could . . . " Oblivious to the fact that Dillis was scowling at the ground beneath the patio, she spun around a few times on the balls of her feet, suddenly carefree. "I think I better go inside and turn on the TV and make sure there's nothing on there about Charlie. It's almost time for the six o'clock news." And with that she opened the sticky sliding glass door with a minor struggle and pranced into the living room, causing Charlie to stir druggedly in his dresser drawer. She bent over him and cooed, "Go back to sleep, Charlie. Everything's going to be just fine, sweetie."

In his opiated dream, Charlie was lifted by gentle hands to recline upon a bosom as soft as a cloud, as the voice of a distant angel sung his praises. He opened and shut his beak, bobbed his head up and down a few strokes, and was still.

Outside, Dillis wondered where he could possibly buy some weed out here in the middle of nowhere.

⌐

The morning after the cat incident Charlie woke up a little nauseous on account of the anesthetic the vet gave him. He felt awkward with a splint and bandage wrapped around his wing, but as he used the wing merely for balance, he only really noticed it when he was walking around—which wasn't often. He took to spending much of his time indoors now, never asking to be let out onto the patio unless somebody was close by. He had no desire to meet that cat again.

Meanwhile the Bishop, having been alerted by Dillis about the cat attack, was at work attempting, as discreetly as he could, to inquire into the possibility of having a chicken baptized. Progress was slow, such a question never having been seriously approached before. He brought it up to a number of canon lawyers of his acquaintance, claiming that it was a hypothetical question put to him by a child in the cathedral youth group, but none of them responded to his e-mails. The timing couldn't be worse. No one in the Church these days, the bishop reflected, was much in the mood for speculation. And now it was beginning to seem that if the question of Charlie's baptism was to be officially approached, it would have to be sooner rather than later, for the cat attack highlighted the precariousness of Charlie's situation. Anything could happen at any time, so there was no time to waste.

Bishop Serxner was almost seventy-five years old, and he couldn't decide if all of this sudden flurry of drama towards the end of his career was pleasing to him or not. Certainly it was fascinating, but it was also extremely frustrating, and the frustration was exacerbated by Father Frank's suddenly unaccountable flakiness. After being bishop for almost three decades, he thought he'd been a highly conscientious shepherd of clergy, checking in on his priests regularly and noting and responding to any hint that they might be burning out or worse, acting out. But after his meeting with Charlie earlier in the week, the Bishop had gone directly to Father Frank's rectory and found him there prone on his sofa with the television on, not drunk, as the Bishop at first, with a sinking heart assumed, but sleeping. Upon being awakened, Frank had announced, sleepily and with an infuriatingly placid countenance, that God was calling him out of the priesthood.

"Have you lost your mind?" The Bishop had exclaimed. "This could be the biggest . . . for the Love of God, this *will* be the biggest upheaval in the history of the Church since the damn Reformation! And *you* brought me into this, Carl! You can't just dump all this on me!"

The younger priest, wrapped in an enviably comfortable looking striped bathrobe, only yawned and leaned back on his sofa. "Sit down, Vinnie," he said. "And don't yell at me. Everything's going to be okay."

"Carl," the bishop spoke through his teeth at first, "For you to all of a sudden *drop out*–well, it's only going to make the whole thing look even more fishy! Don't you have any *consideration?*" the bishop sputtered and was silent. For a moment he felt like taking the cord of Father Frank's bathrobe and wrapping it around the younger priest's unshaven throat.

"Vinnie," Father Frank said. "There is no other way. Believe me. *No other way.* Since the very first time I felt that chicken's beak in my palm, there has been something incredible going on inside of me. At first, I thought it was just the shock . . . the weirdness of it all, but Vinnie, I've been doing a lot of thinking since then . . . a lot of praying . . . and last night, Vinnie, I had a dream." He looked at the Bishop expectantly.

The bishop rolled his eyes. He couldn't help it.

Carl Frank laughed. "I know how it sounds, Bishop. Believe me. I've heard it all before too, you know, all the Freudian and Jungian explanations, I've know that it's all supposed to be ambiguous, that you can't infer the future from dreams, you can only infer your own feelings. But Vinnie, this was not your normal dream. It wasn't even your normal *vision* . . . if there is such a thing as a normal vision. This, Vinnie, was *apocalyptic*. I was standing at the alter saying Mass, and at the moment of consecration, all of a sudden I could feel myself being transformed, into all things, a lily! One minute I was myself, a priest, and the next moment, I was in the middle of a field, and I could feel my roots drinking in moisture from the earth, and I couldn't see or hear, but I could feel myself bobbing in the breeze and taking in the sunlight and I was surrounded by other flowers like myself, and by God, I was a lily! And I'd never felt so complete in all my life! The moment I woke up, I knew I'd received a call from God. I'm telling you, Vinnie, it wasn't like anything that has ever happened to me before in my life. It was so *real*, Vinnie; it was so straightforward. The moment I woke up, I knew what I had to do, and I had peace, Vinnie, more peace in my heart than I've had in years. I don't know, Vinnie, maybe it is all of the stress, maybe my mind had gone haywire, but to tell you the truth, I don't think so. Because it seems to me that if I were cracking up, I'd feel like I was on a *mission* or something. But I don't! It's just the opposite, in fact. I feel like all I really need to do in this world is to be a landscaper. I want to spend my life working with my hands in the dirt, helping things to grow . . . "

Bishop Vincent Serxner' s jaw dropped. He stared at the swarthy, stubbly glowing face of the younger priest on the sofa beside him and searched it for signs of mania, if not full-blown psychosis. But Father Frank's expression was quite calm, if a bit dreamy and the Bishop was struck by the realization that for the first time in their acquaintance with one another, the young priest was not talking to him as if he, the Bishop, his superior, had the answer to everything. Father Frank was owning himself.

The Bishop leaned back in his seat and closed his eyes. There was definitely a shift here, but he mustn't get carried away. One did not forsake one's consecration merely on account of a dream, no matter how numinous. He opened his eyes, stood up, and put his hand on Father Frank's terrycloth covered shoulder.

"A landscaper," he said slowly. "That sounds like a noble calling, but Carl . . . you can't jump to conclusions. I see now that I've let you become too isolated in this parish . . . you need the stimulation of a nearby community of colleagues, but now with all of this business about the chicken coming up, surely you must see that we have to be patient. Change is coming, it's inevitable, so can't you wait? You're going to be at the forefront of a major theological development! You'll probably be made a Monsignor before all this is over with! And besides, who on earth am I going to get to replace you?"

Carl Frank leaned forward and his bathrobe gaped, revealing an unbecomingly hairy chest and stomach. "Vinnie. I'm not going to leave you in the lurch entirely. Whatever I can do to help you . . . and to help Charlie's cause . . . I'll do, but one thing you have to be clear about is that I can no longer function as a priest. It would be . . . a betrayal. All my life, it seems like, I've been waiting for this . . . this one thing to come along that I can do for the Church, and now that it's come, it's like I'm set free. I was meant for this one thing, Vinnie . . . but I wasn't meant to spend my whole life as a priest. I think I've known that for a long time, but I just couldn't admit it. I don't like people, Vinnie. I've got to admit it. You and I get along because we basically agree about things, but about when you retire? I'd go off the deep end, Vinnie . . . "

"Frank, don't be melodramatic."

"Vinnie, you know it's the truth. If this whole thing has taught me anything, it's that things are never what they seem. You've made my time as a priest tolerable, Vinnie. You've taken me under your wing, and I'm grateful. But I've never been happy. And that's not fair to me, you, or Our Lady of Pity. I love the Church, but I don't like it, and I have to have something to like soon, or I'll stop being able to love. Sometimes you have to turn away from the things you love in order to grow up. Do you see what I mean?"

"No," said the Bishop. "But I'm not going to argue with you. You have my support if you feel that God truly calling you be laicized. I just hope you realize that leaving the priesthood is not going to solve all your problems. Neither will being a lily. Carl, I wouldn't be a responsible bishop . . . or friend . . . if I didn't ask you . . . when was your last drink?"

Father Frank grinned like a child with a good report card. "Since the night after I met Charlie. I haven't even wanted one since then!"

"Good for you." Said the Bishop. "Unfortunately, I think I could use one. Carl, why didn't you at least come out to the farm today? It went well enough, but my God, I could have used some backup. The girlfriend is like a little vegan Eva Peron. She's very protective of that bird."

Frank shifted in his seat and looked sheepish. "I overslept. I didn't mean to, but I was up so late after the dream, writing in my journal, and I turned on the TV to keep me awake, but it didn't work, and I fell into the most wonderful, dreamless sleep. I guess it was just meant to be, Vinnie. You know I wouldn't have thrown you to the lions on purpose."

The Bishop rose and Frank followed him to the door. "You know I'll need a letter giving me official notice of your intention to be released from your vows, Carl. His hand grasped the doorknob but was still. He looked back at the younger cleric. "You're not out of the woods yet. I don't have the last word. The Church does."

"God does." Said Carl Frank.

"I suppose you expect me to say 'touché.'" Said the Bishop. "But believe me, the Church can outshout God when it wants to."

"We'll see." Said Carl Frank placidly. "In the meantime, you know I'll do anything I can to help you, Vinnie. You've been my rock."

"Just pray for me." Said the weary Bishop. "And be patient. I have a lot to do with this Charlie business before I can even begin to think about Our Lady of Pity. So if you know of anyone who can take over . . . I mean anyone, even someone right out of seminary . . ."

"I'll ask around. But Vinnie, about Charlie, what's the next step?"

"I have to take it up with the Archbishop. But before I do that, I'm calling in the Franciscans."

"Smart move."

↩

Father Angelo Schiaparelli, OFM, stood on the front porch of the farmhouse in his homespun habit and fingered his rosary beads while he waited for someone to answer the door upon which he just knocked. Brother Sun was beating down upon the young Friar's head with ebullient intensity. Father Angelo considered knocking again, figuring that he had not knocked loud enough, perhaps, the first time, but then the thought occurred to him that there was a good reason that he should be kept waiting. Perhaps he was not yet sufficiently spiritually prepared for this unusual encounter. He turned on the front stoop and regarded the donated Ford Fiesta he'd driven. A prayer for patience, he told himself, and then I'll ring the doorbell. In time, the door would be opened.

He crossed himself and silently recited the third joyful mystery with a concentration of attention that rendered him momentarily oblivious to the heat. This done, he closed his eyes and recalled the events of the previous morning with a similar intensity. The Bishop had called the diocesan retreat center/Franciscan Abbey where Father Angelo acted as Prior.

"Angie," the Bishop had said. "I have a favor to ask you. And it's a doozy."

"Ask away." Angelo had said. "Just don't call me Angie."

"Angelo, seriously. I have a big problem out in Robeson County. It involves a chicken. I thought of you fellows instantly."

Father Angelo was all ears after that. He was a young Friar, but an accomplished one, with a master's degree in Medieval Literature and a knack for arboriculture. Father Angelo had always suffered from an excess of nervous energy. Surviving on only four hours sleep a night, when he was not absorbed in some problem, he had the tendency to wonder if perhaps he was not quite human. He was a short man with a wiry build and a sparse, course, goatlike beard, and he had an excess of body hair, which made him highly susceptible to heat rash, especially in this southern climate.

Father Angelo crossed himself, stood, and knocked, this time very loud, with great energy, and praised God for God's manifold, infinite means of communicating divine will.

⤸

Irene answered the door. "Yeah?" she said.

Father Angelo smiled at the lanky big woman in the doorway. "Good afternoon! I'm Angelo Schiaparelli, of the Franciscan Order of Friars Minor. Bishop Serxner asked me to stop by here and visit with a chicken named Charlie."

Irene opened the door. Even though they had all been made aware by the Bishop that the Franciscans would be involved in Charlie's case, no one, not even Dillis, relished the prospect of the chicken's being carted off to a retreat center for safekeeping. None of them could bring themselves to tell Charlie, either. It was decided that the Friar would come to the farm, introduce himself to Charlie, and break the news. Niniane retreated to her room as soon as she heard the sound of an unfamiliar car crunching up the driveway.

Irene led Father Angelo into the living room, where Charlie was sitting on a pillow by the sliding glass door reading a Norton Anthology of English Literature, having decided to take a break from theology for a while. He raised his head and looked at the friar, and stood up, which in this situation, on account of his lack of lips, was his equivalent of greeting a stranger.

Father Angelo had been told by the Bishop that the chicken communicated by writing in one's palm with his beak. "It's easier," the Bishop had said, "if you just put him on your lap."

Father Angelo didn't feel comfortable assuming so intimate a contact right away. He sat down, lotus style, in front of Charlie. "Good afternoon!" he said, rather slowly, as if he were talking to his hard of hearing immigrant great-grandmother who did not understand English very well. "My name's Angelo Schiaparelli. I'm a priest of the Franciscan Order of Friars Minor, and Bishop Serxner and Father Frank asked me to drop by and see you. St. Francis, the founder of our order, as you may or may not know, is said to have had a very strong rapport with non-human creatures. Do you know what the word 'rapport' means? It happens to be term derived from the French language." He held out his hand, and sure enough, the chicken began to form letters in it with his beak.

No. What does it mean?

The friar was still for a moment as he struggled with a feeling of incredulity he had not foreseen. For as long as he could remember, Father Angelo had imagined himself to be uncommonly attuned to the emotions of animals, and even of plants, hence his hobby of tree cultivation. He had grown up, the youngest son of a large Sicilian family in Staten Island, with one of his immigrant great-grandmothers in the home; and it was this old lady that had sowed in young Angelo the seeds of his vocation. She had been remarkable for her own fervent devotion to the humble, benevolent, animal-loving saint Francis of Assisi, and it was noted by family and neighbors alike that, from the day the old woman moved in with the family until the day of her burial, not one cockroach was ever to be seen in any of the apartments of the large tenement building in which they lived. After her death, however, the bugs that took advantage of her absence were plentiful and large, and even gentle Angelo was obliged to kill them, though never without remorse and the resolve to try to apply the example of the Poverello in such a way that he and creatures like the cockroaches could share the planet in peace. It was not until he was a postulant, working in a Baltimore soup kitchen, that he realized that his great-grandmothers' secret, at least in part, had a lot to do with keeping things clean and not wasting food by throwing it away. Still, Father Angelo sensed throughout his life that there was more to the relationships between the manifold animal and plant species inhabiting the earth than meets the eye, and for this reason he joined the Franciscan order, and for this reason he felt adequate to the task of watching over Charlie while the chicken appealed to the hierarchy for the sacrament of initiation. The Bishop's call had surprised Father Angelo, but he could imagine stranger things. Did not the Scriptures say that all things would in time proclaim the Glory of God? He smiled at the creature before him.

"*Rapport* means, Relationship, especially one of trust or emotional affinity. It derives from the root word in Latin 'porter' to carry, with the prefix 're' indicating a sense of reciprocity, or returning. The founder of our order, St. Francis of Assisi had a knack for finding common ground. He was a poet, by inclination."

I like poetry, scratched Charlie. *Are you a poet too?*

"I am a priest." Said the friar, noncommittally. "May I ask what you're reading?"

Swinburne. Scratched Charlie. *It's great.*

"Love, the first and last of all things made/ the light that has the living world for shade/" Father Angelo quoted. "I am blessed with a nearly photographic memory. I only rarely forget the things I read."

Charlie was impressed. He liked this unusual person! *Niniane said a friar would be coming to see me. She didn't say why. What's happening? Is it because I broke my wing?*

The friar regarded Charlie's bandaged wing. "How does it feel?"

Okay.

"Well, your wing, among other things, *is* one reason I've been asked to come see you. I know you must be wondering, so I'll get right to the point. I am the acting novice master of a small community of friars who run a retreat center on a remote barrier island of this state, and the Bishop has asked us to offer you, for as much time as it takes to discern whether or not the Church can baptize a non-human creature with validity, a place in our community." The friar paused for breath. He was so accustomed to silence in his daily life that when he did talk, he found that his sentences were long and slow and convoluted, like drowsy bodies stretching and twisting themselves awake. "You would be perfectly free there to come and go as you please, and room and board are, under the circumstances, free, with no obligation on your part to participate in the life of the community. The Bishop has asked us, basically, to provide you with sanctuary."

Charlie blinked. *Why?*

"The Bishop is concerned about your safety. You've been hurt."

It was an accident!

"There would be less chance of such accidents on the island. Our cat, Brother Leo, is extremely elderly. You could outrun him easily, even with a broken wing."

I don't want go anywhere!

"I'm afraid you will have to. Your younger friends are also leaving this very lovely place."

Charlie was speechless for a full minute. He looked around the living room wildly. He could hear May in the kitchen, murmuring on the phone to somebody.

Niniane and Dillis are leaving the farm?

"I'm afraid so."

WHY!?

Father Angelo paused. It came to him with a jolt that he was proposing–no . . . he was *initiating* an upheaval in this creature's life that could not be anything but painful. He was come to take this chicken away from the only home, and the only friends he had ever known to a place so remote and inaccessible that it was only fit for persons whom for one reason or another sought the austerity and solitude and intensity and discipline of the monastic life. Charlie, who only wanted baptism, had never expressed any interest in such a life. This, the friar said to himself, is unfortunate. He inched forward, retaining his lotus position, to reassure Charlie through reducing the distance between them. "May I call you Charlie?" He asked.

Yes.

"Thank you. Charlie, I know that this must be very difficult for you. But the situation has evolved in such a way that the Bishop fears, not without reason, that your cause would be hurt by any premature publicity concerning your . . . unique abilities. If word got out before the church provided you with some degree of protection from the onslaughts of the media and the potential violence of curiosity seekers, the consequences for you . . . and your friends . . . could be very distressing. It isn't just for your own sake, though that is important, that there be no trace of any . . . unusual activity on this farm. We must keep everyone's identity a secret until the church has had time to decide how to proceed. That won't be possible with you all here on the farm together, Charlie. We can't be sure that the locals haven't already got wind of you through the receptionist at the veterinarian's office."

What?

"The receptionist saw your friends attempting to get you to communicate with them after you left the animal hospital."

Really?

"Yes, I'm afraid so. So, you see . . . we have reason to think that it may no longer be safe for you to remain in an easily accessible location. The Bishop thinks, and I and your friends agree, that probably the best place for you to be right now would be at our retreat center. The grounds are secured from trespassers, there are no visitors at this time, and the friars are all sworn to vows of obedience to me. There should be no danger of word getting out about you there."

Charlie looked up at the friar's face, at his rapidly blinking brown eyes. Where was Niniane? He realized that she had been uncharacteristically quiet all day. There had been an uneasy air about the household, now that he thought about it, ever since May brought in the mail that morning. As a matter of fact, he told himself, things around the farm had not been the same since he fell off the porch the other day. Yet again Charlie felt that terrible sense that just by existing he was causing problems. His feathers ruffled with agitation.

Are Niniane and Dillis coming with me?

Father Angelo shook his head.

Why?

"Charlie, you are the one who has requested baptism. I don't think your friends–particularly the young lady, or woman I should say, would be comfortable in a retreat center with no other women around. And you know they have their own lives to lead. Niniane and Dillis must return to school and work soon."

But what about May and Irene? This is their farm!

"And it will continue to be. But May and Irene have acknowledged the wisdom of dispersing . . . at least for the time being . . . your little household. I know it's going to be difficult and upsetting for you Charlie, but please know that we will take good care of you. It really is the best thing . . ."

I don't care about that! What am I going to do without my friends?.

"I hope that you will make new friends at the retreat center."

I don't want new friends. I want Niniane and Dillis and May and Irene!

The friar's voice became firm. "Remember your Swinburne, Charlie."

What the hell is that supposed to mean! That, Charlie realized immediately, is something Niniane would say!

"Love has its shadow, Charlie," said the friar with uncharacteristic sternness. "You need to come with me to the retreat center."

⮎

Charlie left the farm that afternoon. It was true that there was no time to waste. A rumor had spread throughout the township, via the receptionist at the veterinarian's office that the inhabitants of the farm, who were already viewed as peculiar on account of their spinsterhood, their lack of family resemblance, and their harboring of a teenage boy and girl who likewise did not look decently related, were pursuing a deviant relationship with a young chicken who had been injured in the process. The morning of Father Angelo's arrival, May had walked out to get the mail only to find a beheaded chick who happened to be one of Charlie's sisters stuffed into the mailbox. She and Irene were used to occasional harassment from the locals, but never before had anyone killed one of their animals.

"I've already looked into a place for Charlie," the Bishop said to May when she called him to let him know about the chick in the mailbox. "A sanctuary. But what about the rest of you?"

"The rest of us can take care of ourselves. Just don't let anything happen to Charlie."

"We won't," said the Bishop. "If nothing else, the Catholic Church knows how to protect its own."

⮎

After their talk, Father Angelo took Charlie in his arms and walked him up to Niniane's room where Niniane was packing. He introduced himself and handed Charlie to her.

I'm leaving. Scratched Charlie into her palm. *I have to. With me around here, the rest of you aren't safe.*

Niniane bent her neck and whispered into Charlie's feathers. "Charlie, that's not true! It's not your fault. It's that goddamn vet's goddamn secretary." Lifting her face from Charlie's soft, seedy smelling feathers, she spoke, in a muffled, phlegmy voice to the friar. "Sorry, Reverend. But I mean it. I want God or whoever's in charge, to damn her, that bigmouthed bitch."

Father Angelo nodded sadly.

Niniane sighed a shuddering sigh and set Charlie on her bed. "I have to leave too." She said, and indicated with a swing of her arm around the room the disarray that was meant to signify that fact that she'd been busy packing. "May says there might be trouble here, so me and Dillis are going back to the city."

Charlie clicked his beak and Niniane came to set down beside him.

I wish you could come with me.

"I do too, Charlie. You wouldn't believe how much I wish I could. But the Man won't let me . . . " She gave Fr. Angelo a quick, scathing sideways glance.

I know. They were silent awhile. Charlie hopped into Niniane's lap. *I wish I could go to the city with you and meet your mom and dad and stay there. With you.*

"One of these days, Charlie. I promise." But Niniane had a feeling that day would never come.

Niniane became aware of the friar regarding them. "Could we have a minute alone?" She said to Father Angelo with not a little irritation.

The friar nodded and walked out into the hallway, closing Niniane's bedroom door behind him.

Niniane bent and pressed her lips to Charlie's now resplendently blood red comb. "Oh, Charlie . . . you're the best thing that ever happened to me. I don't know how I'm going to stand not seeing you every day. I feel like I've known you my whole life."

Charlie had his beak in her palm, but he could not think of anything to scratch into it. He let it rest there. He waited for her to say more.

It was a while before she could continue. "I want you to take care of yourself, Charlie. Make sure they keep you safe. And don't do anything you don't want to do. Don't let them change you, Charlie."

Can't you come see me?

"I don't know. I don't know if that's a good idea, Charlie–at least not right away. It might be dangerous. I'll come if it's safe. *When* it's safe. These things always do blow over. It just takes a while."

Charlie could not cry, being a chicken, but his comb and wattle felt cold and heavy. *I can't believe this is happening. It's like a bad dream.*

"I know," said Niniane. She was far past the point of crying. She held the chicken in her lap and stared, dry eyed and unseeing, out he bedroom window. "The world, Charlie, is cruel. This is . . . " She stopped. She had been going to say, 'this is only the beginning.'

I wish I never heard of Jesus.

Niniane sighed, a very deep sigh. She wished, suddenly, that she were a little girl again, with no chicken to love, a little girl who ate hamburgers without a thought for the feelings of the cow. She wished, with the selfishness that comes of weariness, that she had no human feelings of tenderness and love. "You don't mean that, honey," she said. "You're just upset. Things'll work out, Charlie. They always do." Niniane did not believe a word of what she was saying, yet she could not leave her friend without comforting him.

I'll write. He wrote. *Will you?*

"Yes," she said. "But Charlie, not right away. We have to be careful."

After a while.

"Yes." She said, without the hope that Charlie felt abundantly in his passion for her. "After it all blows over." She stood up, shook herself, reached down for Charlie. "You've got to say good-bye to everyone. And then you better get going."

Chapter Thirteen

The Cloister

BEFORE CHARLIE LEFT THEY all joined hands and wings, at the friar's suggestion, and projected themselves together in a less worrisome future. Dillis removed his glasses afterward and wept openly. "Maybe," he said, not without seriousness, "I'll come be a friar."

No one paid any attention to that remark.

Father Angelo took all their telephone numbers and promised that the Bishop would be in touch. And then, once again, Charlie found himself the passenger in a fast car moving east on an uncrowded interstate.

He said to Father Angelo, who had his hand in the milk crate, *What will I do at the retreat center?*

Father Angelo said, "What do you like to do?"

Read.

"I hope you like to read theology and devotional literature. That's pretty much all we have in our library, although there are a few good novels and collections of poetry."

I've never read a whole novel.

"I'll find you some to read. I think you'll enjoy the experience of reading a novel. They are very much like poems and theology, they require an active imagination to truly appreciate them, and you may find that following a narrative soothes your sense of displacement."

That sounds good.

"Yes. I knew, Charlie, that you would manage to make the best of this upheaval in your life."

I still wish I could stay home.

Father Angelo said nothing but kept on driving.

By the time they arrived at the retreat center, Charlie was fast asleep. Night had fallen as they traveled, and when Father Angelo woke him up Carlie was jolted by the unfamiliarity of just about everything around him. Even the air he breathed had a pervasive, odd, briny odor. He was carried from the car into a building and through a succession of large dark hallways; upon the walls of which hung large studio photographs and oil paintings of men in ecclesiastical garb and with solemn, pinched expressions. Eventually Father Angelo opened a heavy wooden door to a small bare room in which there was a dresser, a rocking chair by a window, and a small, plain twin bed above which was nailed a carved wooden crucifix.

"Voila, Charlie." Father Angelo said, peering at Charlie from the doorway. "Your room—we call them cells—for as long as your visit with us."

From the bed Charlie turned his head and goggled at the entire space. Soon Father Angelo would turn and step back through that heavy wooden door and close it. He wondered how the friar would respond if he asked him to stay. He clicked his beak to summon the friar's palm.

Father Angelo stepped over to the bed and held out his palm. "Yes?"

But Charlie couldn't bring himself to ask for what he wanted. Yet how he dreaded the long night ahead, all alone in this unfamiliar room!

"You're homesick." Said Father Angelo.

The word eddied and flowed through Charlie's mind like a leaf on a stream. Homesick. The word described his feeling perfectly.

Charlie nodded.

Father Angelo laid a steady hand on Charlie's back. "You're used to having Dillis close by as you sleep and dream. I understand. It was difficult for me sleeping in a room by myself when I first entered the community . . . I come from a large family and I always shared a bed with one or two of my brothers. Solitude at night can be intimidating. We will have to keep your door closed at night, for your protection, and because that's the way we must live here, with very concrete boundaries. You may feel uneasy, but try to remember that God is with you and that I will look in on you first thing in the morning."

Charlie nodded.

"It's going to be a long night." The Friar said. "I will leave your light on and bring you a book to read. Not a novel, I think, not tonight. I will bring you something that speaks to your condition of homesickness, something that will console you, in the most ancient, Latinate sense of that word."

The friar left, then returned with a large print copy of *The Diary of Anne Frank*; the heavy pages of which he correctly assumed that the bird could turn without much difficulty with his beak. Charlie read it all at once and found that when he finished it he could not imagine ever really feeling as alone in the world again. Then he went to sleep.

⌒

Back at home with her parents, Niniane was homesick, too. For Charlie. At the request of the Bishop, she'd addressed a statement to the Apostolic Nuncio to the effect that she indeed had raised a chicken which had learned to read, and that she had placed the chicken into the care of the Franciscan Community at St. Alvin's Island, North Carolina. But, for the most part, she spent her days in her room, leafing listlessly through teen magazines, chewing on her hair, staring out the window, and struggling with herself over the question of whether or not she should give in to the temptation to call her beloved mentor Mercedes and tell that sensible, passionate, more seasoned activist and educator everything.

Her parents, having been briefed by May regarding Charlie were unsure how to cope with an even moodier than normal Niniane.

"Niniane, how on earth did this happen?" her mother said.

"I don't know what more I can tell you, Mama!" said Niniane. It was hardly twenty minutes after she woke up her first morning back at home, and her mother had just announced, to Niniane's irritation, that she was taking the day off work to make sure Niniane was all right. "You *know* what happened. I started spending time with one of May's chickens, and somehow he learned how to read."

"Niniane, now really. It can't be as simple as that. I grew up on that farm, you know that, and I know how stupid chickens are. Chickens are not intelligent animals. And now the Catholic Church is involved?! Honey, it just doesn't make sense . . . "

"Mom, I don't want to talk about it anymore. I don't know how I can make it any clearer. He wants to be baptized, that's all . . . It's as crazy to me as it is to you, trust me. Besides, you're the one who's a Christian, not me. I would have thought you'd be happy."

"This has nothing to do with being Christian. I want to understand what is going on! The Catholic Church for goodness sake! And May says that they're discussing this chicken at the Vatican! It just doesn't . . . why the

Catholic Church, Niniane? We've always been mainline Protestant, on both sides of the family."

"*You* have," said Niniane. "Not me. *I* have no idea why he wants to join such a fucked-up church. You'll have to ask him." She turned and looked at her pillow, away from where her mother stood, arms crossed against her chest, in the doorway. True to her vocation as a librarian, Thelma Westvane regarded her daughter's scowling face as if it were a particularly puzzling reference question.

"Don't say 'fucked-up,' Niniane. That's unnecessary." Thelma Westvane lifted her glasses, rubbed the bridge of her nose, and let her glasses fall on their decorative chain to rest on the bosom of her housedress. Perched on the side of her bed, Niniane took a few strands of her long brown hair and took the ends of them between her teeth. This was a childhood habit that indicated real distress. Thelma Westvane sat down on the bed beside her daughter, looked at her face, then at the faded wallpaper behind the bed, then at her daughters neglected, uneven fingernails. "Honey, are you honestly telling me this isn't some revolutionary thing you and Dillis cooked up?"

"Mom!"

"Niniane, he *is* a little strange."

It took Niniane a moment before she realized her mother was referring to Dillis and not Charlie.

"Dillis isn't even vegan, Mother. I've told you that. Can't you keep anything straight about my life?" She sighed. "And he wouldn't lie about something as big as this anyway, Mom. And neither would I. You ought to *know* that. And anyway, do you really think we could fool May and Irene?"

"Niniane, I just don't know what to think . . . "

There was a long silence, until Niniane heaved a sigh. "What does Daddy say?"

Thelma sighed. Horace Westvane could not get it through his bald head that the chicken in question was not merely parroting human script, but that it had a mind of its own. He thought the whole thing was a tremendous joke.

"Oh, you know how he is. He can't take anything seriously."

Niniane hazarded a smile. "And you think *Dillis* is strange."

Thelma hugged her daughter. Niniane looked up at her, and said in a voice just above a whisper.

"I think he likes Dillis more than me, Mama."

Thelma turned. "Your father? Niniane, what are you talking about?"

Niniane stared down into her lap at her hands, their knuckles white and their fingers interlocking. "Not Daddy. Charlie. I think he feels closer to Dillis than me now."

Thelma looked at her daughter. Niniane's position, face down, long brown hair hanging like a veil on either side, hands gripped together one moment tight, the next moment loose, was a familiar one. Niniane had been adopted as a toddler and sometimes needed a great deal of reassurance. Thelma Westvane forgot, for the moment, about Charlie's species.

"Honey, you know how boys are when they get around each other. They put up a front."

⤳

Dillis returned to his part time job at the deli, and found that he could slice, prepare, and even consume chicken meat without any qualms. It seemed to him, actually, that he ate more chicken than he ever had before, for the most part because he could not eat it without thinking of Charlie, and in a sick sort of way it made him feel closer to his friend. He hoped that Charlie wasn't too bored out at that crazy retreat center.

⤳

It did not take long for word to reach the Vatican that an apparently sentient and theologically literate chicken in the United States of America desired baptism into the faith of the Roman Catholic Church. Bishop Serxner felt it prudent to get the process underway as soon as possible. In the interests of preparing the worldwide Catholic community for an immanent inquiry into the teaching of the Magisterium in regard to the spiritual state of non-human creatures as well as in the interest of taking the heat off May and Irene, the Bishop intentionally made a statement to the secular press that the Roman Catholic Diocese of Eastern North Carolina had a remarkable and religiously inclined chicken under observation in an undisclosed and secure facility located somewhere within the state. The media storm that followed was colossal, eclipsing, for a time, all other current events in its degree of frenzy and outrageous speculation. The entire world, it seemed, became intrigued by the question of whether or not a chicken could really believe in God. Tabloid headlines in the languages of every developed country proclaimed the chicken variously as a hoax, an angel, the Antichrist, the Second Coming of Christ, a shapeshifting agent of the Illuminati, and the product of a back alley fertility treatment. The news media converged upon the diocesan offices of the Eastern North Carolina Bishopric like a plague of locusts, and for several Sundays local and national news outlets stationed reporters and camera crews outside of Catholic churches all over the nation to enlist the commentary of 'the average Catholic' regarding Charlie's request. (Most polls indicated that 78 percent of Roman Catholics felt that Charlie should be baptized, while 16 percent disagreed. Among Protestants, the split was somewhat even, with 62 percent in favor of animal baptism.) There were skits on late night talk shows, countless newspaper and magazine columns, websites, chat rooms, and even an academic conference at Harvard Divinity School, all devoted to what was soon known as 'the theological debate of the century.' All sorts of speculation arose concerning Charlie's whereabouts and even his very reality. For the first time since Vatican II, a moratorium was put on access to broadcast or print news at the retreat center. Father Angelo Schiaparelli felt that Charlie might be made inordinately anxious by all the uproar.

⌒

To that end a meeting was held, wherein Father Angelo stated to his community that any contact with the secular press whatsoever would be considered a breach of obedience. "And," he said. "Without converging on him en masse, I want all of us to spend some private time with Charlie, so that we will all have some personal sense of what is at stake. I think every morning he should have a visitor or two. He also needs to be taken for supervised walks on the beach. He spends far too much time alone in his cell, reading."

"Will he participate in the daily office?" One of the newer postulants, Brother Silas, a tall, good-looking, rather cynical friar asked.

"I have left that up to Charlie."

Brother Silas raised an eyebrow.

"Brother Silas." Said Father Angelo. "Do you have a comment?"

Brother Silas looked at Father Angelo. He was aware of all the other friars looking surreptitiously at him, though they were obliged by the rule to attend only to themselves and Father Angelo during such organizational meetings. "No, Father."

"Silas, would you mind visiting Charlie this morning?" Said Father Angelo.

Brother Silas' eyes widened. "Me?" He said.

"Unless you would rather not. But I think it would be helpful for Charlie to talk with you. You're our youngest novice, and the most recent addition to our community–Surely you can relate to how he must feel, a young person in a new situation, far away from the people he loves . . . "

Brother Silas swallowed.

" . . . and far away from the only way of life he's ever known." Father Angelo smiled at Brother Silas, who looked down at the hem of his habit. Brother Silas, he had noticed, was struggling. He was a young man of exceeding intellectual virtues, a historo-critical biblical scholar with the perspicacity of a young Loisy, and no mean homilist. Father Angelo often wondered why Brother Silas had chosen the Franciscan order, as it seemed on the surface that he would fit in more comfortably with the Jesuits. At any rate the young man's spiritual development was retarded by a lifetime of inordinate concern with his striking looks. He was a tall, athletically built, dark haired, blue-eyed, hollow cheeked fellow whose handsomeness was accentuated rather than muted by the austerity of the mendicant wardrobe. Even in the cloister, he seemed doomed to conspicuousness and was the object of numerous romantic fancies. Father Angelo, when he returned to his office, thanked God for Brother Silas and for the inspiration that had come to him to bring together Silas and Charlie in their distinct yet related loneliness's.

⌒

Halfway across the world, in the Vatican, Charlie Chicken was becoming a red-hot topic of theological debate. Bishop Serxner of Eastern North Carolina had been summoned to report on the events surrounding Charlie's emergence to a committee formed in response to Charlie's request for Baptism.

"First of all," said Msgr. Benito Corinni, an Italian prelate who served as a professor of Canon Law, "have we verified the existence of this so called intelligent chicken?"

"Without question," said Bishop Serxner, in Latin, "the chicken exists, and is intelligent. I have seen him and spoken with him."

The group, made up of theologians, canon lawyers, clergy engaged in the study of animal behavior, and one secular veterinarian, met in an opulent, if windowless, conference room near St. Peter's Basilica. Sixteen in number, they were from 10 different countries, and so, during the course of their many meetings, all spoke in Latin, the one tongue they had in common. Bishop Serxner' s Latin was weak from disuse, could not wait until it was all over.

"This is very serious matter," said Bishop Carlos Etchegaray, a Basque Jesuit. "But there is no need to be overly scrupulous. If the chicken is baptized, what harm is done?"

"What if this so called talking chicken proves to be a hoax?" Said Msgr. Corrinni. "Think what harm is done! We must be circumspect. This is as delicate a situation as any Marian apparition. We cannot jump to conclusions."

"With all due respect, we cannot delay in making a decision." Said Dr. Jacques Gallant, an Algerian veterinarian. "Our Blessed Mother may appear as often and as for as long as she pleases, or so it seems, but the lifespan of a chicken . . . " he looked at Bishop Serxner. " . . . is not terribly long."

Bishop Serxner closed his eyes. He turned to face the veterinarian. "Dear Lord." He said under his breath in English. Then, in Latin. "I had not realized that, Dr. Gallant. How long do we have?"

Dr. Gallant shrugged. "It's hard to say with American poultry. Some specimens have been known to live to up to twenty years. In my country, a few years is long. But it has required already many more than twenty years for the Commission to pronounce upon the authenticity of the Medjugorie apparitions of Our Lady."

Bishop Serxner breathed a deep sigh. He leaned forward in his chair and looked at all of the gathered men in turn. "We don't have eternity to decide. Let's pray for a revelation, and the wisdom to discern what must be done." He bowed his head, but the room was silent. Father Yumi, a Japanese theologian, reached across the table to him. "You will lead us in prayer, yes?" he said.

Bishop Serxner thought to himself in English. "When I think of that poor little chicken, leaving this world without the Baptism he's asking for, I just want to blow this whole place to Kingdom Come." But in Latin he said, "Lord, give us strength, give us wisdom, but above all grant us, in the words of your Beloved Pope John XXIII, charity in all things doubtful."

⌒

In the meantime, Charlie was growing used to life at the retreat center. As he had at the farm, he quickly became acclimated to the daily round, and came to attribute his growing sense of peace of mind to the order and regularity of the passing days. And he enjoyed, more than he ever would have imagined, the vast landscapes of solitude. He read voraciously, but at a more leisurely pace than before, often pausing to ponder a certain passage or phrase in whatever he happened to be reading at the time. As Father

Angelo had indicated, most reading matter at the retreat center had to do with theology, but there was a collection of novels, mostly old, sturdily bound editions that easily remained open in front of him as he read sitting on his bed. One called *Wuthering Heights* he found particularly stirring, and he spent much of his first week in the retreat center absorbed in it to the point that he lost a noticeable amount of weight. One of the effects of this experience upon him was that he began to consider the possibility of writing a story one day.

He also spent a lot of time contemplating his potential baptism. The retreat center library had a collection of books under the subject heading of Sacramental Theology, which Father Angelo made available to Charlie by stacking them at the foot of his bed. From these ponderous, ruminative tomes he learned that Baptism had its origin in a late antique Jewish lustration rite, and that Baptism in the name of The Father, The Son, and the Holy Ghost was the most ancient and most distinctive token of Christian identity, preceding the formation of the Church itself as an institution. One slim, readable, rather quaintly lyrical tome entitled *Christian Initiation in the Early Church* authored by a Patristics scholar by the name of Rev. Dr. Lloyd Patterson suggested to Charlie that, based on the Gospel account of John the Baptist's baptism of Jesus, Baptism can be said to abrogate hierarchical distinctions.

He mentioned this one morning to Brother Silas. He and that young brother had rapidly become mutual confidants. From the first of their mandated morning meetings, Brother Silas found that he felt surprisingly comfortable with Charlie. He found the chicken easier to talk to than he had ever found anybody, particularly at the retreat center. But Brother Silas wasn't sure about the ability of any sacrament to disestablish hierarchy. "That's preposterous, it's incoherent," he protested. "Let me see that book."

Taking the book from in front of Charlie, he examined the cover, flipped through the pages, and read the flyleaf. "Well there you go," he said, tossing the book back down on the bed. "This guy's an Episcopalian, not a real Catholic. Episcopalians tend to have a very watered-down sacramental theology."

Charlie was disappointed, for he had rather come to like the little book, and it never occurred to him that the author was not a Catholic. He changed the subject to *Wuthering Heights*, which Brother Silas said was a brilliant, if at times overwrought study of the codependent relationship dynamic.

Sometimes, though, they talked about themselves to one another without the medium of literature or theology. "How do you like it here?"

Silas asked Charlie one afternoon, about a week after Charlie's arrival. He had come to Charlie's room under the pretext of borrowing Charlie's King James Bible for an article he was researching on the various English translations of the book of Habakkuk, but in all actuality he wanted to have a chat with Charlie. Brother Silas was very aware that Father Angelo was very aware that he was spending much more time with the retreat center's visitor than any of the other brothers.

I like it. Scratched Charlie. *I didn't think I would, but I do. I miss home, of course, but I like having all this theology to read.* Before Silas had let himself in, Charlie had been leafing through Volume 5 of the *Notebooks* of Simone Weil, and enjoying in them what little he could understand.

"I guess I like that too," said Silas musingly. "Even when I was in seminary it seems like I never had enough time to really focus. Other people were always bugging me."

Charlie waited.

Brother Silas lay down on Charlie's bed as if it were his own and gazed at the ceiling. He placed the King James Bible on his stomach. "I don't mean to sound conceited." He said. "But I attract a lot of attention. And usually just for the way I look. It can be awkward."

Charlie thought that he could certainly relate to that!

Brother Silas languidly twiddled the belt of his habit. "Sometimes I wonder if I'm some kind of freak. I just don't understand why people are so shallow . . . why do they care so much about the way a person looks . . . ?"

Suddenly the pensive young friar sat up. He reached for Charlie's Volume five of the Notebooks of Simone Weil and leafed through a few pages, but he was not really reading. He closed the book, then put his hand out to Charlie. "You know, you're a good listener, chicken or not." He said, as if he were paying Charlie the highest of compliments. "Maybe *you* should think about becoming a priest . . . now that would *really* blow their minds . . . "

I don't think so. Scratched Charlie.

"Why not?"

I'm not even sure they'll let me be baptized!

"But if they do . . . maybe then you can think about being ordained. You'd be a fantastic priest, Charlie . . . just imagine! You could be Apostle to the animals . . . "

Charlie thought that Brother Silas was beginning to sound a lot like Niniane.

I don't think I want to be a priest. He scratched, hoping to put an end to the discussion. The very idea of becoming ordained made him uncomfortable.

"But why not, Charlie? What else are you going to be? Is it the vow of celibacy that bothers you? That's what gets in the way for most people. But, I mean, if you're a chicken . . . " Brother Silas trailed off blithely.

Charlie let this insensitivity to his intimacy needs pass.

"And after all . . ." The friar continued, "It may well be your destiny. I mean, think about it, here you are, against all odds, a chicken with faith, packed off here to a Franciscan retreat center with a bunch of celibate men . . . Maybe this is God's way of introducing you to the sort of life you're meant to live . . . "

Charlie liked the retreat center, and he liked the friends he was making . . . particularly Brother Silas and Father Angelo . . . but the idea of a lifetime spent in a place like this, so quiet and orderly and polished and completely without the openness and earthiness he associated with life on the farm and with the presence of female humans was depressing. He would feel as if he were giving up if he became a priest.

I don't think so. He scratched. *I think this is temporary. That's what Father Angelo says. I'll stay here until the Church decides whether or not I can be baptized.*

"But say you *are* baptized . . . then what? What are you going to do then, Charlie? What are you called to do? What's your passion?"

Charlie considered a long time before answering.

If I tell you . . . you won't laugh?

The handsome young friar was touched. "Of course not, Charlie! I'd never laugh at you!"

Charlie was still unsure. After a moment he gathered up his nerve and placed his beak into the Brother Silas's palm. *I can't be a priest because I'm in love.* He wrote.

For the next few moments Brother Silas remained so silent and still that Charlie, who had never had the experience of seeing or being near a dead creature began to wonder if perhaps the young man had suddenly been struck dead. Finally Brother Silas released a long, heavy sigh.

"Oh Geez." He said. "I'm sorry, Charlie. I mean, I'm flattered, but . . . I don't know what to tell you. I just don't feel the same way . . . "

At first Charlie was puzzled. Was it typical for young Franciscan brothers to respond to someone sharing their deepest, most painful and hopeless desires by stating that they, for their part, did not share those desires? It certainly didn't seem very compassionate. It was only after a moment, during which Brother Silas shifted not too imperceptively away from Charlie on the bed that it dawned on Charlie that the young man thought that Charlie was in love with *him*! It was too much. Before Charlie realized what he was doing, he jammed his beak into the friar's palm as hard as he could, piercing the skin and causing it to bleed and bleed.

⌒

Father Angelo came immediately when he was called to the infirmary by Brother Lawrence, the nurse practitioner at the retreat center. Brother Silas was sitting on the edge of the infirmary cot, holding his bloody right hand in his uninjured left hand, and a slow tear crept down his cheek.

Father Angelo was not aware of the location and thus the significance of the injury right away. "Brother Silas? What happened?"

Brother Silas lifted his right hand gingerly and held it, palm outward for his superior to see.

Father Angelo had never seen, and never expected to see, even though he had no doubt as to the authenticity of the phenomena, an actual stigmatic wound. He gasped and crossed himself reflexively.

"Not so fast, Father," Brother Silas had said in a flat voice. "It's not what you think. Charlie stabbed me."

It took Father Angelo a moment to take this in. Once he did, he was astonished to feel in his eyes the prick of nascent tears. In the years that he had been in charge of this community there had been squabbles, arguments and even torrid affairs between his friars, but never any violence. And for this first instance of real violence to have happened between two of his charges whom he felt were essentially helpful to one another made him feel terrible. "Charlie stabbed you?" he said, incredulously.

"He stabbed me," said the young friar. "With his beak. The little bastard really stuck it to me. I guess I deserved it." He looked at Father Angelo steadily for a moment, then looked down at the slick, waxed tile floor of the infirmary.

Father Angelo sat down on the cot. He stared at Brother Silas' palm for a minute. "At first glance it really does look very much like . . . you know . . ." he began.

Brother Silas nodded glumly.

There was a silence. Father Angelo let go of Brother Silas' injured hand. "Where's Charlie?"

"He's in his room," Brother Silas said. "That's where it happened. We were in there talking, and I guess I made him mad, so he pecked me. I didn't know he was so touchy!"

"I don't think he's touchy at all," said Father Angelo. "What on earth did you do to make him mad?"

"I sort of implied that he was gay."

Father Angelo stood up. "What!?"

Brother Silas shrugged, then winced. Father Angelo counted to ten to collect himself and then sat down on the cot again.

"All right, what has been going on between you and Charlie, Silas? I want you to be straig . . . . honest with me."

"Nothing, Father," Brother Silas said. "I mean, not what you're thinking. At least, I don't think so . . . "

"Silas, look at me."

Brother Silas obeyed, like Abraham, reluctantly.

Father Angelo took Silas by the shoulders and shook him. "Silas, I want to know right now what would possess you to even comment upon Charlie's sexuality."

Brother Silas scowled like a scolded schoolboy. "We were just talking. All I said was . . ." the friar looked down, embarrassed. "We were talking about vocation. The priesthood, the vow of celibacy. That's all. Is there something wrong with that?"

Father Angelo crossed his arms against his chest. "Silas, if questions of vocation and celibacy are presenting issues for you, you should be discussing them with me, not our visitor! I *am* your spiritual director, remember?"

"I don't have any issues! You told us to talk to Charlie. You told me to spend some time with Charlie, to get to know him, to encourage him. So I thought maybe he should think about becoming ordained, if the Church is so important to him. And he likes talking to me . . . I'm well-read. What are we supposed to do, talk about theology all the time?"

Father Angelo pointed at the friar's bandaged hand. "Silas, it's not a matter of what you're *supposed* to talk about, it's a matter of proportion. If you don't have these issues . . . and the fact that you would even deny such a thing is extremely concerning . . . then why would you be talking with a chicken . . . well, his species is irrelevant . . . but why would you be talking to a visitor about such intimate matters when you haven't even discussed them with your assigned spiritual director, namely *me?* You have been in this community long enough to realize that we are obliged, as long as we're here, to be respectful and careful with one another in approaching matters of vocation and sexuality. When you form relationships, you must form them prayerfully. Is this . . . potentially very inflammatory wound the result of careful and considered speaking?"

Brother Silas' unpunctured left hand involuntarily clenched into a fist. "I suppose not, Father," he said, clipping his words truculently. The infirmarian approached with a syringe. Father Angelo stepped aside.

"Silas, I want you to go to my office as soon as Father Lawrence gives you your tetanus shot. I'm going to speak to Charlie right now."

In the meantime, Charlie was in his room perched on the edge of his bed, wondering if he could somehow manage to flap his useless wings hard enough to lift himself to the top of the six drawer mahogany dresser that stood an easy five feet off the ground. Once there he could jump to his death, and that would put an end to the humiliation and shame he felt. I lost control, was all he could think. I hurt somebody. I made Brother Silas scream. I'm as bad as any of my brothers back in the coop. I'll never be baptized now.

He was debating whether or not it would be more fitting to just stop eating and die that way when Father Angelo came in, picked him up and said "I want to talk to you and Brother Silas together."

Father Angelo sat behind his desk in his office with a window overlooking the shoreline and regarded Brother Silas and Charlie, who were seated in two chairs across the desk from him. In the few minutes between leaving Brother Silas in the infirmary and collecting Charlie from his cell, it occurred to him not to be overly concerned about the dynamic that was emerging between Brother Silas and Charlie, that the relationship, while it had the potential to alienate the rest of the community, could be fruitful for the two of them in that they both, for different and yet similar reasons, tended towards a more ready engagement with books than persons. This misunderstanding, Father Angelo perceived, could only have come about as the result of a burgeoning trust beyond that which either one of them had shown towards anyone else in the community, including himself. His earlier chagrin, he saw now, was an ego-reaction on his own part, fueled by a stubborn surfeit of confidence in his own ability to lead the community. He made a mental note to pray for forgiveness and for renewed faith in himself, and then turned his full attention to the unhappy duo seated across from him. He stroked his beard while Brother Silas rubbed his uninjured palm nervously on the skirt of his cassock and Charlie picked at the feathers of his unbandaged wing. Getting the two of them to talk together when Charlie could only really be 'heard' by one person at a time would be tricky. He searched his mind for a solution and decided that, as his object was to nurture trust, he would have to begin by trusting.

"Brother Silas," Father Angelo said. "I would like you to move your chair closer to Charlie's so that the two of you can communicate more easily."

Brother Silas looked at Charlie, and Charlie looked at Brother Silas. Charlie noted that Brother Silas was paler than usual. My Goddess! The chicken thought. Is he afraid of me? I guess I really hurt him!

Brother Silas moved his chair over until the arm of it was touching the arm of Charlie's. He set his left hand flat, palm up, on the two armrests and waited for further instructions.

"Thank you, Brother Silas," said Father Angelo. "Now, I hope you won't mind translating for Charlie. It seems better that way to me. Unless either one of you objects."

Brother Silas looked at Charlie, who swiveled his head from side to side to approximate the human gesture of negation.

"Great." Said Father Angelo informally. "First of all, just let me say that I'm not here to pass judgment on anybody. I just want to know what's going on. Can I start with you Charlie?"

Charlie nodded and poised his beak above Brother Silas' left palm.

"Brother Silas tells me you pecked him. Is that right?"

Charlie raised his head and nodded.

"Will you tell me why?"

Charlie began scratching on Silas' outstretched palm. Brother Silas dutifully repeated the chicken's words verbatim.

I don't know why I did that. I wasn't thinking. I guess I lost my temper for a minute. He paused and looked up at Silas. *I'm sorry.*

Brother Silas shrugged his right shoulder. "It's not a big deal."

Father Angelo pursed his mouth. "I wouldn't say it's not a big deal, Silas. Obviously it is. What do you think made you so upset as to do such a thing, Charlie?"

Charlie hung his head for a moment. His comb felt so warm he thought it must be glowing.

I was mad, I guess, about something Brother Silas said.

"What was that?"

Charlie looked up once again at Brother Silas. He began scratching, reluctantly.

Brother Silas blushingly repeated the chicken's words. *He said that I was in love with him. Well, he didn't exactly say it, but I know that's what he thought, because I told him I was in love with somebody.*

Father Angelo glanced at the young friar, who looked away. "I see."

"That made you mad, Charlie?"

I guess.

"But why?"

I guess it embarrassed me.

"What's so embarrassing about the possibility of your being in love with Brother Silas?"

Brother Silas opened his eyes wide. He was so taken aback he didn't repeat Charlie's' reply.

"Did Charlie answer me just then, Brother Silas?" Father Angelo rested his chin in his hands.

Charlie scratched again. *I don't know. It was just embarrassing.*

Father Angelo leaned back in his swivel chair. "You know, people who live together closely very frequently develop complicated feelings for one another. It's a perfectly natural part of being a community. The important thing is to figure out how to integrate these feelings, integrate any and *all* of our feelings, in a constructive, christlike manner. I know you haven't made any sort of profession regarding our Order, but Charlie, for better or for worse, I must consider you to be a part of our community for as long as you remain with us, and I hope that if you did find yourself feeling particularly drawn toward or averse to Brother Silas or to any of our Brothers, you would feel safe discussing it with me, because such strong feelings can be helpful guideposts along the way towards self-knowledge and fulfillment."

Charlie suddenly wanted more than anything to be far away from the retreat center and it's no longer merely religious, but indeed overwhelmingly, messily human community.

I would. He scratched. *But I'm not in love with Brother Silas. Honestly. If I made him think I was, I'm really sorry.*

Father Angelo looked at Brother Silas as soon as the friar finished repeating this last reply of Charlie's. "Brother Silas, has Charlie done or said anything before today to indicate that he might be in love with you–romantically?"

Brother Silas' eyes were on his lap. "No. I know now that I just jumped to conclusions. He was telling me . . . " He glanced at Charlie. "He was telling me that he was in love with somebody."

"And you thought you might be that somebody."

"Well, yes." Brother Silas pressed his lips together.

"Charlie, when you realized that Brother Silas had made that assumption, what did you do? I want to hear you say it." Father Angelo smiled and shook his head. "I mean I want to hear Brother Silas say that you said it . . . or wrote it . . . well, you know what I mean . . . "

Charlie paused to recollect. *I hurt him.*

Brother Silas repeated this, in a rather mumbling manner.

Father Angelo raised one eyebrow. "Well, that sounds pretty straightforward to me. So what *is* going on here? I'm afraid I have to ask . . . Silas, are *you* in love with Charlie?"

The handsome friar's jaw dropped. "What?!"

"Are you in love with Charlie?"

"Father, he's a chicken!"

"I'm well aware of that."

"That's *bestiality!*"

Father Angelo tapped on his lips a few times with his index finger. "That's interesting. I wasn't necessarily thinking in terms of sexual expression, but evidently you are. Well, then, are you *attracted* to Charlie?"

"Are you *crazy?*"

Father Angelo laughed. "Calm down, Silas. This isn't an inquisition. I'm just asking."

"Your *accusing* me of something *sick.*"

"I'm asking you a legitimate question. One that I would ask anyone in this situation. Come on Silas, you know your Analytic Psychology. Unacknowledged desire is often projected onto its object . . . "

Brother Silas stood up, jostling the two chairs that were touching. "I can't *believe* this! This chicken stabs me and I get the inquisition . . . "

"Silas, please sit down. I'm not trying to indict you."

"Then what's all this supposed to mean!"

"All what?"

"All this Jungian projection bullshit!"

"*Is* it bullshit?"

Brother Silas made a scornful noise "I thought you were supposed to be a priest!"

"I *am* a priest. And I am at this time your spiritual advisor, and I am asking you to sit *down* and respect my observations!"

Brother Silas huffed and sat down.

Father Angelo leaned forward. "Thank you. Now I want *both* of you to listen to me. I'm not sure what's gone on between you two over the past few weeks, but whether it's love or lust or just male bonding, it's clearly disruptive and it's got to stop. Any sort of particular friendship wreaks havoc in a monastic community. Now, both of you are young and newcomers, and particularly vulnerable to this sort of thing, and I knew that when I suggested you be the first to look in on Charlie, Silas, but I'd never dreamed it would get this out of hand . . . no pun intended. What this tells me, more than anything else, is that the two of you are both extremely lonely. And the erotic element I know of no other way to refer to it tells me that you are both struggling with questions of priestly vocation. I'm more concerned about this in regard to you, Silas, than with Charlie, as you're under my authority as a postulant."

"But I swear to you, I'm not hot for Charlie!"

"But you are boiling over with your projections, which means you're overheated. Now, Brother, this doesn't have to be a problem, but merely a difficulty to be lifted up in prayer. As for Charlie . . . "

Charlie, who had been mesmerized by Father Angelo's handling of Brother Silas, startled so that he nearly fell of his seat. He gazed up at the friar.

"Charlie, there are other ways to express your anger than by pecking."

Brother Silas rested his left palm back on the shared armrests.

I know. I'm sorry.

"I know you are. Nevertheless, violence is violence. I wonder if you would accept a penance, Charlie?"

A penance?

"A discipline to help you internalize the virtue of self-restraint."

Okay. Scratched Charlie.

"Charlie, I'd like you share with Brother Silas the time it takes him to clean and care for and dress his wound until it's healed completely. I want you to participate in the trouble it takes him and the infirmarian to attend to this wound. And I would like for you to include in your daily prayers a prayer for his peace of mind and his vocation."

Okay. Said Charlie.

Father Angelo leaned back in his swivel chair again and he grinned. "This is the most bizarre conversation I've ever had, to be honest." He began to grin. "Brother Silas, you make Narcissus himself look unassuming. What am I going to do with you?"

Brother Silas' eyes widened.

"Is there anything else we need to talk about right now?" Said Father Angelo, picking up a pencil.

Silas and Charlie both shook their heads.

"Then, go in peace to love and serve the Lord." Said Father Angelo.

Chapter Fourteen

Rome

ONE AFTERNOON A FEW days later, Charlie was in his room engrossed in a volume given to him by Father Angelo entitled *Jesus and the Disinherited* when Father Angelo tapped on the door, waited about fifteen seconds, and then let himself in.

"Ah, you're reading Howard Thurman. Good for you, Charlie, I expect he'll give you a great deal of hope and courage . . ." he said, kneeling beside the bed to be eye level with the chicken. "You may need it. I just got off the phone with the Bishop. There's news."

Charlie's comb stiffened. *Are they going to baptize me?*

"They haven't decided yet."

Charlie's comb drooped. *Then what's happening?*

"The Pope wants to meet with you. You're being summoned to Rome, Charlie. To the Vatican."

Charlie froze. Another move . . . just when he was beginning to get used to this strange place! He placed his beak into Father Angelo's palm. *I don't want to go. I like it here, now.* He paused. *Most of the time.*

Father Angelo smiled, "You aren't going to Rome to stay, Charlie. Just to meet with the Pope, and maybe a few other bigwigs. If I were you, I would think of it as an honor. There are many, many human Catholics that would give anything to have a chance to meet the Pope, and he wants to meet with you! I don't want to make your decision for you, Charlie, but I do think that this will further your cause considerably. Do you need some time to think it over?"

Charlie lifted his head and thought for a moment. He recalled that there were many Christians, called Protestants, who did not like the Pope, and did not take into account his opinion regarding much, though they seemed to be in agreement with Catholics on most other things. Among Christians, Charlie did not yet know any Protestants, and imagined them to be a contentious, undisciplined lot. At one point soon after Charlie had learned from Dillis about the practice of Baptism, he had become curious about that group of Protestants known as Baptists; thinking that perhaps they, in light of the name they went by, would be the ones to approach regarding his own baptism. Niniane had told him that her family had always been Southern Baptist, before asserting him that she and May and Irene were of course, no such thing, Southern Baptists being, in the opinion of the women of the farm, notorious for their bigotry. For a moment he considered telling Father Angelo that he would rather stay where he was and perhaps become a Baptist, as this Howard Thurman person he was currently reading was a Baptist and apparently an extremely generously spirited one at that, but the moment this alternative occurred, he dismissed it. He had a sense that Father Angelo, as well as the Bishop and perhaps even Father Frank would take such a defection personally. The Bishop, Charlie knew, was already in Rome arguing for his cause. Father Angelo was kind enough to host Charlie here at the retreat center for free. These Catholics were going to considerable trouble to see that Charlie got baptized specifically Catholic, and Charlie did not want all their trouble to be for nothing. But for a moment Charlie found himself wondering, as Father Angelo waited patiently for him to agree to meet the Pope, whether it truly mattered in the end whether he was Protestant or Catholic? It was the first, but not the last time his miraculous mind dwelled on that question.

He regarded Father Angelo, who sat patiently beside him, his palm open and waiting for the word from Charlie.

Is the pope going to baptize me? Charlie scratched. Maybe if he just went ahead and met the Pope it would all be over with.

"I don't know, Charlie. It's possible, I guess, if he decides it would be . . . prudent."

What does 'prudent' mean?

"It's a virtue, Charlie. In this sense, it means . . . umm . . . " Father Angelo's gaze fell on a passage from the book Charlie had been reading. "It means something like . . . avoiding danger."

Charlie liked the idea of avoiding danger. He had just that morning had the bandage removed from his wing. *When do I leave?*

"As soon as they make the arrangements. I would imagine in less than a week."

Less than a week and he could possibly be baptized. Charlie began to experience a flutter of excitement in his gizzard. He wished he could smile. *Are you coming with me?*

"Charlie, I can't. I have to stay here at the retreat center. I'm in charge here, remember? I know you can't go alone, though. The Bishop is going to meet you at the airport in Rome, but I can't just put you on a plane by yourself. Anything could happen. I thought I'd ask Brother Silas to go and look after you on your journey." Father Angelo arched one thick prognathic eyebrow and suppressed a smile. "I think I can trust you two."

Charlie's comb and dewlap throbbed with embarrassment. Then a thought occurred. *I have to tell Niniane!* He scratched with urgency.

Father Angelo smiled sadly. "I don't see how you can do that Charlie. She can't come here, you know. Leave that to me. I'll make sure Niniane knows where you're going, and why."

How long will I have to stay in Rome? Scratched Charlie.

"Probably not for very long, Charlie. The Pope is a very busy person. He'll probably only be able to be with you for a very short while. Once he's had his time with you, I don't see why you would have to stay any longer at the Vatican. But there's really no way to tell, at this point. The Bishop will know better than me what this trip will involve. I'll ask him as soon as he calls."

When can I go home to the farm?

Father Angelo looked away. He felt sure that the farm would never again be a secure environment for Charlie, that in fact the only safe place for Charlie to stay for the remainder of his life, whether he was baptized or not, would be the retreat center.

"Charlie, do you remember the story of Jonah and the Whale? In the Old Testament?"

Yes. Scratched Charlie. The story was in fact one of his favorites. *Why?*

"It's often the case that a prophet is led . . . by God, of course . . . far from home to accomplish his mission. It's one of the sorrows of the prophetic calling. "

But I'm not a prophet. Scratched Charlie.

There was a pause. "What are you, then, Charlie?" There was no reply from Charlie, and Father Angelo withdrew his hand and stood. "I expect to hear back from the bishop this afternoon. I will tell him that you are willing, and we will make arrangements for you and Brother Silas to fly to Rome. I know that this is difficult for you Charlie; but I also know that God will grant you the strength you need. At least, I will pray for Him to do so. Remember your Swinburne, Charlie . . . "

As the heavy wooden door to his cell closed and clicked shut upon Father Angelo's advice, Charlie wished, not for the first or last time, that he had never even heard of the Roman Catholic Church.

⟿

Arrangements were made through the Vatican to fly Charlie and Brother Silas to Rome in a private jet. A private security company was hired to accompany Silas and his precious cargo to the plane in North Carolina, and an Italian counterpart likewise ensured his safe passage from the Rome airport to the hotel in Vatican City.

Charlie saw it all through the woefully small air holes of the pet carrier. He did not like the sensation of flying inside an airplane as much as he thought he might. Throughout the entire flight he was lightheaded and nauseous. The limousine ride from the Rome airport to their lodgings in Vatican City was much nicer. Brother Silas thoughtfully held the pet carrier on his left knee, which he kept crossed over his right, which raised Charlie just high enough to see, with one eye pressed against one of the air holes of his box, the busy streets of Rome, Italy.

The hotel room itself was the epitome of Mediterranean opulence. Charlie and Brother Silas found themselves overwhelmed by the sheer amount of open space they were granted in this private suite, in which they were protected against witnesses and Charlie was able to roam about and communicate with Silas as much as he pleased. After having been cooped up in a box for the past 20 hours by the circumspection necessary to transfer him safely and secretly from the retreat center in North Carolina to Vatican City, having an entire suite to move around in felt like heaven to Charlie.

It's beautiful here! Scratched Charlie into Silas' hand as the young friar carried him on a tour of their accommodations. *Look at all these paintings!*

Silas set Charlie down on the edge of one of their two enormous beds, and then sat down beside him. Through the east window they could see the spires, domes, and parapets of St. Peter's Basilica.

"It's amazing . . . " breathed Brother Silas. "I still can't even believe it. I can't believe I'm sitting here, in a hotel room in Vatican City! You know what this is, Charlie! It's an absolute miracle! I never once even *dreamed* . . ." He broke off, grabbed Charlie, and squeezed the chicken to his chest in a paroxysm of gratitude.

Charlie submitted to this stoically, then wriggled a bit until Brother Silas put him down on the bed. Charlie preened his ruffled feathers for a moment, and then placed his beak in the young friar's palm. *Be careful of my wing, please.*

Brother Silas grinned. "And to think I thought you were a hoax. You're the best, Charlie. You're an angel!"

Quit it. Charlie's comb was throbbing. He had never before seen anyone so transformed by excitement. Not even Niniane, as far as he knew, had ever felt so overjoyed by anything associated with him. Her pleasure in him had been tempered at first by her fear that she might be losing her own sanity; and then later by a more personal, but to Charlie a disappointingly maternal anxiety. Now, on account of him, Brother Silas was having an experience that, at least so far, was making him profoundly happy. Looking at Silas, Charlie decided that whether or not he was baptized, his existence now possessed intrinsic meaning. But he still wanted his baptism.

Brother Silas lay back on the bed, and smiled up at the high ceiling. Charlie bent over his upturned palm. *What do we do now?*

Brother Silas sat up. They had nothing planned until ten o'clock the next morning, the time set for Charlie's audience with the Pope. "I don't know about you . . . " he said. "But I'm calling room service. It's not every day you get to eat real Italian food. In Italy! I'm getting eggplant parmesan and red wine and dessert!"

Charlie, whose diet consisted chiefly of the feed they'd brought with them from North Carolina, felt a bit left out. *I guess I'll just have the same old thing.*

Silas put a hand on Charlie and pushed down, so that the chicken bounced lightly on the bed. "Come on, Charles. Live a little. I bet a little red wine won't hurt you. And listen, Brother Anthony back home has relatives here, and he told me once that they're always showing hot topless women on Roman cable TV late at night . . . "

When the food and wine arrived, and the late night programming began, Charlie began to enjoy–really enjoy–without any of his usual anxiety–his trip to Vatican City to meet with the Pope.

⌒

After Charlie retired to his carrying case for the night, he had trouble sleeping. Brother Silas, having been obliged to drink almost all of the bottle of red wine, had fallen asleep with the television on, so throughout the suite a pale blue light danced and flickered against the walls and furniture, against all the surfaces of the room. Towards the early hours of the morning, however, Charlie experienced something like a dream. In it, he stood in an enormous, high ceilinged gallery, somewhat like the hallway back at the retreat center, full of dark, solemn portraits, but the space was infinitely wider and more majestic; and there was a hidden and muted but unmistakable overhead source of light. The portraits were of humans, and no details stood out to Charlie, thought there was a sense in which he could see that the faces were all different, and in time, one portrait among many captured his attention. It was an image that gave the impression at once of contemporaneity as well as great antiquity, of a serenely smiling dark haired woman standing with a single candle held in one slim hand. Staring at it, Charlie realized that he could see his own tiny reflection in the gleam of the painted woman's incredibly lifelike eyes; then, in the world of the dream the image of the woman was no longer a painting.

As if he knew that he did not need, as he needed in normal life, any medium through which he must speak other than his own organized thoughts, Charlie asked the painting silently what her name was.

Then without any discernible movement, the lady was beside Charlie, holding him, giving him the impression that she had always held him. She held open her palm, the one that had, in the portrait, held the candle, below his beak, and as Charlie watched, one of the delicate creases in the center of that palm seemed to take on infinite dimensions, becoming a chasm so limitless and dark that Charlie felt himself, body and soul, swallowed and comprehended by that darkness as if it was itself an irresistible, insatiable, willful entity, independent, in the end, of that being of ineffable beauty that Charlie had seen in the painting. Charlie's final thought, as he felt his very self dissolve into the darkness of his dream, was an echo of his question to the beautiful Woman–*who are you?*

Charlie woke up to sun streaming in through the uncurtained east window of the suite, and, giving in to a now irresistible impulse of nature, he crowed; which woke up Brother Silas rather abruptly.

⌒

Charlie and Silas were waiting nervously over a sumptuous room-service breakfast neither one could do much more than sample when a gaunt, sunken-eyed priest in an immaculately starched and ironed black clerical suit arrived at their hotel suite to guide them to St. Peter's Basilica. He introduced himself as Msgr. Klaeber, and he escorted Brother Silas, with Charlie back in his carrier, to a limousine idling in front of the hotel entrance.

A uniformed chauffeur who was wearing mirrored sunglasses against the bright Italian sunshine drove the limousine. Msgr. Klaeber sat in the back of the vehicle, facing Brother Silas and Charlie, who peered out at the austere looking priest through an air hole of the carrying case.

"The Holy Father . . . " Father Klaeber said in heavily accented but perfect English, "Tells me that he very much looks forward to your meeting."

"So do I, Monsignor," said Brother Silas, so rattled that it did not occur to him that the old German cleric had been addressing himself to Charlie. The young friar had a splitting headache, which made him, under the circumstances, overanxious to appear attentive and obedient, lest someone detect that he was hung-over. "And I know that the Pope will be very impressed with our wonderful chicken."

"The chicken," Father Klaeber said agreeably. "Is indeed wonderful." He looked out the tinted limousine window. "Here we are." He said. "If you will stay here in the car until I return? And then, you will follow me and I will take you to the Chapel where the Holy Father will receive you privately. I think it would be best . . . " he said, stepping out of the limousine and leaning his lean, balding head back in before shutting the door "If you did not speak to anyone, Brother . . . . I'm so sorry?"

"Silas." Said Brother Silas, a bit huffily. "Of course, Monsignor. I'm as anxious as anybody that we don't blow Charlie's . . . " here he raised one eyebrow and smiled at the older cleric, " . . . cover."

Father Klaeber smiled, bowed, and made his way up the stairs and into the entrance of the wing of the basilica. Brother Silas exhaled through his nose. "Nazi." He muttered.

Charlie reached for his palm.

What was that you said?

"I said Nazi. I bet he's an old Nazi that they've hidden here since the war."

Charlie remembered Anne Frank. His feathers stood on end. He squawked. *Oh no! What are we going to do!*

Silas pulled the box onto his lap, opened it and peered inside. Charlie's head was wedged in a corner, and he was shivering. Brother Silas groaned, stuck his head in the box, and whispered. "I was just joking, for Christ's sake, Charlie! There aren't really any Nazi's at the Vatican . . . at least not any more . . . "

Charlie gave the friar's hand a quick nip. *Don't joke around*, he scratched, *I'm really nervous*.

"There's nothing to be nervous about," " said Brother Silas, who was too nervous himself to be sympathetic.

↪

Msgr. Klaeber returned to the car and then led Brother Silas and Charlie through the main entrance of St. Peter's into the magnificent sanctuary, and from there into a private chapel were he told them to make themselves comfortable, that the Holy Father would be with them shortly.

Brother Silas took Charlie out of his box and placed him on his knee so that he could look around the space.

It's a lot bigger than the Chapel at home . . . at the retreat center.

"Yes." Brother Silas whispered reverently.

The chapel, which had windows facing west, was filled with a soft, indirect morning light which made the whitewashed walls look innocently open rather than blank. This light made the wooden pews gleam and the golden monstrance on the altar and the gold corpus on the marble crucifix above the altar shine cheerfully.

Charlie looked at Brother Silas, whose eyes were closed. Clearly, the young friar was praying, something which he often admitted having difficulty doing unless he was by himself.

Charlie was still terribly nervous and rather wished that the young friar felt like talking to him rather than God.

Charlie was about to jump off Brother Silas' knee and pace up and down the length of the pew they were sitting on when Msgr. Klaeber strode in holding the arm of an extremely stooped old man clad in yards of vestments as white as the wispy strands of hair that peeked from underneath his beanie. "Gentlemen . . . and gentle chicken . . . I present to you His Holiness the Pope."

Brother Silas immediately stood, then bowed, his left arm bent at the elbow with Charlie resting in the crook of it. "Your Holiness." He greeted the frail, nodding pontiff. "This is such an honor. I'm Brother Silas

DeBassompierre, Order of Friars Minor and this is . . . " he placed his free hand on Charlie's tingling comb. "This is Charlie."

The Pope nodded some more, and with a sort of creaking, wordless vocalization held out his tremulous right hand.

Brother Silas bent and kissed, with great reverence, the Pope's ring.

Msgr. Klaeber bent and whispered a snatch of Italian into the Pope's ear, and the pope nodded more distinctly. Msgr. Klaeber the stood and addressed Brother Silas and Charlie. "I will be back in a half hour or so. My prayers will be with you all in the meantime." And with this he executed a deep bow and a sharp turn, and left the Pope alone in the Chapel with the young friar and the chicken.

The Pope gestured shakily toward the pew they had been sitting on. He said, in very heavily accented English, "Sit, please."

Brother Silas sat, still holding Charlie.

The pope eased into the pew beside the two of them. "God Bless you both." He murmured, as he regarded Charlie. "So this is the miraculous Charlie. How do you do, Charlie?" He held his palsied hand open and palm up under Charlie's beak.

Fine, thank you, Your Holiness, how are you? Scratched Charlie.

The Pope blinked his eyes several times, withdrew his hand, and looked up at Brother Silas. "It is true." He stated. "The chicken is forming English words with his beak. Very remarkable. Very odd to experience. Quite amazing."

"It certainly is, Your Holiness," said Brother Silas. "And that's just the beginning. Not only can he communicate, but he reads theology!"

The Pope's eyes, as bright as those of a much younger man, became even brighter. "Then it is true that he reads theology?"

Brother Silas nodded. "He sure does! Your Holiness."

The Pope blinked. He held the fingertips of his trembling hands together and momentarily still against his lips for a moment and then spoke through them in his quivering, high pitched, nearly incomprehensible English. "Which theologians does he read? Has he been acquainted with the great thinkers of the Catholic Tradition? Has he read Augustine? Aquinas? Von Balthasar?"

Brother Silas was so surprised by the question that it took him a moment to reply. "Well, Your Holiness, I've seen him reading Simone Weil, for one . . . "

"Ah." Said the Pope. "Perhaps he is familiar with her commentary on the *Our Father*?"

Brother Silas opened his palm under Charlie's beak. "I'll have to ask Charlie, Your Holiness. Just a moment . . . "

But the Pope reached out and placed his own hand on Brother Silas' before Charlie had a chance to answer. "I wonder," the old man said. "If Charlie and I might have a few moments alone. There are several questions I wish to ask of this remarkable creature, and I would like for him to be at liberty to answer me with the utmost candidness. You do not mind stepping out into the Basilica . . . ?"

Brother Silas scrambled to his feet. "I would be more than honored, You Holiness." He said, and, bowing, he backed out of the Chapel into the grandeur beyond, leaving Charlie to his private audience with the Pope, from which they emerged a short time later, with the Pope visibly shaken and Charlie no closer than he had been before to the baptism he longed for.

Chapter Fifteen

Home

BROTHER SILAS BEGGED AND pleaded, but Charlie would not communicate with him. Not when they arrived back at their hotel suite, nor during the return flight or during the ride back to the retreat center. What was there to say?

Charlie took to his bed and would not rouse himself to read anything. Father Angelo brought him meals and sat by his bedside for a few minutes several times a day, but it did not seem to make any difference to Charlie, who had become as unreachable spiritually as any other chicken.

⤸

Within a few days it was clear that Charlie was in danger of wasting away. Every few hours Father Angelo or Brother Silas or one of the other friars would let themselves into his cell to pray for him and bring him feed, but Charlie had lost altogether the will to live, and stopped eating. The situation was grave. Father Angelo telephoned Niniane to prepare her, and she became hysterical. She took her mother's car keys without asking and drove straight to Dillis' apartment across town. He took her into his dim, musty bedroom and attempted to embrace her, but she twisted herself out of his arms and sat hunched over on the side of the frameless mattress that Dillis used for a bed, rocking herself and moaning.

"Dillis," she said to him over and over. "He's going to die. We've got to do something."

"Niniane, what can we do?" He protested, but even as he did so, a plan was forming in his mind.

Dillis went to his window and looked out at his Plymouth in the parking lot. What Charlie needs right now, he told himself, are his friends. "To hell with this!" He said. "We're bringing him home!"

Niniane shook her head. "We can't!" She moaned. "He won't be safe in the city."

Dillis walked over to his bed and stood above his dejected girlfriend. His hands were on his hips. "He's not safe anywhere if he won't eat! He might as well be with us. We're his family." He reached for Niniane's arm and led her out to his car.

⌐⌐

By midnight that evening, they reached the gate that closed off the driveway of the retreat center. Dillis parked his car some ways down the gravel road that branched off of the island's two-lane highway. "Stay here," he told Niniane, who had been weepy and quiet for the entire ride. "And I'll check out the scene and figure out how to get in."

She acknowledged him with a slight nod. It was so unlike her to do as he asked that he for a moment he felt like a hero. Shrugging this off, he walked the rest of the way to the grounds. It was very dark out, with clouds obscuring most of the stars. Dillis stood at the tall wrought iron gate that disappeared, on either side into tall grass-patch studded dunes that looked as though they would be teeming with snakes and other hidden dangers. He wondered how they were ever going to cross this boundary to get to Charlie.

He tucked his jeans into his socks, tightened the laces on his sneakers, and took a running start up one of the dunes, but the sand simply gave beneath him until he was knee deep in it. He clambered out, grabbed the rails of the gate and tried to hoist himself up it hand over hand, but his thin arms hadn't the strength to even lift him off the ground more than a foot. He let himself down and sighed, already spent. All along the three-hour drive he told himself that there must be a way into the retreat center. He'd been sneaking into movie theaters and apartment complex swimming pools and on and off the high school grounds for most of his life, and it never crossed his mind that a retreat center would be more formidably secure than those more profit driven places. He bent and brushed sand off the legs of his jeans. That's why they put him here, dumbass, he said to himself. This place is a fortress.

He sighed. He thought he might as well go back to his car and wait in there until morning. Before they left his apartment, he'd gathered up what was left of his last paycheck and snaked two twenty dollar bills from his mother's pocketbook. This thievery did not trouble his conscience in that this was an emergency, but he didn't want to spend anything unnecessarily. His plan was to simply abduct Charlie, take the bird back to Niniane's parent's house, and just in general try to get his mind off of religion for a while.

But how the hell was he going to get over this gate and get to Charlie!

Dillis stood staring up at the shadowy spikes that poked up from the top rail of the gate and did not even see the tall, hooded figure approaching from the other side. A deep, outraged voice cried out and Dillis jumped.

"Hey! What's going on here!" The voice said.

Dillis gave a yelp and looked in the direction of the voice. A shadowy figure was fast approaching, the sandals on its feet made a slapping sound against the paved driveway on the other side of the gate.

"Nothing!" Dillis said. He turned around and started running.

The figure pushed a button on the hitch of the gate and slowly, with a humming noise, the gate began to open inward. "Stop!" The voice called, but Dillis kept running. He was so terrified now that he forgot all about Charlie.

He was almost at his car when the friar tackled him. For a full minute they struggled together on the gravel road until Dillis found himself expertly pinned underneath a panting young friar who looked, in that darkness, with his blazing eyes and dark habit, just like a vampire. Then he heard a shriek. Suddenly there was a thump that pressed the friar against him so that for a moment Dillis could not get his breath. Then the friar rolled off of him, and Dillis scrambled up to see the friar and Niniane on the ground beside him, entwined like shameless lovers in the gravel. "Hey!" He yelled. He caught Niniane's arm just as she reached back to throw a punch.

"Get off me!" The friar shouted. "Get off me! Help! Rape! This is Church property! I'll have you arrested for trespassing, assault . . . I mean it! You're under surveillance . . . "

Dillis pulled Niniane off the writhing, shouting friar who then scrambled to his sandaled feet, shaking dust from the skirt of his habit. He backed away, and took in the image of Niniane, with her long hair, full skirt, and heaving breast. "A girl!" he cried. "What are *you* doing here! This is a restricted area! And *you!*" he turned to Dillis. "Who are you?! Who sent you? The press? I knew that Nazi would leak us to the press! Well, you can forget it. We have a state of the art security system here. You'll never get to him, never. He's under the protection of the Order of Friars Minor, and he always will be."

"No he isn't!" Niniane shouted, her eyes blazing in the darkness. "You and your god-damn church won't even admit he has a soul! That's why he's in there *dying* you Christian idiot! You better let me in there, or I swear to god I'll drive this car right through that gate." She stepped forward menacingly but the friar stood his ground. He grabbed her by both of her shoulders.

"Who told you he was dying?"

"The *Bishop!*" Niniane screeched. Her fists clenched and she wrenched herself out of his grip. "Let me see him! Now! Before it's too late!"

The friar peered at the hysterical girl under the eerie light of the moon. "Who *are* you?" he said.

Niniane had no intention of answering. "Dillis, give me the keys," she ordered.

"Niniane . . ." Dillis said, "You aren't going to drive through that gate . . ."

"You're Niniane?" The friar said. He stepped forward to get a closer look. "Charlie's . . ."

"Friend." She said through her teeth. "Charlie's *best* friend. And I've come to take him home. He's had enough of your goddamn Church. He's coming home with me, where he'll have some *respect*."

The friar turned to Dillis. "Then you're . . ."

"Dillis." Said Dillis. "Look, Father. We really think Charlie ought to come with us . . . we know he won't eat . . . the Bishop called Niniane, and . . ."

The friar interrupted him. "Can I see some I.D.?"

"NO!" Shouted Niniane, but the two young men both ignored her. Dillis pulled his wallet out of his pocket and handed the friar his driver's license. The friar held it close to his face in the dim moonlight, then handed it back. "So you *are* Dillis. Charlie's talked a lot about you."

"He has?"

The friar nodded. "And this is Niniane?" he said, regarding her.

"Yes." Said Dillis.

The friar raised an eyebrow. "The way Charlie talked; I was expecting Helen of Troy . . ."

Niniane bit her lip and looked away. The friar let his hand fall to his side. "I'm Brother Silas." he said. "I accompanied Charlie to his audience with the Holy Father. I wish . . . I wish I could have been more help, but . . ." he sighed. "I was useless . . ."

Dillis touched the friar's shoulder. "Listen . . . can we at least see him ?"
Brother Silas bowed his head. "Of course. Follow me."

⌒

Brother Silas took them through the main gate, then through a smaller gate, which enclosed a sparse orchard, then through a side door, which he unlocked, which opened into the dormitory hallway.

The friar grabbed Dillis by the shoulder, pointed to a closed door, and whispered. "He's in there."

Dillis nodded.

"You're going to have to keep really quiet. *We're* going to have to be quiet. A lot of the brothers have trouble sleeping."

Dillis thought he wouldn't sleep well either if he was a monk or whatever they were. He reached for Niniane, who took his hand. Brother Silas strode ahead of them, unlocked the door to Charlie's cell, and ushered them inside.

Charlie perched on the middle of the bed as still as if he'd been stuffed by a taxidermist. His head drooped slightly, and his eyes were open but glazed. The sudden entrance of the three humans into his room elicited from him no reaction. The foot of the bed was piled with thick hardbound books, and a few of them were open. The sight of this filled Dillis with hope.

He rushed over to kneel beside the bed, reached out and began to stroke Charlie's neck and back. "Charlie." He whispered. "It's me! Dillis."

A slight motion seemed to course through the chicken's inert body. In the darkness it was difficult to be sure, but Dillis thought that maybe Charlie blinked. Dillis looked over his shoulder at Brother Silas, who was standing behind him with arms folded. "He moved!" Dillis said.

Brother Silas said nothing.

Dillis put his hand out under Charlie's beak. "What's wrong, Charlie? You can talk to me . . . "

But Charlie's mind was as empty and fragmented as the shell from which he'd emerged earlier that summer. Only one image remained, and it was upon this image that Charlie, or what was left of him in his depressed state, dwelled continuously. It was the image of that infinite dark chasm which lay in the palm of the hand of the Woman in his dream.

Dillis thought he saw Charlie's head move slightly downwards toward his hand, then stop, but in the dark it was hard to tell. "Let's turn on the light." He said over his shoulder to Brother Silas.

"We better not." the friar whispered. "Father Angelo is always getting up in the middle of the night and wandering around. He'll come in if he sees the light on."

"All right, all right." Dillis said. "Don't you want to get out of here Charlie?"

At that Dillis was sure that Charlie did move.

Dillis turned to Niniane, who stood as if turned to stone, her knuckles against her lips. Not since his days in the coop, before he began to communicate, had Charlie looked to her so much like any other chicken. It was as if he had been reduced, in some horrible, mysterious way, to mere animal flesh, incapable of consciousness or caring. For a moment she was returned to her bedroom at the farm that very first day that he wrote to her, asking herself if she was going crazy. "Niniane?" Dillis stood, feeling like a failure, and came to her. He led her gently to the side of the bed. "You've got to try. He's not saying anything to me."

Niniane let Dillis take her hand and spread it out, palm up, in front of Charlie. That gesture, so familiar, so intimate, so evocative of Charlie himself, undid her, and she bent her head so that her long hair fell forward, a few locks of it draping across Charlie's back. "Charlie," she whispered. "My darling, is there anything I can do?"

Maybe it was the tear of sorrow that dripped off her nose onto his comb, maybe it was faint caress of her hair upon his feathers, or her open palm before him, maybe it was the fact that she knelt by his side and waited for a response from him for as long as she had ever waited for anything that broke the spell he was under, that reached and resurrected what the Pope's denial had crushed in him, the desire to communicate. He lowered his beak to touch her skin and to be so close to her again was like heaven. *You could at least eat me.*

Epilogue

Did he mean it literally? It's difficult to say, for of course Niniane only wept in reply, and Charlie never brought it up again. What can be said, though, is that Charlie did not remain in the retreat center. In the end he decided, against everyone else's better judgment, that the only place left for him to be was the coop from which he had come, where he could blend in and be safe and anonymous as long as he didn't read or write anything. Most importantly, the indifference of his family of origin didn't matter anymore. He knew who he was, and that he was loved.

Hiding Charlie in a pillowcase, Niniane and Dillis and Brother Silas snuck Charlie and a bottle of communion wine out of the retreat center, and Dillis drove the two hundred and fifty miles down the length of the island and inland to the farm on the edge of the coastal plain where Charlie had been hatched. As they drove there wasn't much conversation. Dillis (and a progressively drunken Brother Silas in the backseat) smoked cigarettes and sang along from time to time with the raucous, thumping, screeching sounds that issued from the car's speakers. Charlie just stared out at the night sky from his place in Niniane's lap and he was content just to be held by her. He felt, at least for the time being, that he'd said all he had to say.

Then, with all the solemnity of a midnight mass, the three humans placed Charlie onto one of the posts of the chicken yard fence, where he stood for a moment under the light of the moon, looking like the full grown rooster he had become in the eight short weeks since his hatching.

Without looking back—because he could not bear to—Charlie, with an impressive hop emphasized and prolonged by the flapping of his outstretched wings, descended into the scene of his nativity, trotted into the darkness of the coop, and was gone—his words, rather than his appearance, being distinctive to human beings.

For years to come, until the second coming, the others, Niniane, her parents, Dillis, Father Angelo, Brother Silas, Bishop Serxner, the former Father Frank, May and Irene came together at the farm for a vegan feast every year on June 21st, Charlie's birthday. Thus a number of several Roman Catholics, a couple of witches, a, a secular Jew, two mainline Protestants and a vegan agnostic, despite differences, came together every year to remember a chicken whose only real wish was never to be forgotten.

Coda:

The Friendly Beasts

An Old French Carol

Jesus our brother, kind and good,
Was humbly born in a stable rude
The friendly beasts around him stood
Jesus our brother, kind and good.

"I," Said the donkey, shaggy and brown,
"I carried his mother up hill and down;
I carried her safely to Bethlehem town."
"I," Said the donkey, shaggy and brown.

"I," Said the cow, all white and red,
"I gave him my manger for his bed;
I gave him my hay to pillow his head."
"I," Said the cow, all white and red.

"I," Said the sheep with curly horn,
"I gave him my wool for his blanket warm;
He wore my coat on Christmas morn."
"I," Said the sheep with the curly horn.

"I," Said the dove from the rafters high,
"I cooed him to sleep so he would not cry;

We cooed him to sleep, my mate and I."
"I," Said the dove from the rafters high.

Thus every beast *by some good spell*,
In the stable dark was glad to tell
Of the gifts each gave Immanuel,
The gifts they gave Immanuel.